A Campus Conspiracy

A Campus Conspiracy

Anonymous

First published 2006
by Impress Books Ltd
Innovation Centre, Rennes Drive,
University of Exeter Campus, Exeter EX4 4RN

© the author 2006

The right of the author to be identified as the originator of this
work has been asserted in accordance with the
Copyright, Designs and Patents Act 1988.

Typeset in 10/12pt Sabon by Laserwords Private Limited, Chennai, India

Printed and bound in England by imprint-academic.com

British Library Cataloguing in Publication Data
A catalogue record for this book is available from the British Library

ISBN–10: 0-9547586-7-6
ISBN–13: 978-0-9547586-7-7

For Mark

Author's Note

St Sebastian's University does not exist, and it should not be identified with any institution of higher education in the United Kingdom or elsewhere. Sweetpea College is a similar fiction. All characters in the novel are also entirely imaginary. They have no counterparts in real life.

CHAPTER ONE

Perfectly Proper Behaviour

Term had begun. A slight fog covered the ground as I walked to my first class. Even though it was only my tenth year at St Sebastian's, this was my thirty-first year of university teaching. It was disconcerting to realize that I was now sixty years old, a senior professor. As I passed by the Student Union Building, I caught sight of my reflection in the window. I did look a bit dishevelled. My tweed suit was baggy at the knees and my shirt was frayed at the wrists. My hair had turned grey, and none of my clothes was quite comfortable at the waist any more. Still, I told myself, that is what elderly professors are meant to look like. What counts are brains, not appearance.

The class was in the Arts Building on the first floor, and as I entered I recognized some of the students from last year. But sitting in the front row was an attractive blonde undergraduate. She seemed to have my problem of bursting out of her clothes. Both her shirt and skirt were clearly too small for her and did not appear to cover her very much. Still, at sixty it was not my place to ogle my pupils. As the bells of the cathedral struck eleven I sat down, took out my register and arranged my papers. "Good morning,' I said. "Welcome back. I hope you had a good summer." I then took roll-call. After I finished, the blonde piped up.

"Professor Gilbert," she said. "You forgot me. I'm Lisa."

I looked through the list. "You're right," I said. "Sorry. What is your last name?" She spelled it. I added her to the list. "Right, Lisa," I said. "Anyone else I missed?" There was silence. The course, I explained, dealt with theology and law: essentially it was about Christian ethics. I handed out the syllabus, and told the class that they should get hold of my Christian ethics textbook which had been written specially for the course. I then began my lecture. Unlike the other students, Lisa took no notes. She slumped in her chair, crossed her legs, and stared. There was a gap between the bottom of her shirt and her skirt. I noticed she had a heart shaped tattoo around her belly-button.

Just before the end of the class, I asked if anyone had any questions. The students stirred uncomfortably. I feared I had bored them. But Lisa put up her hand. "Professor," she said. "Are you saying that motives don't matter? I think they do. How can an action be moral if the person's intentions are evil?"

"That's a good question", I said. I briefly mentioned the ideas of the utilitarian philosophers and contrasted them with the views of Immanuel Kant. I told them that these would be the subjects of further lectures. Throughout, Lisa fiddled with her hair. She leaned forward as I explained about Kant's *Critique of Practical Reason* and crossed her arms. I tried not to notice that her breasts swelled underneath the pressure.

When the bell rang, the students gathered up their papers and filed out. Lisa stayed behind. "Professor," she said. "You're my tutor. Can I make an appointment today? I need to ask you about one of my courses."

"Come at three," I said. "I have a staff meeting after lunch." I watched her saunter out of the seminar room and wondered if she were going to be a problem.

As I crossed the quad, I saw the Vice-Chancellor getting out of a new black Jaguar saloon. He was an imposing, balding figure with bushy eyebrows. Professor Oliver Barraclough had previously been a Fellow at King's College, Cambridge before becoming a Professor of Accountancy at Leeds. After a short stint as Pro-Vice-Chancellor, he had been appointed Vice-Chancellor of St Sebastian's. Known as a ruthless cost-cutter, he had abolished all faculties in his first term and created ten departments. At the end of the year, he sent out letters to all staff over the age of fifty-five, encouraging them to take early retirement. A few of the most distinguished professors managed to get new jobs; a number of others were seduced into attractive offers of enhanced pensions with part-time employment; several, like me, tossed the letters into their wastebaskets.

Lunch was being served in the Senior Common Room, located at the far end of the Old College. St Sebastian's had been established as a theological college for missionaries during the Victorian period. Influenced by Oxford-style architecture, the original building was Gothic sandstone with pointed towers. The Senior Common Room was panelled in dark oak. There were small tables with armchairs scattered throughout the room, and in the corner, a waitress served sandwiches and coffee.

I stood in the queue next to the Dean, Dr Wanda Catnip, and her secretary. She was talking animatedly about this afternoon's meeting, giving instructions about the papers which were to be distributed. She was a small, compact, middle-aged woman who was always formally dressed. Her straight, greyish hair was cut severely round her head. Today her suit was brown tweed with a green fleck. Her first degree was from Manchester, but I suspected that she had applied to Oxford and had been rejected. Subsequently she had studied at Hull for a PhD. She had a very slight Northern accent and a definite lisp. I had always tried to be affable to her, but somehow we had never really got on. In private, my wife, who happened to be the daughter of a baronet, mocked her mannerisms mercilessly.

As we waited to be served, Wanda turned to me. "The meeting today is very important," she announced. "We're going to discuss the run-up to the RAE. The Vice-Chancellor wants to come to fill us in." Before I had a chance to reply, she ordered her sandwich, took a pack of salt and vinegar crisps from a basket next to the cash register and strode off. Her secretary followed close behind.

RAE stands for the 'Research Assessment Exercise'. Over the last decade this ordeal has plagued all university departments. Each person's four best publications are evaluated and scored every few years; government money is then allocated on the basis of the result. In the past, departments were ranked depending on the outcome. Those academics who were left out of this exercise altogether were humiliated, and their careers severely damaged.

I ordered a cheese sandwich and a mug of coffee, and sat down next to two colleagues who were engrossed in discussion. Magnus Hamilton was one of the longest serving members of the department. Tall, balding and bespectacled, he was appointed as a lecturer in Old Testament studies. His parents had been killed in a car accident when he was in prep school, and he had been brought up by his Aunt Ursula who had sent him to Winchester. After reading politics, philosophy and economics at Oxford, he went on to do a PhD in biblical archaeology. His supervisor – a distinguished Professor of Old Testament – had given him an outstanding reference, yet he had only published one article in a little-known theological journal twenty years ago. He had never been promoted, and was despondent about academic life. Next to him sat Agnes Flyte, a plump, young lecturer in systematic theology. Invariably dressed in a sweater and jeans, she had short brown hair which emphasized her hooked nose. Her revised PhD thesis had recently been published by Edinburgh University Press and had received glowing reviews in various academic journals. It was quite unreadable.

"Talking about the RAE..." I observed.

"It doesn't really concern me," Magnus grumbled. "I haven't been research-active for years. Always denied study leave. Now they want to change my contract so I'll have to teach all the bloody undergraduates all the time."

"At least they haven't terminated it," I said.

"They would if they could. But they can't. I've got tenure. They have to keep me. Damn Barraclough! He keeps sending me these devious little letters telling me I should think about retirement. He even offered to enhance my pension."

4

"You're not the only one," I said. "I got the same letter. We all did. Not you, of course, Agnes. You've got to be over fifty-five."

Agnes looked embarrassed and picked up a copy of *The Guardian* lying on the table. Magnus continued his diatribe. "Now they tell me I've got to have more postgraduates. I'm supposed to devise some kind of MA programme in Old Testament studies. I've even got to teach during the summer. What has academic life come to?"

"Magnus," I said. "You constantly complain that the university is a crappy place. Why don't you simply retire if you've been given a good deal? That way you'd be free of all this?"

"I've thought about it. But look. Even if I got a full pension, I'd only get about sixteen thousand pounds a year. And then I'd have to pay tax. It just isn't enough to live on. I did once think of doing something else. I read that plumbers earn about sixty pounds an hour. But then I'd have to do an apprenticeship, and it could take years. I know I'm experienced with shit – I have to take such a lot of it here – but I'm the first to admit I'm not very good with my hands and all those spanners and things are very intimidating..."

Magnus was interrupted by the arrival of the Vice-Chancellor who ordered a sandwich and coffee, stopped to have a word with the Dean, and sat at a table nearby. He was carrying a copy of *Private Eye*. Silently he ate his sandwich, and flipped through it.

"Hey," Magnus said. "Maybe he does have a sense of humour after all."

"I don't think so, Magnus. He's simply looking to see if there are any articles about him. He's terrified of bad publicity."

After lunch, Magnus and I walked together to the staff meeting in the Great Hall. On the way, we passed by the Student Union. Several undergraduates were milling about the entrance including Lisa. She was leaning against a pillar smoking a cigarette and waved. "One of your students?" Magnus asked.

"Some girl who wants to see me this afternoon," I replied.

"She'll catch a cold in that outfit," he observed. "Can't understand students these days. Why do they expose themselves like that? I guess they think it attracts men..."

"I suppose it does."

"Better watch out then," he smiled.

About a hundred lecturers from all the departments had gathered in the Great Hall for the meeting. Like the Senior Common Room, the walls were panelled in dark oak and portraits of previous vice-chancellors were scattered throughout the room. For all their academic gowns and mortar boards, they did not look an impressive lot. Dr Wanda Catnip, the Heads of each Department and the Vice-Chancellor sat behind a large table on a platform in the front. Wanda stood up, put on her spectacles which hung on a chain round her neck, and introduced the Vice-Chancellor who, she said, wished to address all of us concerning the RAE.

Magnus, who was sitting next to me, groaned. "Bloody Hell! The man is obsessed!"

The Vice-Chancellor stood up. "Thank you for coming", he said. "This year we are currently preparing for the RAE, which you all know about. I can't stress enough the importance of this. Our funding depends on the results. We want to do even better than last time." He then went on to explain that at the initial stage, each research-active academic would be required to submit a list of publications for consideration. These would be evaluated by referees from outside the university.

"That leaves me out . . ." Magnus muttered.

"Then," the Vice-Chancellor continued, "the Head of each Department will meet with all colleagues to have a preliminary discussion about the suitability of their submissions. These meetings will be arranged by next term. In the meantime, you should think carefully about selecting your best pieces of work. This will help enormously."

Wanda took notes while the Vice-Chancellor spoke. Her eyes narrowed as he outlined what would happen if a decision were made to leave someone out. That individual, he explained, would be required to teach more undergraduates and postgraduates to compensate for the loss of income. It might mean taking on summer school duties.

"That means me," Magnus lamented.

When the Vice-Chancellor finished, Wanda asked if anyone had questions. At the back, Philip McGregor, one of the oldest members of the university, put up his hand. "Vice-Chancellor," he asked, "what if your department doesn't want to submit someone's research? Is there an appeal procedure?" Philip McGregor was a Senior Lecturer in Physics whose career had been held up because he produced textbooks for A-level students. He had just written yet another introductory guide which had had a rather unflattering review in the *Times Educational Supplement*. Even so, his books were said to have enormous sales, and he and his wife enjoyed a nice little extra income from them.

The Vice-Chancellor explained that every opportunity would be given to those who felt they had been unfairly treated. A special appeal committee had been established. Outside opinions would be sought from experts. He stressed that it was his hope that everyone would be able to be included.

"Fat chance!" Magnus moaned.

The meeting continued for another half an hour. Wanda explained in detail the procedure for submitting work to the Research Committee. Her Northern accent became more pronounced, which was a sure sign she was enjoying herself. When it was over, Magnus came to my office for coffee. We passed by the chapel, climbed the stairs and went down the long corridor leading to my room. Magnus slumped into an armchair as I put the kettle on. "You know," he said. "I don't really understand why you want to continue here. You're not like me. Your father made a fortune with his frozen food business; you've got plenty of money. You've married into the aristocracy. You've got a beautiful house in the country. You're a member of a London club. Why waste your time in this stupid place?"

"I like it."

"I don't get it."

"I like the undergraduates."

"You're crazy ..."

"I like the postgraduates ... "

"You really are mad."

"I like doing research."

"You could do it at home."

"Anyway I like my salary. I like the feeling I'm earning my living and being useful to somebody. And the stress is probably good for me. I'd be even fatter than I am if I just stayed at home."

Magnus sighed and looked out the window. "You're not very stout. If I were you I'd just settle for being a gentleman scholar without the students and without the idiotic RAE. You don't fit in here. Look at this room! It's like a film set. All these antiques and oriental carpets. Where did you get them from? Why don't you just take them all home and stuff the university?"

The clock struck three and there was a knock on the door. "That must be my undergraduate," I said. I told her to come in. Lisa entered and sat down in the chair nearest my desk. I noticed she had a dragon tattooed on her back just above the top of her skirt. "This is Dr Hamilton," I said. "Lisa is a first year undergraduate."

"Actually, I'm a second year transfer student," she objected. Magnus got up and left. Lisa wriggled seductively at me as the door shut. I sat down behind my desk. She took out a lighter and a packet of cigarettes. "Do you mind if I smoke?" she asked.

"Actually," I said, "I do. Sorry."

Lisa frowned. "Right," she said, putting her cigarettes down. "I wanted to ask you about the second-year ethics course you teach." She rummaged about in her bag and took out some papers. "You see," she said, "I took the same course at my last university and wrote this essay. But I never took the exam. Anyway, since I got an A, I'd like credit for the course so I don't have to take it here." Lisa leaned forward and handed me the essay.

"Where were you?" I asked.

"I was a first year student at King's, London," she said. "I finished the year. But I didn't want to live in London. My parents have a house there and I wanted some independence. Anyway, I got a place here and they gave me credit for the year."

"But not credit for this second year course?"

Lisa frowned. "No," she said. "But hey look, Professor, I'm sure you can help me, can't you. I can make it worth your while." She slowly crossed her legs, exposing her thighs.

'I'll look at the essay," I said, averting my eyes. "Even though students are allowed to submit an essay rather than take an exam for the course, I'm not sure about this. I'll read your work and let you know. Come and see me tomorrow."

Lisa stood up and smiled. "Thanks, Professor," she said. "You won't regret it."

She shut the door behind her. I looked down from my office window at the students below. I saw Lisa walk off towards the Student Union. She glanced up. I retreated behind the curtains. The phone rang. It was Victoria, my wife. "Darling," she said. "Don't forget to pick up the wine. You know Daddy's very particular." Victoria's father was coming to stay for the weekend.

"I know," I said. "I'll get some claret like we had last time. Should I get a magnum? The Buzzard seems to like big bottles of the stuff."

"Please don't call him the Buzzard."

"But he does look like a buzzard. A craggy buzzard."

My father-in-law – Sir William Dormouse – was over eighty, but still very vigorous. He had inherited an enormously draughty, crumbling castle on the Welsh border. The family was traditionally loyal to Wales. He had been educated at Shrewsbury School and was still active in the Old Salopian Club. Even though he was rather snobbish about my background 'in trade', as he called it, it pleased him to know that I too had been educated at Shrewsbury and that I had read theology at Cambridge. His great-great grandfather, the second baronet, had been a don at Trinity some time in the early nineteenth century. When the elder brother had died in a hunting accident, he had given up his fellowship and returned to live the life of a country squire. The family had remained there, sending their children over the border to public school. Victoria had been to Cheltenham Ladies' College and then on to Girton; her brothers had followed their father to Shrewsbury and Trinity. Victoria and I had met when she was an undergraduate and I was struggling with my PhD.

9

At dinner that night, I told my father-in-law about the RAE. Our two Siamese cats circled the table, hoping that we might share our sherry trifle with them. "The RAE takes place every few years," I explained. "The purpose is to assess the research output of each academic."

"Must be very time-consuming reading all that stuff," Sir William said.

"Well, it is. At least for all the members of the Committee."

"You're on the Committee?" he asked.

"Not me. It's composed of about a dozen experts in each field. They spend about a year reading each person's best work."

"Damn boring."

"It must be. But it's all very important, because money is distributed on the basis of the results."

"Do you get any extra?"

"No, the department does. The Vice-Chancellor is obsessed by the RAE. It's all he can think about. The same applies to the Dean and the Heads of Departments."

"Harry's department did jolly well last time," Victoria interjected.

"Good for them!" he said. "How much extra money did you get?"

"Actually, we got less. You see, all the departments improved like we did. So there was less money to go around."

"Damn stupid," my father-in-law said. 'Don't see the point. Claret's good; I'll have another glass, there's a good girl."

After Sir William had gone to bed, Victoria and I sat in the drawing room. We had bought our house when I was appointed to the Chair of Christian Ethics; it was an old mill house in the country, about eight miles from St Sebastian's. The cats were curled up on the sofa asleep in front of the log fire and Victoria had changed into her dressing gown. She was as slender and dark-haired as when I first saw her at a meeting of the Cambridge Arts Society. "So how was the Faculty meeting?" she asked as she finished the last of the claret.

"Boring as usual. Bossyboots (our nickname for Wanda Catnip) was in charge, and the VC gave us a pep-talk about the RAE. Magnus moaned through most of the meeting. Poor chap! He knows he's not going to be included, and is going to have to teach more courses. He ought to take early retirement, but he told me he can't afford to."

"I can't understand why he's never written anything. You said he was brilliant."

"He came with glowing references, but he simply dried up. It happens. Anyway I meant to tell you about one of the undergraduates in my first-year class. I think she tried to make a pass at me!"

Victoria laughed. "No!" she said, "How very flattering! What did she do?"

"Well she's a transfer student and she came around after the staff meeting. She wanted me to give her credit for my second year course because she'd already written an essay on the subject. I said I'd look at her work, but she kept wriggling and she promised she'd make it worth my while!"

"No!" said Victoria again, "What did you do?"

"I sent her away and told her to come back tomorrow. But actually there's a problem with her essay. I've had one almost identical last year. I think she probably copied it off the internet."

"Oh dear" Victoria looked thoughtful. "Do be careful. She sounds as if she could be a lot of trouble and you don't want to end up as one of those sad old men who are always chasing young girls!"

"I don't think there's much danger of that with you around" I said, and we smiled at each other.

The next day I went into the university for a departmental meeting. The Head of Department, Dr John Pilkington, was a tall, bearded Church historian whose PhD thesis on the medieval papacy had eventually been published by the University of Exeter Press ten years ago. In addition, over a twenty-year career at St Sebastian's, he had written a half dozen articles for learned journals and two years' ago he had been appointed senior lecturer. No one wanted to serve as Head of Department, and he was elected unopposed. A dedicated servant of the university, he volunteered to sit on nearly every committee. It was rumoured that he had ambitions to succeed Wanda

Catnip as Dean. He and his wife, Maureen, lived in a modern bungalow on the outskirts of St Sebastian's. Since he became Head of Department, they hosted the annual Christmas party in their house.

As this was the first meeting of the term, all fifteen of us including Wendy Morehouse, the departmental secretary, assembled in the largest seminar room in the Humanities building. Located across from the Old College, it was a modern structure of steel and glass. Only Magnus and I had refused to have our offices there; it was too ugly. So we still worked in the Old College. I sat next to Magnus who was dunking chocolate biscuits into his coffee. To keep myself from falling asleep, I drew sketches of my colleagues. I began with John Pilkington who, like Wanda the day before, focussed on the significance of the RAE. Convinced that our department was one of the best in the country, he expected us to have an outstanding score.

"Guy's as batty as the VC," Magnus muttered.

"So," Pilkington droned on, "we've got to pull our socks up. If you haven't published your stuff by now, you've got to get going. It takes publishers at least a year to get a book into print, and journals can take even longer. There's just two years left before the RAE deadline."

I passed my drawing to Magnus who giggled and handed it back. I then gave it to Agnes who was sitting nearby. She looked quizzical and hid it under her papers. "You'd better not show it to Pilks," Magnus cautioned.

After a lengthy discussion of other items on the agenda, Magnus and I left the building. Together we walked to the Old College. Magnus was on his way to the corner shop to buy food for the rest of the week. "I say," he said, as we crossed the street, "isn't that the girl who was in your room yesterday?" Lisa was standing on the steps smoking a cigarette. She smiled as she saw us.

"Hi, Professor," she said. "Can you spare a minute." Magnus waved as he left us and walked in the direction of the shop.

Lisa followed me up the steps, and we went by the chapel where volunteers from the town were arranging flowers. When we reached my office, I hung up Lisa's jacket on my door. She sat on my sofa. I placed myself opposite her in a wing armchair.

12

"So?" she asked.

"I'm sorry, Lisa," I said. "Your essay was very good. Really excellent. But it would set a precedent. If you had taken the exam, then you could have credit for the course. But since you didn't, I'm afraid I can't give you an exemption. You'll have to fulfil the requirements here. But if you choose an essay dealing with the same subject, then you can adapt and rewrite what you've already written . . .'

"Come on, Professor," Lisa said, leaning forward and exposing her cleavage, "I said I'd make it worth your while."

I stood up and handed back the essay. "Anyway," I spoke more severely than I felt, "although it was very good, I do have to say that your paper was very similar to one I read last term. You are aware, aren't you, that all essays submitted for formal assessment have to be gone through by the departmental secretary? They are checked against anti-plagiarism software to make sure that no one had copied material directly off the internet or anything like that. I'm sure you wouldn't think of doing such a thing, but . . . "

Lisa turned bright red. She interrupted me, "How dare you suggest I would copy an essay!" She snatched the paper out of my hand, grabbed her jacket and turned on her heel, "You'll hear more about this!" she said and she flounced out of the room.

I was disturbed by this encounter. Had I done the wrong thing to warn my student of the dangers of plagiarism? Was she upset that I had rejected her advances? Or was she just a spoilt child used to getting her own way? I picked up the telephone and rang Magnus's mobile.

"Look," I said, "something very upsetting has happened! I think I may be in trouble!"

"What have you done?" Magnus was interested. "Did you hit Wanda? Or even better, the VC?"

"No . . . Nothing like that. I've just had the most extraordinary encounter with that student."

"I thought she might be a problem. What did she do? Try to seduce you?"

"Well actually, yes. She wanted to get credit for my course on the basis of a single essay she wrote at her last university.

And she said she would make it worth my while if I agreed. I had to admit it was a very good essay, but the problem was that there was no proof she had written it and it was very similar to an essay another student wrote for me last year."

"So you said no?"

"Yes. And I warned her about the dangers of plagiarism from the internet."

"I wonder what she meant about making it worth your while." Magnus's voice took on a faraway expression. "She really didn't have many clothes to take off."

"Don't be absurd, Magnus. I don't know what she meant and I don't care. What matters is she bounced out of the room slamming the door and she gave me to understand that I hadn't heard the last of it."

"Why don't I come round and you can make me a cup of coffee? I've just finished shopping and I'm exhausted."

Within a couple of minutes there was a knock on the door and Magnus appeared. He was loaded down with three plastic shopping bags and a huge sack of cat litter. Like Victoria and me, Magnus was very fond of cats. His large middle-aged tabby was called Pushkin. He was known to be extremely fussy and would only eat the most expensive cat food and use the most rarified cat litter. Magnus tossed his bags into a corner and stretched out on my sofa.

"I think you may have missed a splendid opportunity," he said.

"Don't be stupid Magnus. I'm sixty. I'm not interested in the undergraduates."

"Well she did look a particularly toothsome young thing . . ."

I frowned. "What I'm concerned about is what she's going to do next. I was hoping for a nice quiet term when I could get on with my new book. I really don't want to have to deal with Wanda Catnip and accusations and counter-accusations and heaven knows what."

Magnus took a sip of his coffee. "I don't think you have any cause for worry. She'll get over it. After all you didn't do anything wrong . . . or did you?" He looked at me slyly over his spectacles.

"No I did not. I acted perfectly properly and that's what I'll say if I'm asked."

"I'm not sure acting 'perfectly properly' is what goes down well in this establishment," remarked Magnus gloomily. "In my experience deceit, vanity and self-aggrandizement are far more successful."

CHAPTER TWO

There's Nothing They Can Do

When I arrived home, I told Victoria what had happened. She was dismayed. "Are the students really like that?" she asked in amazement.

"It's never happened before."

"Well, I'm glad to hear it. What a horrid, spoiled girl!"

"But what if she wants to make trouble? The last thing I want is a student complaint."

"But you didn't do anything wrong. You just warned her of the consequences of plagiarism. And anyway, your colleagues will support you. Magnus would."

"But he doesn't have any influence. If anything, his support will just make matters worse. If there's a hint of a complaint, Pilks will want to set up an official inquiry. Bossyboots will be frightful. She'll take the matter through formal proceedings. She loves that sort of thing."

Victoria giggled. She put on her special Catnip manner, "Now Harry, this is a very serious matter..." She reverted to her usual tone. "I don't see what the girl has to complain about. You rejected her advances and told her not to copy her work off the internet. That's exactly what you're supposed to do."

"The VC would love a complaint, however ridiculous. He's only concerned about money and he's longing to get rid of anyone who's over fifty and expensive. He'll make any excuse to suggest early retirement again."

Throughout dinner, we continued to discuss the incident. Our cat, Cleo, sat on my lap and tried to lick cream from the silver cream jug.

"Look," I said, "I think we just have to wait and see. So far nothing's happened. This girl, Lisa, fled from my office, and hopefully she won't come back to class. She doesn't want a fight. What would be the point? She won't gain anything by making a fuss." Eventually I let Cleo finish the cream. She then jumped down and was instantly sick over our Heriz carpet.

The next day I arrived early for class. On the way to my office, I stopped in the Porter's Lodge to collect my post. One of the letters was marked Private and Confidential. It was from the Head of the Department. This was bad. When I got to my office, I opened it. It read:

Dear Harry,

Yesterday a second year student, Lisa Gold, came to see me about an incident that took place in your office in the afternoon following the staff meeting. She has accused you of sexual harassment. As you know, this is a most serious offence. I am therefore treating this matter as a disciplinary case under Provision 24 of the University Statutes. I am scheduling a meeting to discuss this accusation for next Monday at ll:00 in my office. You are entitled to bring a representative to the meeting. I shall be accompanied by the Dean. Please let me know if this date is convenient.

Yours ever,

John

Dr John Pilkington,

Head of the Department of Theology

A formal disciplinary case! I had never faced such a thing! I sat looking out of my window at the trees which were now shedding their leaves. Why didn't Pilkington come to see me? Surely he could have informally discussed such an accusation before proceeding. John Pilkington and his wife had entertained us at his house at Christmas, and we asked them to our annual drinks party. We had not been on bad terms, even though we were not particularly friendly. It was true that Victoria was patronizing about their bungalow in private. She thought his wife was suburban; she made fun of their neat lawn and tidy hedges. But these comments were made only to me. Could the Pilkingtons have found out what she thought?

What would be the implications of such a formal complaint? Pilkington had already told Wanda because she was going to be present at the meeting. Could they really believe I had been so foolish? And what about Barraclough? Had he been informed too? Probably everybody would soon know. I looked at the envelope marked 'Private and Confidential'. This was to be a private and confidential matter. But it wouldn't be. Everyone would soon know. The Professor of Christian Ethics accused of sexual harassment. What a story! What humiliation! What disgrace!

After my classes I went to the Senior Common Room for lunch. Pilkington was standing in the queue ahead of me talking with Wanda. When they saw me, they smiled. Surely they must have discussed Lisa's complaint, but they gave no indication. They were engrossed in a conversation about the RAE. I ordered a tuna sandwich, coffee and a packet of shortbread biscuits and sat down in an armchair next to Magnus who was deeply engrossed in *The Times*. He was reading the obituary column. "Look at this," he said. "My supervisor, Rupert Berry, just died. He was a fossil thirty years ago. I had no idea he was still alive."

"Magnus," I whispered. "I just got a note from Pilks. That girl put in a formal complaint. She said I harassed her sexually and they're going to investigate it."

Magnus looked up. "Really," he said. "She is a tough little so-and-so. Perhaps you should have been more accommodating!"

"Come on Magnus!"

"Just a suggestion. By the way, what did Victoria say?"

"She was very cross...not with me, but with the girl."

"You know," Magnus said turning over the pages of *The Times*, "Berry never wrote much. I think he only published his PhD thesis and then he got a Chair."

Exasperated, I spluttered: "Magnus, you're not taking this very seriously. I'm in trouble. Real trouble. Pilkington wants to investigate this affair under some University Statute."

"Probably Provision 24. That's Discipline leading to Dismissal. I looked it up when Pilks sent me a note about not getting my essays marked on time. He actually mentioned it in his letter?"

"You think I might get a warning?"

"Could be worse than that. Sexual harassment is gross misconduct. You could be fired on the spot...but there's no proof. It's just that girl's word against yours. Do you think she's done this before?"

"Don't know. She's new here. Maybe she did the same thing at her previous university and that's why she transferred. Perhaps she's a nymphomaniac."

"Lucky you," Magnus grinned. "Sorry, couldn't resist. Really, I am sorry. This is unlucky. But not a tragedy."

"No?..."

"Well, there's no evidence. So there's not much the university can do about it. There's no proof unless you recorded the whole thing. You didn't did you?"

"Of course not."

"What a pity. I would have enjoyed hearing it. No doubt Victoria would have been interested too. Oh well. I wouldn't worry about it too much. You'll just have an unpleasant interview, and that'll be it." Magnus paused. "Maybe in future, you ought to have someone in the room with you if you're talking to an attractive girl. You can't be too careful around here," Magnus sighed as he began the *Times* crossword. "You don't know a synonym for crooked?" he asked.

"Try Barraclough," I replied.

19

When I got back to my room, I looked up Provision 24 in the Staff Handbook. Magnus was right. Pilkington was referring to the formal disciplinary procedure. Any complaint, it read, should first be investigated informally by the Head of Department. If there is a prima facie case, then there should be a meeting with the person against whom the complaint has been made. He or she has the right to bring either a union representative or a friend.

Pilkington had clearly skipped the first stage. For years I had been a member of the UCU (the University and College Union). Hesitantly I rang the local president, a Senior Lecturer in Women's Studies. She wasn't in, but I left a message on her answerphone. Later in the afternoon, she called back. I asked if I could come and see her.

Penelope Ransome's room was on the ground floor of the Humanities building. Her door was covered with posters defending gay and lesbian rights. I knocked, but there was no answer. Down the hall I heard Penelope talking to her department administrator. Several minutes later she emerged wearing jeans and a multicoloured jumper. Her hair had been streaked green since I last saw her. She wore dangling silver earrings with a cross.

We sat in her small office. Essays and papers were piled high on the floor. The air was thick with cigarette smoke. I explained what had happened and showed her Pilkington's letter. "Look," she said. "I've had a lot of experience with these cases. It's her word against yours. She won't be able to prove a thing. But you did say she would make bending the rules worth your while?"

"Yes, but I firmly ignored that part of the conversation," I said sheepishly. "I just warned her of the dangers of plagiarism, and she flounced out of the room."

"You didn't kiss her?"

"Certainly not!"

Penelope took out a packet of cigarettes and offered me one. I refused. She lit up and took several puffs. "Well," she reflected, "you'll simply have to explain and in the end, nothing will come of it."

"Are you sure?"

"You're a professor. The university may want to get rid of you, but they don't want a scandal. You won't enjoy the interview, that's for certain. You say Pilkington isn't much of a friend?"

"I don't think he's an enemy."

Penelope stood up. "I'll be there on Monday."

"Thanks," I said. I got up and left. On the way out, I saw a group of students huddled together talking in hushed tones. When they saw me, they looked away. I wondered if they had already heard about the complaint against me.

On Monday I put on my best suit. I found that the waist was even tighter than when I had last worn it and resolved for the hundredth time that I really had to do something about my weight. I arrived at the university a few minutes before the meeting with Pilkington. Penelope came up looking agitated. Over the weekend, she told me, there had been a union rally about part-time employment in London; she was one of the speakers and was exhausted. I was a bit disappointed to see that she had made no special efforts to dress for the occasion: she was wearing an old leather jacket with a hole in one sleeve and a bright green jumper. Her earrings were pink and black with dangling silver bells. Surprisingly, she had the latest sleek mobile telephone which she placed on the table. "Just in case I get a call," she announced. Pilkington was late. He was wearing a brown suit with a wide polyester striped blue tie. I noticed that his socks were sludge green. He was accompanied by Wanda who was wearing a mauve two piece suit and a cream blouse, offset by a paisley silk scarf. Her lipstick was a strange shade of mauve which made her seem paler than normal. Neither looked friendly.

Before we began the meeting, Pilkington announced that he had spoken to the Vice-Chancellor about the accusation we were to discuss; he had been instructed to tell us that the university was taking the matter very seriously and that the Student Union would be informed of the outcome. Wanda took some papers out of her black leather briefcase as Pilkington continued. The meeting was to be an informal discussion, he explained. Although Provision 24 was being invoked, this did not mean that disciplinary action would necessarily follow. On the contrary, he went on, it was his intention to see if the matter could be resolved without recourse to formal action.

He then read out a statement from Lisa in which she alleged that I had fondled her breasts and kissed her. This, she stated, was clearly sexual harassment which, according to university regulations, was a grave offence and should result in dismissal. Pilkington then turned to Wanda.

"I am most perturbed by this situation," she announced. "As Dean, it is my responsibility to ensure that students are not subjected to irresponsible action on the part of staff." So, she said, she felt it necessary to sit in as the Head of Department's representative. Although she did not intend to contribute very much to the discussion, she wished to make notes of what was said.

I hoped that Penelope would respond, but she remained silent. I realized I would need to defend myself.

"So Harry," Pilkington began, "can you tell us what you think happened?"

This was all most embarrassing, but I tried to respond calmly. "Nothing happened," I said. "The whole thing is a pack of lies. She asked if she could see me about the course I am teaching. She wanted to get credit for it on the basis of a single essay she wrote at her previous university. Then she said, whatever that meant, that she would make it worth my while."

"What do you think she meant?" asked Wanda.

"I didn't know, and I didn't want to know. I told her I would read the essay and see her about it later. When I examined it, I realized that she had almost certainly copied it off the internet. So when I saw her again I told her she would have to fulfil the obligations of this university to get credit for the course, and I warned her of the dangers of plagiarism. She stamped out of the room slamming the door and that was the end of it. I in no way harassed her sexually. If anything, she harassed me."

"So it's not true that you kissed her and touched her breasts?" Pilkington asked.

"Certainly not!" I said

"Then why did she say she would make it worth your while?"

"I have no idea!"

"You don't think you encouraged her to think you were attracted to her?" Pilkington could be very persistent. I felt myself go red, but I was determined to give no quarter. "Certainly not!" I said again.

"So," Pilkington continued, "This whole thing is a complete fantasy on Miss Gold's part?"

"That," I said, "or a malicious lie!"

At this point Penelope interceded. "Look," she said. "I think my colleague has made it clear that he had no intention of trying to seduce this undergraduate. It's her word against his. And since there's no evidence one way or another, you'll have to leave it. Natural justice demands that Harry is deemed innocent of these charges. That is, unless the girl has got concrete evidence which demonstrates Harry's guilt."

Wanda made notes while Pilkington looked on as Penelope stressed my innocence. It all seemed so unfair. There was no substance to these damaging charges, and yet I was compelled to endure this ordeal. My truthfulness was being challenged. Both Pilkington and Bossyboots were junior colleagues. I was senior to them in the university hierarchy. This seemed to make no difference. They sat in judgment because they were my line managers. Penelope was right. There was simply no proof to support Lisa's claim. Without witnesses, she would fail. But it was unpleasant and I felt that I should not have to endure it. After all I was Professor of Christian Ethics and a clergyman. Presumably I had some integrity.

When Penelope finished, Pilkington put his papers into his briefcase and adjourned the meeting. Before we left, he announced that he would discuss the matter with the Vice-Chancellor and report back to me in the next few days. He stressed the confidentially of our discussion. He and Wanda remained behind; Penelope and I walked to the Senior Common Room for coffee.

"What do you think?" I asked.

"It was OK. I think they got the point that there is no evidence to support your student's claim. There is the unfortunate aspect of her propositioning you. I wonder if you should have left that bit out."

"But she did try to make a pass at me."

"'I know. But they wouldn't know. You could have simply said she made the whole thing up. I know you're an expert on morality. You probably don't think you should tell lies. But sometimes it's necessary. After all, no one saw anything. You're a senior member of the university and they'd be more likely to believe you than a second year undergraduate. My point is that it would have looked better."

Standing outside the Old College, Penelope took out a packet of cigarettes and her lighter. "Got to have a smoke before we go in," she said. "Damn university won't let anyone smoke inside. The entire place is littered with these 'No Smoking' notices. Want one?"

"No thanks," I said. "You're sure it's going to be OK?" I asked.

"Don't worry about it," she said. "You'll be all right. Barraclough knows the rules. He won't want a strike on his hands. And he hates bad publicity. But, I have to tell you Harry, I feel instinctively that the Dean and your department head have got it in for you. If I were you, I'd look out."

Magnus was in his usual place drinking coffee and reading *The Times*. I ordered coffee and a blueberry muffin and joined him. "Well, how did it go?" he asked.

"Could have been worse," I said. "I probably shouldn't have mentioned that she propositioned me."

Magnus looked amused. "How did Wanda take that?"

"Not well, I thought. Pilkington was very inquisitorial..."

"He must have loved it."

"Penelope was silent until the end. But then she told them there was no substance to the case, no evidence. I think they got the point. She thinks both Bossyboots and Pilkington have some kind of grudge against me. Do you think she's right?"

"Of course she is. You're a professor. They know you've got a private income. Your room is full of antiques. You live in a country house. You're married to a baronet's daughter. Come on, Harry, be realistic."

"This makes a difference?"

Magnus shook his head. "Pilks lives in a suburban bungalow with his dowdy wife. Bossyboots never married. What do you expect?"

"Are you sure, Magnus? Victoria always tries to be nice to them."

"You may be an expert on ethics," he said, "but you really don't know anything about people."

The next evening I went to the Acropolis, my club in London. My father had persuaded some friends to propose me while I was still a young lecturer. The price of the subscription was monstrous, but, as I tried to justify it to Victoria, she belonged to the Women's Institute and it was my only real extravagance.

I was there to attend the monthly meeting of a small discussion group. The members all belonged to the club and we gathered together first for dinner and then went up to the library where one of us read a paper. That evening the topic was: Astrophysics and the Beginning of the Universe. Most of those who belonged to this venerable group were retired; I was one of the younger members. The speaker, Sir Robert Manson, was the Emeritus Professor of Astronomy at Oxford who had won the Nobel Prize over twenty years ago. After about thirty minutes most were asleep – some snored loudly. By the end I was the only one awake. After our meeting, I went to the drawing room with the Bishop of Bosworth who also belonged to the group. More than thirty years ago we had been postgraduate students together. I had never expected him to rise to such a lofty position in the Church – at Cambridge we had rowed in the same boat, and he had been a jolly, beer-drinking sportsman.

"Charles," I said, as we sat down in green leather armchairs, "I've got a problem."

"What about a drink?" he asked.

"Not for me," I said. "But go ahead."

Charles walked over to the bar and ordered a double whiskey. He returned carrying a dish of olives. "This is rather embarrassing," I said. "I've been accused of sexual harassment by a student..."

"Oh dear," he said.

"Well, it is bad. But there's nothing to it. One of my students propositioned me and I ignored her."

"Dear, oh dear," Charles said, shaking his head. "It could happen to any of us."

"Anyway, she said I kissed her and tried to fondle her breasts. It's a complete lie, but of course the university had to have an inquisition about it."

"And what happened?"

"Well, it's my word against hers, so there's nothing they can do, but I'm really upset by it."

"And this happened while other people were looking on?"

"Don't be ridiculous. It was in my office. No one was there except us."

"Not even the cleaner?"

"No, Charles. Please be serious. I've had a meeting with the Dean and my Head of Department. They want to investigate."

"Nothing to worry about there," Charles said as he ate his olives. "Similar thing happened to me once. I was a curate. One of my parishioners did much the same. She said she needed pastoral help. Actually what she wanted was an affair. I told her no. She was furious and went to the Bishop. There was an official interview. But there wasn't any proof. So the whole thing was dropped. But I did get a warning: the Bishop told me never to interview a woman on my own. Rather good advice. I've always followed it."

"So you don't think anything will happen?"

"Not in the end... I say, George," Charles called out to the waiter who was hovering nearby, "can I have another one of these? Sure you won't join me?" he asked. "That talk rather stultified the brain. I've got a meeting of the Mothers' Union tomorrow, and I've got to have a clear head."

On the way home from London, I sat near two students from St Sebastian's – they were wearing university scarves. One had curly brown hair and wore an earring in her nose. The other had a shaved head with about four silver earrings in one ear. I had never seen them before, and they didn't pay any attention to me. They were slightly drunk and were shrieking about something that had happened to one of the new students. I was curious to hear what they were saying. "So she took off her sweater," the brunette exclaimed, "and he

26

just stood there. But then he jumped on her and grabbed her tits."

They roared with laughter. Could they be talking about Lisa and me? This was horrifying. "Anyway," she continued, "this old guy tried to seduce her, and she complained to the Student Union President. So there's going to be some kind of trial." I got up from my seat, went to another carriage, and opened *The Spectator*. I couldn't concentrate. Clearly news of this disaster had circulated amongst the undergraduates. Perhaps my students had already heard.

The next morning I received a summons from Pilkington, inviting me to come to his office. I phoned Penelope to ask if she could come as well, but she wasn't in. When I arrived, Pilkington was already behind his desk; Wanda arrived several minutes later looking flustered. We both sat in armchairs as Pilkington began. He was more informally dressed than at the previous meeting on Monday: he was wearing a grey sports jacket and a red tie with green spots. Wanda took paper out of her handbag and began making notes.

"I've just been with the Vice-Chancellor," Pilkington began, "and we have come to the view that it is best if this student complaint goes no further. There is no evidence, and it's simply your word against hers." I sighed. Magnus and Penelope were right. This was a relief. "But," Pilkington went on, "we're very perturbed by the situation. It's vitally important that students are happy here, and student complaints like this are harmful."

"But," I interjected, "I didn't do anything wrong . . ."

"That's not the point, Harry," Pilkington interrupted. "Accusations like this get around, and it does no one any good. The VC was adamant about this. We must be careful not to alienate student opinion. I understand he has been on the phone several times with the Student Union President; he has had to reassure him that this allegation will be investigated properly. Students are now asked to fill out Student Satisfaction Surveys, and this case may do us a lot of harm. The *Times Higher Educational Supplement* is going to rank universities on the basis of student satisfaction, and we want to do as well as we can."

"Look, Harry," Wanda said, her Northern accent was very pronounced. "As Dean I want to protect all the departments

27

from any kind of criticism. We've all got to be careful. In the future, you should make sure that you don't see any female undergraduate or postgraduate on her own. Take someone with you. Take John if you need to. But don't do this alone. We can't afford to have another incident like this."

"And, Harry," Pilkington broke in, "we don't want any more formal complaints. Be careful in the future..."

"Speaking of the future," Wanda interrupted, "can I ask you about the letter that the VC sent all staff over fifty-five. You did get it, didn't you?"

"You mean the one about early retirement?" I replied. "I did. But I threw it away. It's simply out of the question."

"Are you sure?" Wanda inquired. "Of course we don't want you to leave. But, it's important that younger members of the department have opportunities to take on senior roles. Are you sure?"

"I'm sure, Wanda. I don't want to retire. I'm far too young. I like my job, and I plan to stay at least until the official retirement age."

Wanda looked unconvinced. "There's a lot you could do without university responsibilities," she said. "You'd have time to do research without teaching and you could avoid administrative duties – though you seem to be good at that anyway. You and Victoria could travel. You should think about it."

"I have. But I'm not ready to go," I said. The meeting had come to a close, and I stood up to leave.

"Well, Harry," Pilkington said, "let's get back to work." I wandered out of the Head of Department's office in a confused state. At least the ordeal was over quickly. Lisa was not going to be a problem. Rumours would die down and life would continue. But I did have a sinking feeling about this last meeting. Had they agreed with the VC that I should go? Had this issue become a means of getting rid of me? As a senior professor, I was one of the most costly members of staff. I earned more than any one else in the department. My leaving would be a major saving, and the money could be used for other purposes.

When I got back to my office, I phoned Penelope to tell her about the meeting. She listened patiently, but cut in when I told her about Pilkington's and Wanda's comments about

28

early retirement. "This isn't good," she declared. "They're not supposed to mention anything like this in the context of a disciplinary matter. The union doesn't like it. We've never agreed to anything like this. Anyway, keep me informed."

When I put the phone down, I heard a knock on my door. It was Magnus carrying more shopping. "Has anything happened yet?" he asked.

"It won't go any further. I've just come back from seeing Pilkington. There isn't enough proof."

"That's what I told you," he said, as he slumped into my wing armchair. "Shall we celebrate?" He took two cans of Budweiser beer out of his bags and a chocolate sponge cake. "Got this at the Farmers' Market cake sale in town," he announced. He took a pen out of his top pocket, attempted to cut the cake with it dropping crumbs on my carpet in the process and handed me a piece.

"Thanks Magnus," I said, getting out a couple of glasses. "This is very good of you."

"Don't mention it. I didn't have breakfast, and this is my favourite," he said, as he stuffed cake into his mouth. "Most delicious!"

CHAPTER THREE

It Sounds Like a Conspiracy to Me

I was relieved to see that Lisa had disappeared from my first year course on ethics. To my amazement, however, it appeared that a great many students from other departments had switched courses and were now enrolled in my class. There were even postgraduate students who asked if they could audit the course. Overnight the group was so large that another lecture room had to be found. Instead of being the target of suspicion, I had suddenly become a curiosity. Women students far outnumbered the men. When I told Victoria, she was amused.

"The Don Juan of the Theology Department!" she mocked.

"This isn't funny," I said. "Pilks and Bossyboots were horrid. They told me I had to be careful. They had even discussed the matter with the Vice-Chancellor. Really, Victoria, you've got to be more serious."

"Well," she said, "you must admit it is ironic. You're charged with sexual harassment. As a result, women are lining up to get a glimpse of the St Sebastian's stud."

"This is no joke," I said.

"Come on Harry, Lisa's done you a favour. The students have always liked you, but this is the icing on the cake."

While the students gossiped about Lisa's allegation, St Sebastian's staff were preoccupied by the introduction of a new pay scale. Several years previously it was agreed by the unions and university management throughout Britain that academics would be shifted to a new pay structure based on roles within the institution. Each university was free to devise its own scheme, but it had to conform to national standards.

Wanda sent out a note to everyone requesting that they attend a meeting where this would be discussed. Magnus and I joined over a hundred staff assembled in the Great Hall to listen to a talk by the Director of Personnel. Julie Hummer was a beaky, large woman with curly grey hair; she wore an eau-de-nil two piece suit with a cream blouse. Throughout a complex PowerPoint presentation, she explained how it would work. In essence, we were all to be transferred from the previous, age-based pay scale to a new scale based on responsibilities.

Afterwards Magnus accompanied me back to my room. "That was about the stupidest thing I ever heard," he complained.

"The PowerPoint presentation was rather good," I objected.

"Look, Harry. The whole idea is ludicrous – people being paid for what they actually do... You must be joking!"

"Well," I said, "there is a logic to it."

"But it's impossible to implement. Senior staff dump all the awful jobs on lecturers. They're the ones who do all the work. The whole system's based on exploitation."

"But, Magnus," I said, "you don't do any administration. You've refused for years."

"That's why I never get promoted," he sulked.

"But, don't you see? It's a vicious cycle. You won't take on administrative roles because you think professors or readers or senior lecturers should do the work. And so, you don't get promoted because only those who put up with the drudgery do. Then, when they get the senior positions, they promptly give up all administration. The new system does seem a bit fairer."

I handed Magnus a cup of coffee and a chocolate digestive biscuit.

"Well," he said, "things may not be exactly looking up for you with this new system."

"Oh?" I said.

"Julie said salaries would be based on roles. But you're not Dean or Head of Department. So, they might conclude that you don't earn your professorial salary. And they'll either make you Dean or Head, or reduce your pay packet."

"Do you think they might?" This aspect of the matter had not occurred to me.

"With Barraclough," Magnus mused, "anything is possible."

The next day I had a phone call from a Rabbi Wally Wachman whom I had met at a conference of the Council of Christians and Jews in London a year previously. I did not know him well, so I was surprised by his call. He was the senior rabbi at the largest synagogue in Finchley. A graduate of London University, he later gained a PhD from Manchester in medieval Jewish philosophy. I had a vague recollection of him as a stout jolly person with a flowing grey beard. His PhD had been in Maimonidean ethics, and he had given a paper about medical issues.

"You may not remember me," the rabbi said, as he introduced himself on the phone, "We spoke a year ago at a CCJ Conference in London. I gave a very dull paper on Maimonides and you asked a very sensible question."

"Of course I remember. It was a most interesting paper," I said. "How are you, Wally?"

"I don't want to interrupt you, but I thought I should get in touch. The Golds are members of my congregation," he explained. "And they have come to see me about their daughter Lisa, who is one of your students."

I had a sinking feeling. He went on. "They told me that their daughter Lisa has had some trouble at your university."

"Trouble of her own making. I'm afraid she told a pack of lies about me," I said.

"Oh dear! Anyway, I'm sure you are distressed about it. The point is that something similar happened here several years ago at the synagogue. It didn't involve me. It was my assistant,

Rabbi Fine, who had the problem. Lisa was in his confirmation class. She had misbehaved and Fine talked to her afterwards. Apparently they had a most disagreeable conversation about her attitude. She is not what I would describe as an industrious student. But then – and this is why I called you – she accused him of trying to seduce her. Of course, there were no grounds for this accusation. Rabbi Fine is a most moral and upright chap. He's married with three children. But when Lisa complained, I had to listen. The president of the congregation, who is a close business associate of the Golds, intervened, and Rabbi Fine was dismissed. Mercifully, I managed to get him a job in Florida where he has rather a good congregation. Even though I am sure he was innocent, the president insisted he had to go."

"But surely there are employment laws?" I said.

"Yes. But if he had stayed, we would have lost the Golds, and in any case rumours get around. No smoke without fire. That sort of thing. Fine would never have got another job in the British Jewish community. The Golds are big donors – though I have to say they tend to promise more than they deliver. At that stage they had pledged a sizeable contribution to the building fund. The president had to take action, otherwise we would have lost the money. We're in the middle of a big building programme, and we are dependent on the goodwill of individual donors. It isn't always easy and, alas, sometimes principles go out of the window."

"Thank goodness universities aren't like that."

"Oh," he said. "I thought they were going the same way. Well, I felt you might want to know. Lisa's no doubt got you into trouble."

"Well, frankly she has. But I think it's all right. I've been told that it was my word against hers, and I do have tenure. But, it's terrible about your assistant. How has he taken it?"

"He's done very well. They're lucky to have him. But he did have to start again in the States. I hear from him occasionally. I understand he's now doing his own radio programme, and is taking a course in psychological counselling. But the point is, I didn't want you to feel bad about your difficulties with Lisa. I thought knowing about Rabbi Fine might help."

"Wally...Can I ask a favour? You wouldn't be willing to testify to all this, in case there are problems?"

There was a long pause. "Can't really," he replied. "The Golds would be furious if they knew I was telling you this, and my job would be on the line if I put it in writing. I hope you'll understand."

The call ended with mutual expressions of esteem. Later in the afternoon, I went to the library. On the way in I ran into the Registrar, Dr Robert Sloth, and his wife. After finishing a PhD on John Galsworthy at Goldsmiths' College, London, he joined the Registry at the University of Southampton, where he met and married his wife, Jenny, who was working in the library. Dr Sloth had a large office next door to the Vice-Chancellor and reputedly spent every afternoon asleep on a sofa. He always snored at university meetings except when he was in the chair. He was clutching a stack of books. I waved. He smiled. I glanced at the titles as he passed. One of the books had a photograph of a university on the cover: it was entitled *Risk Management in Higher Education*.

It was my turn to take chapel services for the week. Since Barraclough had ruled that the university could no longer afford a full-time chaplain, the chapel services were conducted by a rota of part-timers. Magnus and I met up for a drink before Evensong. I told him about my encounter with the Registrar.

"Risk management is the new buzz word," Magnus announced. "I read about it in the *Times Higher* last week." I had a vague recollection of the article, but I had skipped over it to look at the reviews, just in case someone had written about my last book.

"'Universities can't be too careful," Magnus said. "But you can be sure Sloth will never understand it. He's incapable of finishing anything he starts. How big was the book?"

"Looked quite thick," I said.

"Well...Sloth by name and sloth by nature. He really should get some sort of concession for procrastination," Magnus announced. "Didn't his doctor say he had some kind of disease?"

"Narcolepsy," I said.

"Oh. I thought it was necrophilia," Magnus smiled.

For the rest of the week there was no mention of Lisa. However, the following Tuesday there was an official envelope marked Private and Confidential in my pigeonhole. It was from the Vice-Chancellor. I was summoned to a meeting later in the day in his office. He said that Robert Sloth would be accompanying him. I immediately phoned his secretary to ask what it was about. She said she didn't know. I asked if I should bring a union representative. She wasn't sure but would check. Before lunch I received an email from Barraclough stating that it would be an informal meeting, and therefore there was no need to bring someone from the union. But he didn't say what it was about. To be on the safe side, I phoned Penelope. She told me not to worry, but if anything emerged that concerned the union I should phone back.

At two o'clock I knocked on the Vice-Chancellor's door. He was sitting at his large mahogany desk; the Registrar was in a leather armchair opposite. Barraclough's office was located on the floor above the chapel overlooking the cathedral. The room had been freshly painted a sickly pale green and there were acres of emerald green carpet on the floor. In the corner of the room was a Victorian long-case clock. There was a highly polished reproduction Sheraton dining table in the corner surrounded by dining chairs – this was used for official meetings as well as interviews of candidates for jobs. Over ten years ago I had been interviewed here for the Chair of Christian Ethics. Without standing, he gestured that I should sit next to the Registrar. He was holding a letter in his hand.

"Harry," the VC began, "I just had this letter from the father of one of your students: Lisa Gold." The Registrar sighed. He looked as if he was about to go to sleep. "I have heard about this matter from Wanda," Barraclough continued, "and I know what happened. I understand this girl's allegation has been dealt with . . ."

"Look," I interrupted, "I'm sorry. But Lisa is deranged. I understand from her rabbi that she's done this before."

Barraclough looked puzzled. "You've spoken to her rabbi?" he asked.

"He phoned me. But the point is – I'm completely innocent."

"That's neither here nor there. I want you to hear what her father has written to me." He read it aloud.

"Dear Vice-Chancellor,

I have just had a most distressing conversation with my daughter, Lisa, who is a student at your university. You may know that she transferred this year from London where she was not particularly happy. She was anxious to live in a small campus community where she would receive individual attention. However, it appears that she has had a very unpleasant encounter with one of your teachers. She tells me that this person, Professor Gilbert, tried to seduce her in his office. She says that he molested her. I am very shocked about this, and I expect the university to conduct a thorough investigation. This is all most distressing because I had intended to make a sizeable gift to the university on Lisa's graduation in memory of my dear mother. I know Lisa's grandmother would have been very proud of her granddaughter if she had been alive. But, after hearing how students are treated in your university, I have regrettably decided that this might not be the best way to remember Mother.

Yours sincerely,

Freddy Gold, MBE

Gold and Gold Manufacturers."

Sloth shook his head. "We could have done with the money."

"So, Harry, you see what we are facing. The loss of a substantial donation," continued the VC.

"But..." I stammered.

"Now, Harry," Barraclough was not going to let the matter go, "there is no question of taking action here. But I do want to discuss the letter I sent you some time ago about early retirement. I have had no reply. Are you sure this is something you wouldn't like to consider? You are reaching retirement age, and we could make you a good offer."

"'Look," I said. "I'm sixty, and that gives me five more years. As a matter of fact, the government is considering abolishing retirement age altogether because of the European Directive outlawing age discrimination. So I might be able to continue after sixty-five. I have no intention of leaving at present."

The Registrar sighed again. Undeterred, the VC went on: "No one denies you have done a great deal for the university in the time you've been here. We are all most grateful for your contribution. But most academics retire by the age of sixty-two. Are you sure you wouldn't like to have more free time, liberated from teaching and marking essays?"

"I like it here," I said indignantly.

"Good. I'm glad you do. I'm not suggesting you leave us altogether. I'm simply indicating a change in contract might be beneficial to everyone. Part-time teaching. You could keep your room..."

"Vice-Chancellor," I said, "I'm not interested. There's no reason I should go just because some over-indulgent father is offering a bribe to get rid of me."

The Registrar looked up. He had been doing some calculations on his pocket calculator. "Do we know what kind of manufacturing Mr Gold is involved in?" he asked.

"I understand he is in the corsetry business," the VC said. "His company is the biggest bra manufacturer in Europe."

When I got back to my office, I phoned Magnus and told him what had happened. "The bra business," he chortled. "That's even worse than your Pa with his frozen fish fingers."

"My father was an importer of high class comestibles," I said with some dignity. "At one stage he was the sole supplier of black caviar into this country. He inherited the business from my grandfather who had a licence from the Romanovs themselves."

Magnus was not interested, "And you told the VC you aren't planning to retire. Well, well. Perhaps the administration's sagging spirits could be lifted by a visit to Mr Gold's factory."

Later in the afternoon I phoned Penelope to tell her about my discussion with Barraclough and Sloth. She was appalled. "You mean they actually suggested you take early retirement because this girl's father offered to give the university a donation?"

"The VC didn't put it quite so baldly," I said. "But that was the gist. The Registrar simply sighed every time Barraclough mentioned the loss of money. But this Gold character didn't actually promise he would make a contribution. He simply said he didn't think he would in light of his daughter's allegation."

"That's blackmail."

"It's certainly a threat with menaces. I guess that's what blackmail is."

"And the VC fell for it?"

"He did."

Penelope groaned. "What's the university come to?" she asked. "This simply won't do. I'd better contact our regional union rep to tell him about this."

"Will it do any good?"

"Possibly not. But I'm duty bound to keep him informed. By the way," she asked, "what does Lisa's father do for a living?"

"He's a bra manufacturer. Actually, according to the VC, the biggest in Europe."

Penelope giggled. "No kidding! Well, that's a switch. I wonder if business is holding up."

"Very funny, Penelope," I said. "First it's Magnus; now it's you making jokes. Don't you see it's all very distressing...."

"Of course it is. Sorry, Harry. But you've got to admit, this is rather amusing: a bra manufacturer with a busty daughter who accuses the Professor of Christian Ethics of making a pass at her. Wait until I tell the committee."

"Do you have to?" I asked.

"Not if you don't want me to. But, the thing is, Harry, if we are to confront university management, we've got to have a clear case of misconduct. It seems to me that you've got one. Barraclough can't go around suggesting to professors that they give up their jobs just because some stupid undergraduate makes damaging, unfounded charges about her teachers. It's a question of fairness. The union has got to stand up to management. Let me speak to our regional rep, Morris O'Murphy. He doesn't care what he says to people."

Over the weekend Victoria and I went to London. My father-in-law had come down from Wales to attend an old regimental dinner at his club. We stayed at the Acropolis, and the next day he took me to lunch while Victoria went shopping at Peter Jones. The Burlington Club was located near Sloane Square in a small Victorian building with pillars at the entrance. When I arrived, Sir William was standing in the hallway talking to an upright white-haired gentleman wearing a red carnation in his button-hole. As we climbed the stairs to the dining room, he told me about the dinner the night before. "Glorious food," he announced. "I hope lunch won't disappoint." We sat at a table overlooking Sloane Street.

"So," he asked, "how's the RIP going?"

"No, William, it's not RIP, it's RAE."

As the waiter took our orders, I explained that we hadn't yet been told the criteria against which publications would be measured. He looked confused. "What do you mean they haven't told you how all that stuff will be evaluated?"

"Well, they just haven't," I said. "I know it's stupid."

"And when is the judging going to take place?" he asked. He spoke of it as if it were some kind of agricultural show.

"In about two years' time. But it can include anything published in the last five years."

Sir William looked out the window for about a minute without speaking. "By Jove," he eventually blurted out, "it's just like the Caucus Race!"

"The Caucus Race?"

"In *Alice in Wonderland*," he said. "There was no fixed course. Everyone ran in whatever direction they liked. And they went on running until the Dodo said, 'Stop!' Then the question arose, who won? The Dodo declared: 'Everyone has won, and all must have prizes.' Your RAE seems to work in exactly the same way. I hope the judges are equally generous!"

I was amused, "If I remember rightly everyone got a sugar comfit from Alice's pocket and Alice's prize was her own thimble!"

At that point the wine waiter arrived with a bottle of claret and poured some into Sir William's glass. "So," he said, as he tasted the wine, "everyone must have prizes! Why don't you tell whoever is in charge that's the only solution?"

I heard no more from the Vice-Chancellor about Mr Gold; it appeared that the issue of Lisa's complaint had been dropped. Lisa did not reappear in my class, which had nearly tripled in size. I ordered more copies of my textbook for the library, and informed the University bookshop that they should stock my book as well. However, after several days a number of students complained that the books had not arrived in the library. I checked the library holdings. They were right: there were only four copies, and all had been checked out. I wrote a note to Jenny Sloth, the Registrar's wife, who was in charge of ordering books at St Sebastian's. A couple of weeks later one of my students came up after class. "Professor," he said, "there's still only four copies of your book in the library."

I did a library search on my computer. He was correct. I then sent an email to Jenny asking if the books had been ordered. I asked her to email me back. There was silence. I sent her another email. Again silence. Yet again students complained about the situation. I sent another email. There was no response. In desperation, I wrote Jenny a letter. I emphasized that I had contacted her several times and that she had failed to respond. Although the book was available in the bookshop, I didn't want students to feel they had to buy it. It was her job, I stated, to ensure that orders were filled promptly. The situation, I concluded, was becoming intolerable.

The next day I saw Pilkington in the departmental office collecting his post. He looked grave when he saw me. "Harry," he said, "are you free to come up to my room?" We walked up the stairs in silence. This was ominous. I wondered if Mr Gold was continuing his campaign. Pilkington hung up his coat on the back of his door. He sat down at his desk and gestured that I should sit opposite. He took a letter out of a folder on his desk and handed it to me. "I got this yesterday," he said. It read:

Dear Dr Pilkington,

I have had a most upsetting letter from Professor Harry Gilbert. As you know, the library has been extremely busy. We have just completed a major recataloguing of the books which took over three months of labour. The reading room was painted over the summer, and we had to remove all the books in the reference section. It is only now that we have been able to put them back on shelves. Five library staff were on leave for the summer, so we have had a particularly hectic time. Several weeks before the beginning of term, we ordered books for the new students. As you know, academic staff were asked over the summer if they would supply us with details of what would be needed.

I had a recent request from Professor Gilbert to order copies of his introductory textbook on ethics. This order should have been sent in months ago when we sent out order forms to each teacher. Since I received his order, he has been sending me continual emails demanding a response. As I said, all the librarians are extremely busy at this time of the year, and we cannot be expected to jump to attention whenever an academic sends in an order, particularly when it is late. I regard his behaviour in this matter as both irritating and insensitive. Such an attitude is particularly unwelcome from someone who professes to be an expert on Christian ethics. When I received the enclosed letter, I was upset for nearly two hours. Professor Gilbert must understand that he cannot treat staff in such a fashion. Therefore I would like to make a formal complaint to you as his line manager.

Yours sincerely,

Jenny Sloth

"I don't understand what's going on, Harry," Pilkington said. "First it's a student. Now, an assistant librarian. And she is the wife of the Registrar. The VC's bound to hear about this."

"This is ridiculous, John," I replied. "My student enrolment tripled in the first week of term, and I had to order more books for my class. It's Jenny's job to get them. I'm sure she's very busy. But so am I. So is everybody. What was I supposed to do? The students were beginning to get upset. After all, you yourself are always talking about the importance of student satisfaction."

"That's as may be," said Pilkington magisterially, "but it doesn't alter Jenny's feelings. I cannot understand why you can't be more tactful."

"There's nothing to be tactful about. The books didn't arrive, and that's that. Jenny should have ordered them. That's her responsibility. I can't order them."

"Well, whatever the case, I now have to deal with this matter as a grievance. This morning I looked up the statutes. Staff grievances are dealt with under Provision 14. There will have to be a preliminary informal meeting, and you can bring a representative."

Once again, discipline was being invoked. Would this ever stop?

Later in the afternoon I phoned Penelope to tell her about Jenny's letter. She was in the middle of a tutorial and told me to ring later. When I eventually reached her, she was rushing off to a lecture. "Look," I said. "This is urgent. Can you come to see me when you finish? I've had a disturbing letter from Jenny Sloth."

"The Registrar's wife?"

I explained briefly that she was making a formal complaint. "I'll show you the letter when you come," I said.

At a quarter past four, Penelope knocked on my door. She was carrying a bright purple bag full of books and student essays. She sat on my sofa looking exhausted. "Would you like some coffee?" I asked.

She looked at my decanter. "I think I'd really like some of what's in that," she said.

I poured her a large glass of sherry. "So," she said, "what's this about the letter?"

I showed it to her. She sipped her sherry and looked perturbed. "Bloody hell," she muttered. "This is ridiculous. There's nothing here. You asked her to order books for your students, and she's making a formal complaint. Everyone knows the woman's a lazy cow. But what do you expect, married to that dozy imbecile?"

"So, you think there's nothing to worry about?"

Penelope hesitated. "There shouldn't be. But she is the Registrar's wife. Sloth knows about the affair with the student and that girl's father. Jenny must also know that Lisa's father had planned to give the university some kind of donation."

"Do you think this is a conspiracy?"

Penelope took a mobile phone out of her bag. "I think I'd better check with the regional officer," she said. She dialled his number and left a message for him to ring her back. Picking up her bag of books, she walked to the door. "I'll get back to you as soon as I hear from Morris," she said looking over her shoulder. "I'll send you an email. Don't worry too much. You've got the union on your side."

After she left, I phoned Magnus. "You won't believe this," I said.

"The girl has reappeared?"

"No, it's worse. Sloth's wife is now complaining about a book order. I had a meeting with Pilkington."

"Sloth's wife? You mean that little rodent who works in the library. I've had a run in with her before."

"Well, she's written a formal complaint."

"I'll be straight over," he said.

As the cathedral bell struck five, Magnus knocked on my door. He was wearing ear muffs and a large scarf wrapped around his duffle coat. His nose was bright red. "I've got an awful cold," he sniffled as he sat on the sofa. He picked up Penelope's empty glass and looked at it. "I see you've had a visitor."

"Penelope – the union president," I said.

"Isn't she involved in some campaign about gay rights? I've seen some startling posters on her door."

"I think so. But you'd better read this," I said, handing him Jenny's letter.

"Can't concentrate without a drink. Can I have a new glass?"

Magnus shook his head as he read the letter. "Incredible. She's too busy to order books! How long does it take, for heaven's sake? This doesn't look right."

43

"No?"

"No doubt Sloth has something to do with this. He knows about Lisa's father. Probably you're being ganged up on by the VC and the Registrar. Maybe Sloth got his wife to write the letter. Looks like a conspiracy to me."

"I did wonder."

"Well, no doubt she's offended. Must hate criticism. And she knows her husband will defend her." Magnus scratched his head. "Maybe she's a bit deranged... but on the other hand, the VC does want you to take early retirement. They probably want to put you under pressure to leave."

"But I don't want to go. I like it here."

Magnus finished his sherry. I refilled his glass. "A tricky business," he ruminated. Then he looked up, "You may like it now," he said. "But you might not in a few months time."

CHAPTER FOUR

The Vice-Chancellor Looks Guilty

Over the weekend we had a large party in our house for over fifty friends and neighbours as well as some academics from the university. This was our annual 'at home', catered by a local firm. Victoria ordered invitations. I made arrangements with the caterer and purchased three cases of non-vintage champagne from the wine merchant. Normally the Vice-Chancellor, the Sloths, the Pilkingtons and Wanda came, but this year they all sent apologies. We rearranged the furniture so that we could put glasses and drink in the dining room, and have sufficient space in the drawing room. When the guests arrived they parked their cars down the drive. By six there was also a long line of cars along the country lane leading to our house.

Very quickly the house was full of people eating and drinking. Victoria and I took plates of canapés around; we were also busy introducing guests to one another. Our two cats hid under the bed upstairs, waiting for everyone to leave. Usually, Victoria and I enjoyed the evening, but this year I was less enthusiastic. With a formal complaint pending, I was in no mood for a celebration. After the last guest left, we washed the dishes, hoovered the rooms, and put rubbish bags at the end of the drive for collection.

"Why didn't the VC come?" Victoria asked. "He normally does, and gets rather drunk. It's the only time he ever seems to be human. And what about that dreary little Miss Catnip? I don't think she's ever missed before? What's going on?"

"I don't know," I replied. "It doesn't look good. Magnus thinks there's a conspiracy against me. Penelope from the union is suspicious too. She's consulting the regional officer."

"Oh God," Victoria said. "These academics – do they have nothing else to do?"

Eventually we collapsed in bed. I turned on the television. "Harry," Victoria said, "you aren't in very good spirits tonight."

"Do you think anyone could tell?" I asked.

"No. But I know you. Are you very bothered?"

"I suppose so."

"Look, Harry. You don't have to continue in this job if you don't want to. You inherited loads of money. Daddy won't live forever, and even though Billy will inherit the Castle, there's a trust for each one of us."

"I know," I said. "And I'll get a good pension. But I like my job; I've got friends at the university; I like my students; I enjoy teaching; I like doing research. Why should I give it all up, just because a student's father blackmails the university, and the wife of the Registrar is too lazy to do her job?"

"We could travel..." Victoria continued, "though I hate leaving the cats."

"We can travel anyway. There's nothing to do outside term except deal with graduate students. Where do you want to go?"

"I don't know, Harry. But we could go abroad if you retired."

We had recently purchased a satellite dish which enabled us to watch the channel which specialized in repeats of popular programmes. My favourite American detective offering, 'Homicide Life on the Street', had just started. This episode was about a college professor who had murdered one of his colleagues.

"I'll think about it," I said, as I turned up the volume.

46

"Do we have to watch this?" Victoria asked.

"Shhh," I said. "This is important – it's research. You never know when it might come in handy."

During the weekend I had an email from one of my postgraduates. Ronald Grundy was a third year PhD student who had previously been an undergraduate at the university. After he got his first, I had worked hard to make sure he had received an Arts and Humanities grant to work on the current Anglican debate about homosexuality. The present Archbishop of Cannonbury had been an undergraduate when I was a postgraduate at Cambridge and we had kept up contact. I bumped into him fairly regularly and we exchanged Christmas cards. When Ronald began his research, I had contacted the Archbishop and asked if they could have a session together. It was subsequently arranged that Ronald could use restricted archives.

Ronald said he wanted to see me to discuss his latest chapter. I emailed him back saying that I would be free on Monday morning at eleven o'clock. As I was driving into the parking lot on Monday, I saw Ronald talking to Wanda. They were in animated conversation standing on the steps of the Old College. When they saw me, Wanda headed off in the direction of the Vice-Chancellor's office. Ronald waited for me on the steps. He followed me to my room. I sat behind my desk and he spread out papers on the sofa. He showed me his notes, and asked for suggestions on how he should structure the chapter. After an hour's supervision, he left.

I then went to the Porter's Lodge to collect my post. There was a large envelope marked Private and Confidential. It was from Pilkington. He was summoning me to an informal meeting to discuss Jenny's letter, and he had enclosed the Grievance Procedure regulations. The meeting was to take place in a fortnight's time, and I had the right to bring a union representative. He explained that he would initially meet with Jenny. He concluded by saying that his intention was to sort out our differences informally. He hoped to avoid a formal procedure which could take several months.

I immediately phoned Penelope. I read her the letter. She said she would go to the meeting with Pilkington. But she suggested that I should get together with the regional union representative who was planning to visit the university at the end of the week for a discussion with the new pay-scale committee. She said she would try to arrange for me to see him at ten; the pay-scale meeting was to begin at eleven. Later in the day I got a message from the regional officer, Morris O'Murphy, who said he could see me at the arranged time.

On Friday morning, I arrived early. Victoria had baked a chocolate cake which I brought with me. I knew I shouldn't eat it, but I was having a bad time. I put on the kettle, assembled the letters I had received from Jenny and Pilkington, and waited for the regional officer to arrive. At 10:30 I heard a knock on my door. Morris O'Murphy was rotund and bespectacled. He had a red moustache and was wearing a turtle-neck sweater. In a strong Irish accent, he apologized for being late. "Bloody British Rail," he said. "Always lets one down. And then I couldn't get a taxi.'" He plopped down on my sofa. I handed him a cup of coffee and a large piece of cake. "Great!," he said as he put the whole lot in his mouth.

"My wife made it," I said. Morris slurped his coffee, and crumbs fell on his sweater. He eventually put the mug on the floor, pulled papers out of a tattered briefcase, took a large pen out of his pocket, and started to concentrate. "Ridiculous letter from Mrs Sloth!" he announced. "Can't see what she has to complain about. There's simply nothing here. No mention of bullying or harassment. Nothing."

"So you think I've got nothing to worry about?" I asked.

"Well..." he paused. "I understand from Penelope that she's the Registrar's wife. Always a bad idea to employ husband and wife in the same institution! Still can't be helped!"

"Does that make a difference?"

"It shouldn't, but it does, I'm afraid."

"That's not fair!"

"Who said things were fair?"

"Hell..."

Morris shook his head. "You see," he explained, "in most cases, it's simply a matter of power. This is a conflict between a professor and somebody who works in the library. Normally, the person in the library would be told to stop complaining. But, since she's the wife of the Registrar, this isn't going to happen. And Penelope tells me the VC may also be involved in this."

"It's possible," I said.

"Because of the case with the student and her father?"

"I'm afraid so."

"So, the situation is completely different. Management has more clout than professors. But," he went on firmly, "the union has more clout than management."

"It does?"

"Of course! No VC wants a strike or for the university to be black-listed by the union."

"There could be a strike?" I asked incredulously.

"Not really," Morris said with a grin, as he put his papers back in his briefcase. "But we can always threaten one. Anyway, keep me informed. Penelope will go with you to the meeting. Try not to worry. Sorry, but I've got to go to this pay-scale meeting. The VC's going to be there. He's terrified he might have to find more money."

"Maybe that's why he's so anxious to have early retirements," I said.

"Oh, yes, Penelope told me about that, too. Disgraceful! The union won't have offers of early retirement connected with discipline. The VC should know that. Look," he said as he stood up, "the union is here to help you." He fished in his pocket and took out a UCU lapel pin and pinned it on my jacket. "Just regard it as an amulet to ward off the evil eye," he smiled slyly, all Irish charm. "I don't suppose I could have another piece of that delicious cake before I go, could I?"

Since the surge in attendance at the beginning of term, my class had diminished in size. Some students dropped out, no doubt disappointed by the lack of scandal. Others were simply bored with the topic. Only occasionally did I see Lisa walking across campus. Invariably she looked in the other direction. Magnus and I continued to have lunch in the Senior Common Room; frequently Agnes sat with us, but this made it impossible to discuss the impending meeting with Pilkington.

On the day of the meeting, I arrived fifteen minutes early. I waited outside Pilkington's office above Wendy Morehouse's secretarial room. She was busy photocopying. I paced back and forth, rehearsing what I planned to say. Concerned that Penelope had forgotten, I phoned her on my mobile. She replied that she was sorry to be late, but that her cat had been sick over the hall carpet and she had had to clean it up. I knew all about her cat. His name was Rufus and he had come from the same breeder as Magnus's Pushkin. Pushkin was a fusspot and Rufus was famous for his hypochondria. His being sick was just what I needed.

I heard voices inside Pilkington's room and tried to listen in to what was being said. When the door opened, Jenny Sloth came out clutching a red leather briefcase. She was wearing a blue suit and high heels. She was followed by one of the library assistants. Both glared at me as they passed.

I heard footsteps and panting – Penelope was clutching a yellow and green file in one hand, and a cat basket in the other. "Got to take him to the vet," she announced. Pilkington looked startled as we entered. "Sorry," Penelope said. "cat's sick. I called the vet, and I've got to take him there after the meeting." I looked into the basket: Rufus stared back at me with his deep green eyes. I tried to stroke his nose, and he pointedly stood up and turned his back on me. This was not an auspicious start.

Penelope put her cat in the corner, where he growled. We sat around a table covered with papers. Pilkington picked up a folder, and took out a letter. "Well," he began, "I have spoken to Jenny and the matter is more serious than I first thought. As you know, the university regulations specify that all complaints must be dealt with informally. You should regard this as an informal discussion initially. What we need to ascertain first is why you sent this letter to Mrs Sloth. I understand you had already sent a series of emails to her about library books."

I explained that there had been an increase in the number of students attending my course, and I wanted to be able to supply them with textbooks. My book was written for the course, and the lectures were designed to explain their content. I emphasized that I knew an order form had already gone to the library over the summer, indicating how many books would be needed. But the increase in numbers had made it necessary to obtain more. I went on to describe the delays that had taken place as well as the students' impatience with the lack of books. I also pointed out that student satisfaction with an important issue for the university.

When I finished, Pilkington picked up his pen and pointed it at the library regulations. "It says here," he stated, "that all books should be ordered before the beginning of term." Penelope interrupted, stressing that circumstances had changed.

Pilkington took no notice of Penelope's comment, and pulled out a series of emails. "So you sent these emails?" he asked.

"Yes," I replied. "But only because no notice was taken of the request. The students were becoming increasingly agitated."

"But you did pursue Mrs Sloth...and repeatedly sent her emails...."

"What else could I do?" I asked.

"And then you sent her this inflammatory letter," he continued.

"Only because she would not respond to my emails."

"Really, Harry. You have shown little tact in the way you handled the entire matter. You must remember that you are a professor and Mrs Sloth is an assistant librarian. Your outburst was deeply threatening..."

"Threatening...?"

"Quite frankly, I think you were abusing your position as a professor in this university."

Penelope's cat had become increasingly distressed, and began meowing. He was trying to claw his way out of the cat basket and made wailing sounds. "I'm sorry, Penelope," Pilkington said crossly. "This is an important meeting, and you can't deposit your cat in my office if it continues to be uncontrolled."

"Could he go in your secretary's office?" she asked.

"I happen to know Wendy's allergic to cats," Pilkington said. "I'm afraid we'll have to postpone this meeting if he stays."

Penelope shook her head. "Well, John," she said. "I really am sorry, but I've got to take him to the vet at twelve o'clock. There's nowhere else for him to go."

Pilkington looked confused. Penelope's cat continued to wail. "The meeting will have to be adjourned," he announced standing up. "I simply can't concentrate with that wretched cat screaming."

51

Penelope got up, scooped up her papers and marched off with her cat. I followed behind. On the stairs she stopped. "I am sorry, Harry," she said as she turned around. "But that man is totally insensitive. Rufus isn't himself, and he's got to see the doctor." She stalked off, and I heard Pilkington's door slam.

Later in the day, I received an email from Pilkington asking that we resume the discussion without Penelope's cat. He suggested we meet on Friday at three o'clock. I phoned Penelope and left a message asking if she could come. She emailed me back, mentioning that Rufus had vomited up a hair ball and was now much better.

On Friday I met Penelope in my room before the meeting. She brought photographs of Rufus, since I had asked after his health. We walked across the campus to Pilkington's office. When Pilkington opened his door, he looked relieved when he saw there was no cat. I asked if he had any pets, and to our astonishment he replied that in his view the only reason to keep an animal was to eat it. Penelope thought this was a joke in bad taste. Pilkington, however, was serious. Citing Thomas Aquinas' opinion that animals lack souls, he maintained that animals were created only for the benefit of man. Penelope disagreed – loudly and vehemently. This was yet another inauspicious start to our meeting.

"Now that we are not being interrupted," Pilkington began, "I think we can address the issues raised by Jenny's letter."

"Look," I said. "It wasn't my intention to upset Jenny. I think she should have ordered books for my students. That's her job. But I don't want to make this a matter of principle. I'm quite willing to write an apology for upsetting her, although I think I will have to say that the books should have been ordered."

Pilkington looked troubled. "You must apologise," he said. "You were very tactless. I've talked this over with Wanda and the VC, and in our view we think you were misusing your position as a professor. But an apology is not enough. I'm afraid I am going to have to issue you with an oral warning." He opened the Staff Handbook which was lying on his desk. "This has been an informal meeting so far," he continued, "but given the gravity of the situation, I'm proceeding from Provision

52

14 (Grievance) to Provision 24 (Discipline). This states that an oral warning can be given in situations where there has been serious misconduct. As Head of Department I am empowered to issue such a warning as long as I've consulted the Dean and Vice-Chancellor. They both agree that this would be the correct action given the circumstances. Of course you have the right of appeal. But I would strongly urge you not to invoke it."

Penelope was outraged. "This is ridiculous," she said. "As an officer of the union, I must protest in the strongest terms. There is simply no reason for issuing an oral warning. The regional officer of the UCU will be very annoyed when he hears. Jenny Sloth should have ordered books for Harry's students. She didn't answer his request. He emailed her. This was quite proper. There was no response. So he emailed her again. And then he wrote her a letter. Throughout he has acted professionally. You would have been the first to criticize if he had ignored student complaints..."

"Well," Pilkington interrupted, "that's not the way the Dean and the Vice-Chancellor see it." He sat at his desk and frowned at us. "You can do as you wish," he said. "Don't think I take any pleasure in this matter. You should be relieved this isn't going to be a written warning. In any event, an oral warning lasts for a year and will be cancelled assuming there is no repetition of similar behaviour. I will confirm in writing that I have given you an oral warning. It takes effect immediately."

Penelope and I stood up and walked to the door. Enraged, Penelope complained all the way to my room. "The man's an idiot," she said. "He's nothing more than a little creep. And what about his attitude toward animals... he's a complete barbarian," she announced loudly. "Rufus should have bitten him when he had a chance."

Pilkington's letter arrived the following week. He informed me that I had been given an oral warning which was effective from the date of the meeting and would be in force for a full year. Any similar offence, Pilkington stated, would be regarded with the utmost seriousness. He went on to emphasize that both the Dean and the VC had been consulted and had authorized this action. He concluded by saying that I had the right to appeal against his decision – if I did wish to do so, I should write directly to the Registrar.

I phoned Magnus and asked him to meet me for tea in the Senior Common Room. When I arrived, there was a table in the corner. I put my coat on a chair and ordered lemon tea for us both plus two toasted teacakes each. I felt guilty about the tea cakes, but I thought they might cheer us up. The SCR was empty except for two Law lecturers who were poring over papers spread out on their table. When I read the letter to Magnus, he groaned. "They fixed it up," he said. "They've decided you've got to go. No doubt about it. Are you sure you don't want to take a retirement deal?"

"But this is entirely unfair," I replied. "I spoke to Penelope earlier today. She said I should appeal against Pilkington. She tells me that the Appeal Committee is chaired by the Vice-Chancellor and two other members drawn from Senate. What-ever I finally decide," I declared, "I'm going to clear my name."

Magnus slumped in his chair and ate his tea cakes. They were sticky with butter which dribbled on to his Harris tweed jacket. "Delicious," he mumbled. Wiping butter from his chin, he spread open *The Times*. "Look here," he said gazing at the obituaries, "the Regius Professor of Theology at St Patricks has just died. He was only fifty-nine. He was at my college at Oxford. Biggest crawler in my year. How he became Regius Professor, God only knows!"

"Didn't he write a book about divine omniscience?" I asked.

"It was his PhD thesis."

"So he must have known that God would know!" I said brightly.

"The only thing that chap knew about was how to play his cards right. Regius Professor! He only wrote one book, for Christ's sake."

"Magnus, you've got to concentrate on the matter in hand. What am I supposed to do?"

Magnus flicked through *The Times*. "There's only one thing to do," he said. "Wait and see."

Victoria and I had planned to go to London on Sunday; she had a commission to write a review of the Chelsea Antiques Fair for

Country Life magazine. Over the last few years she had written a regular column about antiques for the *St Sebastian Gazette*, and had recently published several articles for *The Times*. This was her first publication in a glossy magazine. We arranged to stay at the Acropolis on Saturday night and have lunch at the fair. Our room at the club was spartan, not unlike my schoolboy room at Shrewsbury.

We had dinner in the coffee room and coffee afterwards in the drawing room. We sat on a green leather sofa near the door. Victoria was reading the magazines and I was enjoying myself looking up my own entry in the latest *Who's Who*. Suddenly I heard a familiar voice. It was Barraclough who was with a group of elderly men. As he passed, he greeted us briefly.

"Looks rather guilty, don't you think?" Victoria commented.

"More than a bit," I said.

"Who are those men?"

"I've never seen them before. Perhaps they're fellow Vice-Chancellors."

Barraclough and the others had assembled by the drinks table. They were joined by several churchmen, including the Provost of St Sebastian's Cathedral. Barraclough and the Provost were speaking animatedly, but I couldn't hear what they were saying. "Harry," Victoria said, holding up her magazine, "look at this house." It was a Georgian cottage in the Cotswolds. "Don't you think it's lovely?"

"Victoria," I said, "I don't want to move. Please."

"Just thought you might be interested, that's all."

Gloomily I looked over at Barraclough and the others who had seated themselves near the library. "I wonder what the Provost and the VC are talking about," I ruminated. "Probably me."

The next day Victoria and I took a taxi to Chelsea. We had been sent invitations to the fair from *Country Life* and we had lunch there with Vanessa Mandril-Fortescue, one of Victoria's old friends from Cheltenham Ladies' College. She lived just off the King's Road in a small town house. Her husband, James, had just retired from the City and had been given an enormous golden handshake. She was at the fair looking for a pair of Queen Anne chairs for their new cottage in Gloucestershire. "Come round to the house for tea," she said as we finished lunch.

"We'd love to," Victoria said. "I want to hear about the cottage. Perhaps you can persuade Harry to move near you. There's a delicious little place for sale in Upper Honeycomb."

"That's very close," Vanessa said. "It would be absolutely lovely. Are you thinking about retiring, Harry?" she asked.

"Not really," I said. "Victoria simply saw this cottage in *Country Life*..."

"You know," Vanessa interrupted, "I'm always running into people I know in the Cotswolds. Nobody seems to live in London nowadays. It's full of foreigners and tourists."

After lunch I wandered from one stand to another. Victoria was busy taking notes and talking to exhibitors. Vanessa had disappeared in search of her chairs. At one stand I saw a small Georgian chocolate pot that I thought would look splendid in my office. I asked the price; it turned out to be an Edwardian reproduction of a Georgian design and was two hundred pounds. The previous week I had received an advance for a new book on Christian attitudes to Third World debt. I didn't think Victoria would mind, so I bought it.

She had just finished taking photographs of a Welsh dresser with her digital camera. "This is a present for you," I said.

"You mean for you," she smiled.

"Well, actually it's for both of us."

She looked in the bag. "A chocolate pot? That is pretty!"

"Don't you think it will look good in my office?"

"Well scarely a present for me, but it's certainly a very nice shape. How much was it?"

We had a rule that whenever we went out to dinner or bought each other presents, we gave an equivalent sum of money to Christian Aid. I was a little defensive. "I paid for it with the advance for my new book."

Victoria laughed, "The book about Third World debt – very appropriate. Now, Harry, look at this delightful dresser. Don't you think it would look perfect in that cottage?"

As I wandered around the exhibition, I caught sight of a vaguely familiar figure. Wearing a sombre black suit and a hat, Rabbi Wachman was examining a small silver spice-box with

Hebrew letters. I went up, tapped him on the shoulder and asked him if he was about to spend Mr Gold's money. He recognized me and laughed. "Oh dear," he said. "I'm afraid that wretched Lisa gave you a lot of trouble. In fact the whole lot of them are difficult. The father promised a vast donation to the synagogue. We got the first instalment, but endless excuses are being made for the non-arrival of the rest." He sighed. "I shouldn't speak ill of my own people, but they're not an easy family."

"Good of you to tell me about the girl," I said. "It made me feel a lot better. I was afraid I had given her the wrong signals, but if she is in the habit of doing this then no man is safe." The rabbi smiled and we parted amicably.

Later, after tea in Vanessa's house, we went to the evening service at Westminster Abbey. We took our bags with us so that we could catch the train back to St Sebastian's. On the way home, Victoria talked incessantly about Vanessa's new country cottage. "Oh Harry," she said, "you really should think about leaving that horrible university. This business with the Registrar's wife is awful. You'll absolutely hate going through an appeal."

"I know," I said gloomily, "but I can't let Jenny Sloth get away with it."

"What difference does it make? We've got quite enough money. You don't have to stay on until you are sixty-five. Why not make the break now? We could get a place in Gloucestershire, or somewhere nice. You could go to your club more often. And we could go travelling. Why put up with the gruesome Pilkingtons and that awful Wanda Catnip?"

"I'd miss Magnus," I said.

"You can see him anyway. And just think of all the new friends we'd make."

I stared out of the window as the train passed through the outskirts of St Sebastian's.

CHAPTER FIVE

No sign of Peace on Earth and Mercy Mild

The appeal was set for the week before Christmas. It was to be heard by the Vice-Chancellor and two members of the Senate. This committee was sent all relevant papers including the correspondence between Jenny Sloth and me, a report from Pilkington and Pilkington's letter about the oral warning. The procedure would be non-adversarial: first the committee would meet with Jenny and her representative, and then with me and Penelope. Then they would meet with Pilkington. The Registrar was responsible for sending out all relevant documents and for overseeing the appeal. During the last few weeks, I had looked up grievance procedures at other universities on the internet. I also arranged to have a meeting with Morris O'Murphy at his office in London.

Several days before the appeal, I caught the train in the morning, had lunch at my club, and took the underground to Paddington where the offices of the union were located.

It was a grey, cold day when I set off; by the afternoon, it had begun to rain. Morris's office was located in a modern building overlooking the station. The elevator was festooned with posters. The lift stopped at the third floor. A black woman wearing African dress greeted me at reception and directed me down a long corridor. Morris's room was at the end. The door was open; Morris was sitting at his desk eating a chocolate bar and drinking a mug of coffee while talking on the phone. He gestured for me to sit down. I took papers from my briefcase as he discussed one of his cases.

"So, the point is," he stated, "you've got to hand over your computer for the authorities to check it. They're alleging that you downloaded pornography after giving Hotlips UK your credit card number. They're going to-take the computer apart. I'm in touch with the Vice-Chancellor, and I'll let you know when he gets back to me. In the meantime, try not to worry."

Morris looked tired as he hung up the phone. "Now, he's in real trouble," he sighed. "Can't understand why a distinguished academic would want to watch that stuff. So, how are you feeling, Harry?" Morris was wearing a wooly sweater which was too tight for him, a light green tie the colour of the walls of his room and there were ink stains on his shirt. Compared with him I felt positively chic. His desk was strewn with paper including a file marked 'Harry Gilbert vs. St Sebastian's University'.

"I'm fine," I said. 'But this case is troubling. Do you know the Registrar is supposed to be in charge? How can that be allowed if his wife is involved?"

"Well, he is the Registrar: it's his job. In theory he's supposed to be objective. Anyway, the appeal is actually against your Head of Department, not Mrs Sloth."

"But his wife is the one who brought the complaint."

"I know, I know. There's nothing we can do about it. The Vice-Chancellor is determined to follow university regulations to the letter." Morris opened the file, and took out the Staff Handbook. "I've looked at this carefully," he said. "Mrs Sloth didn't say you bullied or harassed her. Otherwise, the case would be more serious and could result in a written warning. Her claim is that you were insensitive, that you lacked tact. Basically, she is arguing that you put undue stress on her, and

59

the Head of Department thinks that this was an abuse of your position."

"But what was I supposed to do? She wouldn't order books for the students. And they had begun to complain."

Morris got up, refilled his electric kettle, and asked if I'd like to have a cup of coffee. He took a jar of instant coffee from a shelf, unscrewed it, and poured some into two mugs. "Milk?" he asked. He poured in powdered milk, opened up a biscuit tin stamped with the union logo on it, and offered me a chocolate digestive. With admirable self-control, I refused. "Sugar?" he asked. When I shook my head, he took out four sugar lumps and dropped them into a mug for himself.

"That's quite a lot of sugar," I observed. "It'll rot your teeth, Morris."

"Already has," he grinned, as he helped himself to three biscuits out of the tin. "Now where were we?"

"Student complaints."

"Oh yes. Well, Mrs Sloth is arguing that you could have phoned her or gone to see her, rather than send her what she regards as hectoring emails."

"But everyone sends emails," I said.

"Yes, of course, they do. But she thinks you were unnecessarily overbearing. And Dr Pilkington agrees."

That evening I went back to the Acropolis for a talk dinner: Baroness Wingbat was speaking about artificial insemination. The dining room was packed. I was seated next to a visiting African bishop who was in London for a conference at Cannonbury Palace. He had been in committees all day discussing the issue of women bishops. He told me the Archbishop looked drained; the threat of division in the Anglican world was an overriding issue for everyone. I was gratified to hear that my book about Christian ethics was being used in African seminaries. During the discussion after dinner, I saw Barraclough at the far end of the room sitting next to a golden-haired youth. I had never seen him before – who was he? Perhaps Barraclough had a secret life . . . it was an enticing thought, but sadly improbable.

Afterwards, in the drawing room, I looked at the candidates' book. I was dismayed to see that Barraclough and the Provost of St Sebastian's Cathedral had proposed the Registrar for membership. I looked to see if anyone was watching, and then wrote in very small letters near Sloth's name: 'Unsuitable. Too Lazy and Horrid.' Perhaps this would discourage others from supporting him.

During the afternoon, I had visited a bookshop off Piccadilly Circus and bought *The Art of War*. This ancient manual was written over two thousand years ago by Sun-Tzu, a Chinese general. On the back of the book was a statement which intrigued me: 'Ultimate excellence lies not in winning every battle but in defeating the enemy without ever fighting.' Could the Vice-Chancellor, Pilkington and Catnip be defeated without a battle? Sitting on the train reading this slim volume, I hoped no one would observe me and I hid the book behind my *Times*.

The next day there was a letter in my pigeonhole from Pilkington: the envelope was handwritten. Was this another official summons? Instead, it was an invitation to Pilkington's annual Christmas party. It had a drawing of Father Christmas, a reindeer and glitter. I wondered what Victoria would make of it.

When I arrived home that evening, I put it on the hall table – Victoria had gone to a meeting of the local Women's Institute in the village hall. She was a loyal member; she always said it was the way to get to know normal women and to learn useful things. With considerable effort I cooked spaghetti with tomato sauce, made a small salad, poured myself a glass of Muscadet, and went upstairs to watch television. As I sat on the bed, trying not to spill my wine, the two cats joined me. They peered into my spaghetti bowl. I was anxious to see a repeat of 'Homicide Life on the Street'. Eventually Victoria arrived home, and I heard her giggling up the stairs.

"Father Christmas and his sleigh at the Pilkingtons'," she announced. "This is their worst card yet. Why don't they just send out At Home cards? I suppose the only charitable thing is to call it retro-kitsch. Really, Harry, your colleagues! They may be fearfully brainy, but their aesthetic education has been sadly neglected."

"Do you think we ought to go?" I asked. "Given this appeal, it will be embarrassing."

"Of course we must. You can't show you care about their silly plot. Anyway I always enjoy seeing their house – it's truly hideous. This time, you must go to the downstairs loo... it is the most extraordinary shocking pink colour! And take a good look at the hall carpet."

"What's wrong with it?"

"Harry, you must be blind. Its shag pile with beige swirls. Have you not honestly noticed?"

"I do remember their sofa and matching sludge armchairs and the lampshades with the fringes. But maybe it's because they don't have much money..."

"Nonsense! Frilly lampshades are not cheap. And anyway, it's always so clinically clean. Maureen Pilkington must spend a fortune on hoover bags. We must go. I wouldn't miss it for the world. Will Little Miss Bossyboots be there too?"

"She's normally invited. Last year even Barraclough made a brief appearance. Are you sure about this?"

"Absolutely! Just write back and tell them we'll be delighted to come. Anyway, the appeal will be over before the party."

"Victoria," I said. "Is your father going to have us all for Christmas this year?"

"Of course. And you're supposed to give the sermon again in the village church. Have you forgotten?"

I looked in my diary. It was true. I had been invited nearly a year ago by the local vicar, Henry Rowlands. He had the living in the village church near the castle. My father-in-law had rowed in the same boat as Henry's father at Trinity. Last year I had helped at the service, and he had asked me to preach. I pondered what I should say. Perhaps it wouldn't be appropriate to speak about forgiveness and reconciliation – there was no sign of peace on earth and mercy mild in my life this year.

As Chairman of the Appeal Committee, Barraclough had asked the Professor of Chemistry, Ralph Randolph, and the Reader in Twentieth-Century History, Patricia Parham, to hear the appeal with him. Professor Randolph had been a lecturer at Sussex before coming to St Sebastian's; small and bespectacled, he had a strong Lancashire accent. Dr Parham was a revisionist historian who had written a controversial book on Holocaust denial and was frequently interviewed by the BBC. A strong supporter of gay rights, it was rumoured that she was living with a female car mechanic.

I was told to submit a brief account of my dealings with Jenny Sloth to the Committee. First, they would see Mrs Sloth, and then me. Afterwards they would write a report which would be submitted to Council in which they would make a recommendation. If the appeal were upheld, the oral warning would be cancelled; otherwise, it would remain in force for the rest of the year. In a letter describing the procedure, the Vice-Chancellor explained that the appeal hearing was scheduled for the Monday of the last week of term at two o'clock. Although I would be allowed to have a representative at the meeting, I must inform the Vice-Chancellor at least a week in advance who would be performing this role.

I sent the letter to Penelope and a copy to Morris O'Murphy. Penelope emailed me and asked me to come to her room to discuss how we should proceed. On the day, I arrived several minutes early. Penelope was on the phone and asked me to sit down. Several piles of essays were scattered on her desk alongside an overflowing ashtray, a mug of coffee and a wilting orchid. On the floor were stacks of books. Penelope's computer and printer were placed on a table in the corner of the room alongside piles of floppy disks. The walls were covered with photographs of Rufus the cat as well as several gay rights posters.

"The bugger . . ." she splurted. "If he thinks he can get away with that, he's got another think coming . . ." Eventually she hung up. "A complete shit!" she declared.

"Another union case?" I queried.

"No, it's my brother-in-law. He just walked out on my sister."

"Oh," I said.

"The thing is," she continued, "he's got a new girlfriend, nearly twenty-five years younger than him. And he wants to go to live in Greece."

"What does he plan to do for a living?" I asked.

"I can't imagine. He's an accountant and certainly can't speak the language. Imogen is distraught. She has two little girls and a large mortgage. If that bastard goes abroad, he can escape the Child Support Agency." Turning in her chair to face me, she added: "At least you have the union to support you. My sister has no one, except me."

I felt guilty. My problems seemed trivial compared with those of Penelope's sister. Penelope began to search through the files on her desk. Eventually she found mine under a large pile of documents.

"Right," she said. "How are you feeling, Harry?"

"OK, but what do you think of the Committee?"

"Could be worse. Randolph is a creep, but Patricia is all right. She's been a real supporter of the gay campaign. She's bound to have sympathy for whoever is victimized." Penelope hesitated, "The problem is I know she wants a Chair...."

"Was my letter to the VC satisfactory?" I asked.

"Very good explanation, I thought."

"But will it get anywhere?"

Penelope paused. "Well, I can't promise. You see, Harry, it's not a question of fairness. There's no natural justice at St Sebastian's. That's the problem. Instead there's a little cabal which includes the VC and his managers who make all the decisions. In theory the Senate and the Council are supposed to take charge. But it's really Barraclough, Wanda and the department heads who are in control. That's why the union is so important. We're your only protection."

"Against tyranny?" I was amused.

"And tyrants..." Penelope was serious.

"How has it come to this?"

Penelope shrugged. "Who knows? The union was tricked into accepting pay deals on unacceptable terms. I can't imagine how the new pay structure is going to work out. The VC is going to cut corners wherever he can to save money. All he wants is to get rid of people."

"He can't get rid of everyone," I countered.

"No, of course not. But he'll aim for those with the least security or those who are the most expensive."

In the afternoon, I had a telephone conversation with Morris O'Murphy. He was on the train from London to Manchester. He was handling a complicated case about sexual harassment involving a senior administrator and an undergraduate. We had a poor connection, but I did manage to explain about my meeting with Penelope and told him about the members of the Appeal Committee. He told me to keep in touch. Later in the day I went to see Magnus in his room. Unlike me, he was not naturally tidy. His bookcases were overflowing, and there were stacks of papers scattered on the floor. On the walls were maps of ancient Israel. In the corner was a large clay statue of a fertility god with an enormous phallus. Magnus used this as a peg for his coat.

He was drinking a mug of coffee and eating a ginger nut biscuit while on the phone to the local garage. "Look," he said, "you promised those tyres would get here today. Do you expect me to take the bus? I don't care if you have to go to London to get them, I expect to drive home."

Exasperated, he hung up. "Damn. Those people never keep their promises."

"Do you want a lift?" I asked.

"Do you mind?"

I pushed several books off a chair as well as copies of the *Journal of Old Testament Studies* and sat down. Magnus handed me the biscuit tin. It had a picture of a country cottage and ducks in a pond. "So," he said, "what's the news?" I told him that Ralph Randolph and Patricia Parham were to be on the appeal panel.

"I wouldn't trust Randolph," he said. "Sneaky little shit. He'll try to please Barraclough. But Parham might be good news. By the way, isn't she living with some woman car mechanic? Maybe she could have got me some new tyres," he mused.

"You really think Randolph would uphold the oral warning?" I asked

Magnus took another biscuit from the tin. "Help yourself," he said.

"No Magnus, thanks."

"Look Harry," he continued. "Randolph knows if he supports you, the Registrar will be pissed off. And so will the VC. He's nearing retirement, and they'd be sure to go after him. In addition, Chemistry has been under threat for years. It's too expensive."

"What about Parham?"

"I understand she just published a new book about homosexuality in the Third Reich. She's bound to apply for a personal Chair. She has to have Barraclough's support. You can't get anywhere in this place without it."

"But this has nothing to do with the merits of the appeal."

The garage rang to tell Magnus that the tyres had arrived. When he put the phone down, he looked at me critically. "Harry," he said. "You're supposed to be an expert on ethics. But right and wrong have nothing to do with this. It's not about justice; it's about politics. An oral warning won't kill you. It's just a rap across the knuckles."

"But it's not fair!"

"Who said anything about fairness?" Magnus ate the last biscuit.

That night I told Victoria about my conversation with Penelope. "I forgot to tell you about the Registrar," I said. "Barraclough and the Provost of St Sebastian's Cathedral have put him up for the Acropolis."

"Sloth? Have we got to meet that ghastly little man at the club?"

"So, you see, they're all in this together."

Victoria did not understand. "But that has nothing to do with the appeal."

"On the contrary," I explained, " it has everything to do with it. The Provost is Visitor of the University; he's technically Barraclough and Sloth's boss. If the Provost is matey with Sloth, Barraclough is bound to reject my appeal to protect Sloth's wife. No wonder that lazy idiot has survived in his job so long. I had no idea he had friends in high places. Anyway Magnus thinks I should just accept the inevitable and live with an oral warning. It only lasts a year."

"So why don't you, and just drop the appeal?"

"I won't," I said.

"Why? If you're going to lose..."

"Even if I lose, there's the principle. I can't just give in to injustice. Otherwise what am I doing teaching Christian ethics?"

"You're earning an honest penny."

"Yes, but..."

"Look, Harry. Ethics has nothing to do with the way the world works. Or how Christians behave either. Some of the worst people I know are clergymen."

I was insulted. "How can you say that?" I said. "What about me? What about my Christian ethics textbook?"

Victoria kissed me. "You're a darling. And the book's a nice little earner. But really, Harry, you don't live in the real world."

Penelope and I arrived at Barraclough's office ten minutes early for the appeal. We sat outside in a corridor; the door to the office was closed and we could hear voices inside. Eventually Jenny Sloth emerged followed by Malcolm Fishman, the Librarian. They looked pleased with themselves and smiled slyly as they passed. After several minutes the Registrar summoned us.

The Vice-Chancellor was sitting at the head of the table; the Registrar sat on his right, and Randolph and Parham on opposite sides. Barraclough had a pile of paper in front of him consisting of letters and emails. Randolph was wearing a shiny navy suit and a green tie with blue stripes. There was an indefinable chemical smell emitting from him. Parham was dressed in red dungarees. She looked as if she had been helping her friend mend motor car engines. Her fingernails were encrusted with grime. As usual, the Vice-Chancellor was dressed in a grey suit and was sporting his Acropolis tie. I wondered if I should have worn mine. Sloth looked nervous.

Barraclough began by telling us that he had interviewed Pilkington about the warning and had just met with Mrs Sloth. He briefly outlined the nature of Jenny's complaint, and read out relevant correspondence. He then recounted Pilkington's explanation of the need for the oral warning. At this point, Penelope went on the attack. She pointed out that Mrs Sloth had not done her job, and it was not unreasonable for academic staff to remind colleagues if a duty had been neglected.

Barraclough emphasized that the question was not whether staff could make requests, but rather how such requests should be made. "Dr Sloth," he said, "tells me that poor Jenny was most upset by it all, and has had to have several days off with stress-related illnesses."

"For heaven sakes," Penelope interjected, "she was being asked to do her job! Nothing more, nothing less!"

"In this case," the Vice-Chancellor continued, as if Penelope had not spoken, "the objection was to Harry's lack of tact. And after all, this is not a unique instance." I looked astonished. No one had ever complained before. "There have already been complaints this term from a student about Harry's behaviour."

"Untrue and unsubstantiated," I interrupted indignantly.

"So we know Harry has a tendency towards this kind of behaviour," continued Barraclough magisterially.

"My staff are always complaining about how rude he is," said Sloth. During this discussion, Randolph looked out the window, and Parham fiddled with her hair. Neither made eye contact with me or Penelope.

The Vice-Chancellor then asked me to present my account of events. I stressed that the number of students in my first year Christian ethics class had risen dramatically at the beginning of term. Randolph smirked and muttered something to Parham who frowned. I then explained that I had initially asked Jenny to order additional copies of my textbook. I had had no response. As a result, I sent her additional emails and eventually wrote a letter asking that she deal with the matter. It was her delay, I said, which had created the current problem. In my view, there were no reasonable grounds for an oral warning. I had acted properly throughout. Jenny, on the other hand, had neglected her responsibilities as a librarian.

The Vice-Chancellor took notes as I spoke. He took the Staff Handbook from the bottom of his pile of papers, opened it to the section dealing with discipline, and read out the regulations. The difficulty, he said, was that although there was an attempt at an informal solution to the problem, this had not been achieved.

Penelope shifted in her chair. "Look," she said. "Dr Pilkington gave no opportunity for an informal solution. Professor Gilbert was willing to apologize for upsetting Mrs Sloth, but Dr Pilkington insisted this would not be sufficient. He was determined to issue an oral warning from the start."

Barraclough looked through his papers and pulled out a letter from Pilkington. He read it out loud:

"Dear Vice-Chancellor,

It is with regret that I am writing to you about an unfortunate incident involving a member of my department. Several weeks ago Professor Harry Gilbert contacted one of the librarians, Mrs Jenny Sloth, requesting additional books for his Christian ethics class. This was due to an increase in student numbers at the beginning of term. This was followed by a series of emails and eventually a highly critical letter. As you know, the library is extremely busy at the start of term. Mrs Sloth was unable to respond immediately to Professor Gilbert's request due to the pressures of work. Professor Gilbert, however, was insensitive to the situation. Instead of patiently waiting for a response, he adopted a hectoring tone throughout. I have always been concerned for the welfare of my department as well as for staff throughout the university. It appears to me that Professor Gilbert has misused his position as a professor in acting in this tactless way. It is for this reason that I have had no option but to issue an oral warning."

Yours ever

John

Dr John Pilkington,

Head of the Department of Theology"

Neither Randolph nor Parham had said anything during the meeting. The Vice-Chancellor asked if they would like to ask any questions. There was no response. He then asked if I wanted to make a final comment.

"Look, Vice-Chancellor," I said. "I have been an academic here for ten years. Prior to this year, I never had a complaint from either staff or students. I have always tried to be courteous; it was never my intention to cause offence. I'm sorry if Jenny was upset by my request for books. I only had the welfare of my students in mind. I told my Head of Department that I was prepared to write an apology to Jenny. But, I must stress that

I don't think I was wrong to persist in asking for these books. Nor do I think my requests were in any sense abusive. The real question is why Jenny is so sensitive. I'm sorry she had to take time off for stress. If she does find being a librarian overly taxing, then she ought to consider whether she should continue. I consider myself totally innocent in this affair. Furthermore, I think you would be creating a serious precedent if you uphold the Head of Department's warning to me. It would mean that any member of staff – either academic or non-academic – who did not want to do a particular job, could issue a formal grievance against the member of staff who made the request. Do you really want this to happen?"

"You can hear how arrogant he is," said Sloth. For once he was fully awake. "How dare he suggest my wife should give up her job – that's just typical of him! Rich and arrogant!" He realized he had gone too far and lapsed into silence.

"We are not here," the Vice-Chancellor said with dignity, "to determine how I should manage the university. The question is whether Professor Gilbert behaved in an offensive fashion. The Committee will give its decision, and I will communicate it to you in writing." He stood up and escorted Penelope and me to the door. He thanked us for coming, and slammed it shut behind us.

Forlornly I walked back to my office with Penelope. "That didn't go very well, did it?" I said.

"They want to get rid of you," she said. "You're expensive, and they probably have someone in the wings. I know the signs. Keep a close eye on your graduate students." Fleetingly I thought back to the scene of young Grundy with Wanda. I told myself I was being paranoid.

I found Magnus in the Senior Common Room. He was struggling with the *Times* crossword. "Damn difficult today," he announced. "Can't seem to make any sense of most of it. So, how was Barraclough?"

"Terrible," I said.

"Didn't go well then?"

"I didn't have a chance. How could I, with Sloth running the show?"

"How were Randolph and Parham?"

"They just sat there. They didn't even look at me."

"Oh dear. Well, Harry, you'll just have to live with an oral warning. It could be worse. You might have to teach summer school."

Later in the afternoon, I had a brief note from Barraclough telling me that my appeal had been rejected. I wasn't in the mood to do anything, but I had to attend the Talks Dinner Committee at the Acropolis at six. I caught the train and arrived a half hour late. Afterwards I stayed for dinner and sat at the Club Table. When I went up to the drawing room, I looked in the candidates' book to see if anyone had supported Sloth. To my surprise the page with his name and supporters had been removed. I saw the secretary of the club standing by the bar and went over to speak to him.

"I was looking for a candidate's name in the book," I said. "But it seems to have vanished."

"Who's that?" he queried.

"Dr Sloth. He's the Registrar of my university."

"Oh yes," he said. "He was a candidate. But his supporter and seconder have asked that his name be removed."

"Really?"

"Yes, there seems to have been a problem about his page. I'm afraid someone defaced it. I think his supporters thought there might be opposition to his election."

"Oh dear!" I said.

"Well, someone was certainly determined he shouldn't be a member."

This was cheery news. I felt much happier and decided to have a little celebration. I ordered a glass of champagne and took a bowl of peanuts to eat as I read the latest issue of the *Church Times*.

CHAPTER SIX

Better to Sleep than to Fight

Over the next few days I looked at Pilkington's party invitation on the mantelpiece. I was in no mood to attend, but Victoria was insistent. "If you don't go," she said, "it will look as though they've won. And I want to have another peek at their extraordinary decor. Don't forget to use the downstairs loo so you can see what colour it is."

"Really Victoria, you are a snob!"

"I am not! I love my friends in the Women's Institute. It's just the Pilkingtons. They're ghastly. I wouldn't miss their party for anything."

On the day, I reluctantly drove to the party, picking up Magnus on the way. He lived in a small flat near the university. It was littered with books and potsherds from the Middle East. In the dining room was a massive Assyrian sculpture. When he brought it home from Iraq, customs thought it was a bomb and Magnus was detained at the airport. On the way, he told us that he had just had a Christmas present from his aunt. She sent him a hundred pound premium bond. "If I win," he announced, "I'll take the early retirement deal."

"But Magnus," Victoria said, "it's like the lottery. The odds are about twenty thousand million to one."

"That bad?" he asked.

"Nobody ever wins the big prizes, Magnus," I said. "Well somebody does. But it won't be you."

Cars were lined up outside the Pilkingtons' bungalow, stretching down the street. Their house was part of a small, modern estate on the outskirts of St Sebastian's. When we rang the doorbell, one of the department postgraduate students opened the door. I noticed that the hall carpet had not improved. The dining room was crowded with members of the university. In the corner, I noticed Wanda talking to Jenny Sloth and the Provost of St Sebastian's Cathedral. Victoria marched over to say hello. I felt a stab of pride. Victoria was wearing a wine-red velvet dress. I happened to know she had bought it at an Oxfam shop in Knightsbridge, but it had once been very expensive. It was cut simply and showed off her dark slenderness to perfection. She looked like an elegant butterfly among the dowdy polyester moths of the other wives.

Magnus and I took glasses of wine from the dining room table. "Probably cheap plonk," Magnus muttered. He was right. Maureen Pilkington was handing out canapés from a large tray. They seemed to be pieces of cheese and pineapple on orange sticks. Magnus took three. I shook my head. They did not look worth getting fat for. Maureen greeted us as she passed. "Look Magnus," I said, "I promised Victoria I'd go see the downstairs loo. I'd better get it over with."

"But we just arrived."

"I know. But Victoria thinks the colour is extraordinary. She said I had to look."

Magnus looked amused as I made my way through the crowd. The door was ajar and I entered. Victoria was right, their lavatory was the colour of chewed bubblegum. I wondered what it said about Pilkington's anal obsessions. On the way out, I saw Barraclough leaving. As in the past, he was making a brief appearance. I didn't look forward to running into the Registrar, and hovered over the drinks table. Magnus had refilled his glass, and was looking for alternative hors d'oeuvres in the kitchen. He came out with a plate loaded with plastic-looking vol-au-vents. Throughout the evening, I managed to avoid Wanda and the Sloths. They were also keeping their distance. By the time we were ready to leave, Magnus had drunk at least six glasses of wine and looked increasingly morose. On the way home, he warbled: "An old don's life is not a happy one."

On Saturday, Victoria and I went Christmas shopping in London. We bought a large stilton for my father-in-law from Fortnum and Mason, ties for Victoria's brothers from a shop in the Burlington Arcade, and scarves from Liberty for the sisters-in-law. There were also tokens for the five nephews and nieces. As we walked up South Audley Street, we passed a travel agency which was advertising skiing holidays in Aspen, Colorado. "Harry, why don't we go?" Victoria said. "You deserve a treat."

Inside the shop we looked at several brochures, and eventually decided on a seven-night package holiday including meals. The hotel, the Aspen Siesta, was next to the ski lift and overlooked the town. We were to arrive at Heathrow on 27 December and fly to Denver and then on to Aspen. I hadn't skied since I was at Cambridge, but Victoria assured me that I would remember everything. Victoria hadn't been on the snow for many years either, but was undeterred.

The day before Christmas, we loaded up the car with presents and set off for Wales. Our neighbours promised to look after the cats while we were gone, and we booked a kennel for them for our trip to the States. When we arrived at the Castle, Sir William was decorating a gigantic Christmas tree in the drawing room with the help of his grandchildren. Victoria's brother, Anthony, was seated at the piano practising Christmas hymns. Her sister-in-law, Joanna, was preparing tea. Victoria's eldest brother, Billy, and Selina, his wife, were walking their undisciplined bearded collie.

In the evening there was the usual Christmas party for all the children in the village school. By tradition the owner of the castle was the chairman of the governors. Billy had taken on this duty, but Sir William still insisted on giving the party. Over the years the number of children in the school had dwindled, but each child was still given a carefully chosen present off the tree. Because the children did not know me, it had become my duty to dress up as Father Christmas. I wore the old, slightly musty-smelling costume which had been in the family for generations. To my annoyance, I noticed it was tighter than last year.

After the party we had dinner. It was noisy – everyone talked at once. Victoria struggled to tell the family about our forthcoming trip. After dinner, the grandchildren disappeared and Sir William insisted we play Scrabble. I had the lowest score and was teased about losing. Aided by a large bottle of claret, Sir William put all his letters down on a triple word score and was particularly triumphant.

On Christmas day I preached a sermon on humility in the village church. Sir William sat in his usual pew with Victoria, Billy, Selina and young Will, the oldest grandson. The rest of the family stayed at home, preparing the food. After a delicious lunch we opened our presents, and later Victoria and I took Buggins, her brother's dog, for a walk across the hills. Snow had fallen in the morning, and had covered the ground. As we walked towards the village, past grey stone cottages, Victoria brought up the issue of retirement again.

"Harry," she said. "It's so lovely in the country. I do think we ought to consider buying a little house in the Cotswolds." Victoria had been looking through old issues of *Country Life* since we arrived. "The university is awful. I can't see how you're possibly going to enjoy teaching if you have to worry all the time about this wretched oral warning."

"It'll only last a year," I said. "And it doesn't really matter."

"But what if someone else complains? Then it could get worse."

Victoria was right. But I was determined not to let Pilkington and Wanda Catnip drive me out. "Look," I said. "I'm going to retire in a few years anyway. Why should I give up a job I like just because Barraclough wants me to leave?" In the distance we heard the honking of geese. Buggins shot off, chasing after a rabbit. Country life was delightful. I wondered if Victoria had a point.

After Boxing Day we left the castle for one night at home. Our plane was to leave Heathrow at eleven o'clock in the morning of the following day. We parked in the long-stay car park, and headed for Terminal 4. Crowds of passengers jostled us as we made our way through immigration. Eventually we went to an airport lounge. Victoria ordered a gin and tonic and settled into a comfortable armchair. I sat in front of one of the computers and checked to see if there were any emails. One was a Christmas greeting from Magnus who had gone to see his aunt who lived in East Anglia. It included a cartoon of Father Christmas who looked remarkably like Barraclough. Wanda Catnip had sent the entire academic staff a letter about university developments last term and concluded with a sentimental holiday greeting. There was also an email from Pilkington asking for marks from last term.

When our plane was announced, Victoria and I walked to the gate. A half hour later the plane took off, and I looked through the magazine to see what films were being shown. Our package holiday included economy-class tickets. Behind me was a little girl who giggled and kicked against the back of my seat. I turned around and glared at her parents. They glared back. "Do you want to change seats?" Victoria asked.

I shook my head. "If I can endure Catnip," I said, "I can put up with this."

The flight seemed interminable, but I was able to sleep after the meal despite being poked from behind at regular intervals. When we arrived in Denver, we changed planes and flew to Aspen in a small jet with several other skiers. One of the passengers, a tall distinguished-looking man, was accompanied by a well-dressed, brown-haired woman wearing a mink coat. He was carrying a leather bag stamped with a college crest. They were seated across the aisle, and immediately they started chatting with Victoria. It emerged that he was the President of a small Southern liberal arts college in Virginia. Sweetpea College was founded at the end of the eighteenth century by an Ebenezer Sweetpea, a plantation owner and philanthropist who had established the college for young Southern gentlemen. In the 1970s, women had been accepted for the first time, and it was now fully coeducational.

Victoria told them that I was the Professor of Christian Ethics at St Sebastian's. The husband, Oscar Billstone III, had been a Rhodes Scholar at Oxford. Subsequently, he had studied at Harvard for a PhD. His first job was at Princeton, where he became Dean. Six years ago, he was appointed President of Sweetpea. His wife, Nancy, was from an old New England family and had been educated at Mount Holyoke College. She had still been a student when she met Oscar. They had two children. The son was a stockbroker in Wall Street; their daughter worked at the Metropolitan Museum in New York, specializing in Flemish painting. They, too, were staying at the Aspen Siesta. By the time we landed, we had made plans to get together for dinner.

The Aspen Siesta is an old hotel located outside of Aspen. Surrounded by trees, it overlooks snow-covered peaks. The sun was setting when we arrived. We unpacked and quickly fell asleep, exhausted from our journey. Later we met the Billstones in the dining-room. Over dinner, Oscar told us about his experiences at Oxford while his wife looked on admiringly. They asked where Victoria and I had met, and about her background. When they learned she was the daughter of a baronet, they looked at each other. "Thomas would be fascinated," Nancy said. "He's one of the trustees of the college. He adores the English aristocracy."

"We're not really aristocratic . . . " began Victoria, but Nancy was in full flow.

"Thomas is from an old American family. His mother was a prominent member of the Daughters of the American Revolution in Virginia. His great-great-great grandfather, Thomas Jefferson Porpoise I, owned the plantation on which the college is located. He sold the land very cheaply to Ebenezer Sweetpea. Thomas is actually Thomas Jefferson Porpoise VI. His family have been major benefactors to the college for over two hundred years. Our collection of Paul Revere silver was a recent bequest. Thomas went to Harvard and specialized in art history, but he has always been loyal to Sweetpea. I wonder if he's heard of Victoria's family."

"I doubt it," Victoria said." My father isn't a peer; he's just a baronet. He's in *Debretts*, but we're not an old family. Mr Porpoise sounds grander than us."

"That's not what the old Buzzard would think," I said.

77

"Please, Harry, I don't think Oscar and Nancy want to hear about my father."

"But we do," Nancy said. She clearly meant it.

"Well, he lives in a draughty castle on the Welsh border. It's desperately cold in winter, and whenever we visit we have to carry a hot-water bottle everywhere. Daddy refuses to put in central heating. He thinks it's self-indulgent."

"And expensive," I added.

Oscar took out a small notebook. "I'll write a note to Thomas. What's the family name?"

"Dormouse," Victoria said. "The crest is a dormouse couchant. And the motto is *Melius dormire quam pugnare.*" Nancy looked mystified. "'It is better to sleep than to fight,'" I said.

Everyone giggled. Oscar diligently wrote down what I said. "Thomas will be enchanted – you must meet him when you come to Sweetpea."

The next morning, Victoria and I set off for the slopes after breakfast. We hired boots, skis and poles, bought our lift pass, and rode the chairlift to the top of the mountain. I was having a difficult time with the moguls. I fell several times while Victoria skied ahead. As we came round to the other side of the mountain, Victoria plunged into a large gulley and took a spectacular fall. I skied over and saw she was in severe pain. "Harry," she cried, "I think I may have broken my ankle."

I reached down to help her. She couldn't stand up. "It really hurts," she said. "I hate to be a bore, but I think you'd better get the ski patrol." I skied down to the bottom as quickly as I could and found one of the ski instructors. Eventually the ski patrol brought Victoria down in a sled. One of the paramedics examined her ankle; it was swollen, but he was sure it wasn't anything more than a sprain. Victoria hobbled off to the lodge. "Don't worry about me," she said. "I'll have some hot chocolate, and then I'm going shopping." I could see this was going to be an expensive holiday.

The rest of the day, I skied by myself. Late in the afternoon I returned to the Aspen Siesta. Victoria was sitting by a fire in the lobby of the hotel talking to Nancy. She was also drinking a large cocktail, nibbling olives and wearing a turquoise necklace

I had never seen before. "Look what I bought!" she said. "There was this charming Indian shop in the centre of town. Isn't it lovely?"

"How's the ankle?" I asked.

"Swollen."

"Are you OK?"

"Fine," she said. "Come and have a drink."

For the rest of the holiday Victoria sat in the lounge of the Aspen Siesta reading a stack of novels she had bought in town. She was perfectly happy. Several evenings we joined the Billstones for dinner at local restaurants. They refused to allow us to pay. All costs, Oscar announced, were part of his entertainment allowance as President of Sweetpea. They seemed intrigued about my account of the personalities at St Sebastian's, but I was careful not to say anything about my recent difficulties.

Victoria and I were due to go to New York for one night before returning to London, and we planned to meet our new friends there. They were going back to Virginia before we left Aspen, and then Oscar had to fly immediately to a meeting in New York; Nancy was planning to join him. "This time," I insisted, "you must be our guests." We were staying at the Harvard Club, which had reciprocal relations with the Acropolis and we agreed to meet there at seven.

The Harvard Club is just off Fifth Avenue. When we arrived, we went to our room and unpacked. Then we joined the Billstones for a drink in the bar, before going in for dinner. Once our first course arrived, Oscar told us that he had called Thomas Jefferson Porpoise on his return. He was keen to meet us, and Oscar had been instructed to invite us to the college. "Every year," he said, "we ask a distinguished academic to give the Porpoise Memorial Lecture. I know it's last minute, but we have a vacancy for this spring. This year's lecturer was supposed to be Professor Norman Rattlesnake from Yale. But he's just won the Nobel Prize and he's got to go to Sweden to collect it. Would it be insulting to be a substitute?"

"I'd be honoured," I said. "Could Victoria come?"

"Of course – that goes without saying."

79

The next morning, Victoria and I strolled down Fifth Avenue. Our plane was to leave in the evening. Near the Harvard Club we came across an antique shop selling Russian art. In the window was a seventeenth-century icon of St Sebastian shot with arrows. We went inside, and a small gentleman dressed in a black suit greeted us. In a strong eastern European accent, he told us that this particular icon was Cretan. The shape of the rocks in the background, he said, indicated its origin. Victoria loved it. While I looked at the rest of the shop, Victoria discussed the price. "Harry, it will look spectacular in your office," she said.

"But we can't afford it," I objected.

"Yes we can. It'll cheer you up. When we get back to St Sebastian's, we'll have a little party to show it off." I could see I was going to be sending an enormous cheque to Christian Aid that month.

When our plane arrived back in London, we went straight to St Sebastian's. We were relieved to find that the cats were well. The next week I hung the icon between the Gothic windows in my office and sent out invitations to a drinks party. I explained that I had just purchased an icon of St Sebastian, and the purpose of the party was for people to see it. It was to be a little gathering for the first day of term; I hoped Barraclough, Catnip, the Pilkingtons and the Sloths would come, along with Magnus and other colleagues. On the day, Magnus arrived early. "Good grief," he said, "how much did that cost?"

"It was a present from Victoria," I said.

"Chap got shot with arrows," he observed. "How very suitable! He's just like you . . . a martyr of the university."

"Worse for him," I said.

I handed Magnus a glass of champagne as Victoria put out nuts and olives. Slowly the room began to fill up. Barraclough arrived with Catnip and the Sloths. Pilkington had earlier sent his apologies. Barraclough immediately strode over to the icon. "Most impressive," he said. "I hope you're planning to bequeath it to the university."

"I'm not dead yet," I said.

"Well . . . 'Be Prepared,' as the boy scouts say."

"Actually," interrupted Victoria coldly, "it was paid for with money from the Dormouse Trust. Harry has the obligation to return it to my brother Billy when the time comes." She busied herself with her guests. "The vulgarity of that man is unbelievable!" she said to me in a not very quiet voice as she passed.

I opened bottles of champagne as Victoria flitted about. A little crowd stood around the icon. Among the admiring comments, we overheard Jenny Sloth mutter to Wanda Catnip: "That's the most ridiculous thing I've ever seen. Who do the Gilberts think they are?" Victoria was delighted. "See, I told you it would be a great success!" she said.

On the opposite side of the room hung an old engraving of the club. I saw Sloth gazing at it and went over to talk to him. "That's the Acropolis in London," I said.

"I know," Sloth replied. "The Committee wanted me to join, but I thought it wasn't worth the money." I smiled to myself as I went around refilling glasses.

Amongst the guests was Ronald Grundy, my research student. He was standing next to Wanda, helping himself to olives. I went over to say hello. "Harry," Wanda said, "I've been meaning to ask you about your first-year class on Christian ethics. You know that Ronald has a student bursary, and he has to do some teaching. I wondered if he might take one or two seminars with your students. Perhaps near the end of term."

"That's fine with me," I said. Ronald looked pleased. "Come see me and we can discuss it."

"Cool!" he exclaimed.

"Thanks, Harry," Wanda said. "As Dean, it's my responsibility to make sure that teaching arrangements are made for postgraduates who have bursaries. Could you let me have a note about this?"

As I walked away, I saw that Wanda smiled conspiratorially at Ronald. What, I wondered, was that all about?

Ronald was due to have a supervision the next week and had sent me a chapter of his thesis. He was doing well and I had taken a lot of trouble with him. As well as his Arts and Humanities Research Council grant, I had persuaded the department to give him a small bursary. The thesis was coming along nicely and he expected to submit it by the end of the summer. When he came to see me, I asked him about his future plans.

"I hope to hand in the thesis soon," he said. "My money will run out by the end of the summer, and I'll need to look for a job."

"Have you thought where you'd like to live?" I asked.

"I like it here, but it all depends what's available."

"Well," I said, "I don't think there's currently an opening. It all depends whether the department is able to advertise for a new lectureship. And then I'm not sure it will be in your field. What we need is another Church historian."

"I know," he said. "I'll probably have to look elsewhere. But St Sebastian's would be my first choice."

The next few weeks were uneventful, except for difficulties with my new laptop. At the beginning of term, the University Information Technology Unit had set up a new machine in my office. For some reason, it crashed the first day I used it. Nothing I could do would help. I tried to turn it off and on again, but with no success. Magnus came to look at it, but we couldn't get it to turn on. I contacted the IT Unit and told them what happened. The Head, Simon Evans, explained I'd have to wait for someone to come around since they were extremely busy at the beginning of term. I complained that I wasn't able to receive emails or do any work. This produced little sympathy. I phoned several times in the following days to ask for assistance, but I was continually told I'd have to wait.

I hesitated writing a letter: I didn't want to cause any more problems. But I was worried about not being able to respond to emails. It was exactly the sort of thing which would get me into trouble. Eventually I wrote a letter by hand to Simon, explaining the urgency of the matter. Two weeks passed with no response. I then asked Magnus if he could send an email for me. Again, there was no reply. In desperation, I sent a fax from the office fax machine. I stressed the urgency of the situation. I was bewildered, I said, not to receive any response from the Unit. All the new technology, I stressed, was designed to facilitate communication rather than hinder it.

The next week I had a letter from Pilkington, marked Private and Confidential. He asked to see me in his office, and told me I could bring a representative. I phoned Penelope immediately. She wasn't in, so I left a message on her answerphone. I told her to phone me rather than send an email since my computer wasn't working. Later in the day, she contacted me. She had just been playing squash and was exhausted. "Look," I said. "I don't know what this is about. But I've just had another threatening summons from my Head of Department. He didn't say why, but he told me to bring a representative." Penelope said she was free on the date Pilkington suggested. She insisted I ask him what it was about.

When I phoned him, he was out. I left a message that he could reach me at home. That evening, he rang. "Harry," he said sternly, "I'm afraid we've had another complaint. This time it's via the Registrar. He tells me you've been harassing the IT department about your computer."

I had a sinking feeling. "Look," I said. "I didn't harass them. I've been telling them that my new laptop doesn't work. They keep putting me off. I can't receive emails or do any work. What am I supposed to do?"

"I don't think we can get very far on the phone. Come to my office. We can discuss it then."

"This is ridiculous," I said.

"I'm just doing my job, Harry. Simon Evans mentioned to the Registrar that you were nagging him about your computer. Sloth took it up and insists I investigate. I have to tell you, you already have an oral warning. This is becoming increasingly serious. The next warning will have to be a written one if you have repeated the same offence."

Exasperated I went to see Magnus. I had brought him back a US Marshal badge from our visit to Colorado, and he was wearing it on the lapel of his tweed jacket. He was writing a review of a book on the Minor Prophets for the *Expository Times*, and books were spread out over the floor. I had to step over several piles when I walked in. I took a large Hebrew lexicon off a chair and sat down.

"You won't believe this," I said. "Now I've got trouble from the IT Unit."

"Bunch of idiots," Magnus said. "Couldn't organize a booze-up in a brewery."

"That's just the point. My computer still doesn't work, and they won't come to fix it. And now, Simon Evans has complained to Sloth that I'm harassing him."

Magnus smiled. "Exactly what he deserves!"

"Magnus, be serious. I didn't harass him. I simply phoned him and asked if he could fix the damn computer. And we sent him an email. And then I faxed him. Now, he's complained and I've got to have another formal interview with Pilkington."

"Does Wanda know?"

"Pilkington didn't say anything about her. But I wouldn't be surprised."

Magnus took out a pack of Camels, and lit a match. "You don't mind if I smoke?" he asked.

"I thought you gave it up."

"I did. But what the hell. You only live once."

"So, Magnus . . . what's going on?"

"They want you to leave. They're putting you under pressure to go". He shook his head. "Another complaint. This time from Evans. He should be shot. No wonder the place is falling apart. Have you told Penelope?"

"She'll come with me to the meeting."

"What about that O'Murphy chap in London?"

"I haven't phoned him yet. Do you think I should?"

"Can't do any harm. Might even do some good. But, frankly, if I were you I'd just quit. You don't want to be like those kids in America who shot the teachers. The Professor of Christian Ethics can't end up on trial for murder. Although frankly, it would be quite a way to go."

At five I left my office. As I walked towards the car park, I saw Lisa Gold walking with Ronald Grundy. They were holding hands. I dropped behind so they wouldn't see me, but I could quite clearly hear what they were saying. Ronald was wearing a grey duffle coat and trainers and was holding a squash racket. Lisa was dressed in a skimpy white skirt and an Aran sweater. She was also clutching a racket. Ronald was in the middle of discussing his job prospects.

"So, you see," he was saying, "there's a chance for me here. At least if I play my cards right. That's what Catnip said, anyway."

"Did they actually offer you a job?" Lisa asked.

"Not in so many words," he said. "It all depends on Gilbert. They think he's past it. If they can get rid of him, they'll need someone to take his classes."

Lisa smiled. "That shit! I think my father can take care of that," she said. "He never takes no for an answer."

On the way home, I puzzled over what I had heard. Penelope was right. Even my research students couldn't be trusted.

Over dinner I told Victoria. I described what I heard Ronald say to Lisa. "Nasty little bitch," she said. "First she tries to seduce you; then she seduces your research student. She must be desperate."

"I don't think I'm that bad ..." I began.

"That's not what I meant. She clearly has a weakness for academics. God only knows why! I could tell her a thing or two!" We laughed.

"But you like academics," I protested.

"Hardly, Harry. You know I don't fit in. Do you think I could ever be a friend of that sad little Miss Bossyboots? Or that idle cow Jenny Sloth? Or, heaven forbid, that stout matron Maureen Pilkington? I mean, I try to be polite but I'd go mad if they were my only friends."

"What about Magnus?"

"Magnus is a darling. But the rest are not exactly my cup of tea. Lisa may be poisonous and delusional, but from what you've described, she does have some style. I can't imagine why she'd want to spend her life in a university."

85

CHAPTER SEVEN

The Happiest Day Since I Came Here

Eventually the Information Technology Unit did come to fix my computer. When I switched it on, there was a large picture of Wanda Catnip on the university homepage announcing that she had been promoted to a personal Chair. The announcement went on to say that her Inaugural Professorial Lecture would take place in several weeks time. There was also an email from Magnus. It read: 'The witch has her reward from Barraclough. A disgusting spectacle. What is the world coming to? Magnus.' There was an email from Morris O'Murphy too. He asked me to phone him about the disciplinary meeting which was to take place at the end of the month. When I reached him, he was on the train to Birmingham, and I arranged to see him on his next visit to St Sebastian's. He was coming to meet with the Pay Scale Committee to discuss the implementation of the new scheme.

On the day, he arrived late in the afternoon with Penelope. He was wearing a brown suit and a wide brown and green tie with the union insignia. Penelope looked very different from usual in a smart tweed suit. They looked drained.

Morris sat on the sofa. Penelope slumped in the armchair opposite. I gave them each a large glass of sherry. "Barraclough was at his most opaque," Penelope moaned.

"Man's an ignoramus," Morris declared.

"So it didn't go well?" I said.

Morris groaned, and then looked astonished. "Who's that guy shot with arrows?" he asked, looking at the icon.

"That's the real St Sebastian," I said. "We got the icon in New York. It was painted by a Cretan artist in the seventeenth-century."

Penelope looked bewildered. "I never knew St Sebastian was used for target practice," she said.

"That's not quite the story," I replied, "He was a native of Milan and was martyred. He is traditionally portrayed standing in the middle of archers, being shot through with arrows. But he is supposed to have recovered from the onslaught through the ministrations of a kindly widow. But then he was clubbed to death."

"Just like you, Harry?" Morris grinned.

"That's what you're here to prevent," I said.

"Quite so," Morris said. "I'm afraid there's not a lot we can do though. A precedent was set with the oral warning. All the Head of Department has to do is prove that the same offence was repeated."

"But this is ridiculous," Penelope protested. "The oral warning shouldn't have been given in the first place..."

"That's true. But it was. And we can't do anything about it. Harry lost the appeal. So, if this computer person can show that Harry behaved in a similar way, a written warning could be issued."

"There's nothing I can do?" I asked.

"You can always appeal against the warning, but I don't think it will do much good."

"This is hopeless," Penelope complained. "We're supposed to protect our members."

"I think all you can do at this stage is to explain why you needed a functioning computer. You should stress that you had to reply to emails. And then hope your Head of Department gets the point. In retrospect, it would have been better to have done nothing. You have been given an oral warning. In that situation, it's best to tread very carefully. It's a pity you didn't call me before you sent out your letter to the Head of IT."

"I don't think the Head of IT was that bothered," I commented. "The matter was seized on by the Registrar. It was he who instituted proceedings."

"So that's it? Even though there's clearly a conspiracy against Harry?" Penelope asked.

"I'm afraid there's little we can do at this stage. We'll just have to wait and see how the Head of Department plays it. You see," he went on, "disciplinary hearings are like a game. You won't know how the other side intends for things to go until the meeting itself. Maybe they'll be co-operative. Often they're not. It all depends what the game plan is. And we don't know what they're up to."

"I'm afraid I do," I said gloomily.

"You haven't got anything to eat, have you?" asked Morris. I handed over the biscuit tin.

With a sense of foreboding I met with Pilkington at the disciplinary meeting. Penelope was to accompany me, but she was late since she had to take Rufus in to see the vet again. He was still having trouble with fur balls. Wanda was already seated when I arrived. Reluctantly, I congratulated her on her personal Chair. She was clearly elated. Pilkington fidgeted while we waited for Penelope to arrive. Flustered she knocked on the door fifteen minutes after the meeting was due to start.

"Sorry," she said. "I had to rush Rufus to see the vet this morning. And I wanted to take him home afterwards."

"Is he OK?" I asked.

"The vet says he has to change his diet. So, I bought an expensive bag of prescription cat food. You can't get it at a supermarket. It has to be got from a vet. You know," she said with astonishment, "it costs nearly twenty pounds."

Pilkington looked impatient as Penelope told us about her cat's difficulties. "We're here," he began, "because there has been a formal complaint by the Head of Information Technology. He said that Harry harassed him about fixing his computer. Has it now been repaired?" he asked.

"It has," I said. "But this is after weeks of nagging..."

"So you do admit nagging Simon Evans."

"Well, yes..." I said. "But he should have fixed it immediately. Instead, he did nothing, even after I sent him a note and an email. I eventually sent him a letter, but still nothing happened."

As always, Wanda took extensive notes. Whenever Pilkington criticized my contact with Simon, Penelope interrupted, pointing out that it was the role of the IT unit to repair computers.

After a half hour's discussion, Pilkington concluded by referring to the oral warning that had recently been given. "The Staff Handbook specifies," he said, "that a written warning is to be given for any repetition of the same offence. I have discussed the matter at length with the Vice-Chancellor," he continued, "and we are both of the opinion that you have behaved in the same fashion as before. I'm afraid nothing has been said today which convinces me otherwise. Therefore I regrettably have no option than to issue you with a written warning. As you know, a written warning lasts for two years. If there is a further repetition of similar behaviour, then the matter will go before a disciplinary committee. And, I must warn you, Harry, that it could result in your dismissal from the university."

"This is totally unwarranted," Penelope objected. "I want to put on record that the union does not accept this judgment, and as union president I will be encouraging Harry to appeal against your decision."

"You have every right to do so," Pilkington said. "But as you know, the Vice-Chancellor would chair such an appeal. And quite frankly, I can't imagine the decision would be any different from the previous case. You will simply be wasting everyone's time."

Wanda had not said anything since we arrived. But at this point, she indicated that she had something to add. "As Dean, I want to give you some advice, Harry. It would be far better for you to concentrate on improving your attitude than staging a fruitless appeal. As John said, you are free to do as you wish. But the real question is whether you will be able to exercise self-restraint in the future."

Penelope was furious and began putting her notebook and pen back into her handbag. "Come along, Harry," she said. "I can see there is no point in continuing the discussion." I got up and followed her out of the room. Later in the day there was a letter from Pilkington in my pigeonhole. I read it and stormed off to Magnus's room. He was asleep in his battered armchair in the corner surrounded by books. His overcoat was draped as usual over his Canaanite god. "What's up?" Magnus asked as I entered.

"Read this," I said.

He looked grave as he read Pilkington's letter. "So you've finally been given a written warning. Astonishing!"

"But Magnus, I didn't do anything wrong. It's not my fault. It's theirs."

Magnus nodded. "You're right. But what do you expect from that shit? He's determined to get you to leave. And so is Catnip. They've convinced the VC. Sorry, Harry, but there's nothing you can do about this. That is, except take early retirement. Did the VC make you any kind of deal?"

"Not yet," I said.

"He made me a lousy offer. You might do better."

"But I don't want to go!"

Magnus picked up a short article that was lying on the floor. "You know, I just wrote the most damning review of Professor Macpherson's new book on Second Isaiah. It made me feel a lot better. Do you want to see it?"

"Thanks, Magnus," I said, "but I'm not in the mood."

"Pity! It's one of the most vicious things I've ever written. Quite a tonic for depression! You ought to try it!"

When I arrived home, I was furious. Victoria poured me a glass of whiskey, and our blue-point Siamese, Cleo, sat on my lap and purred as I recounted my interview with Pilkington. Our other cat, Brutus, was busy chasing a paper ball. Victoria waited impatiently for me to finish, and then showed me the latest issue of *Country Life*. There was a picture of her holding a Georgian teapot and a short article about collecting tea-time porcelain. "That's splendid," I said.

"It arrived this afternoon. Plus a cheque for five hundred pounds."

"Well done! I'm really pleased!"

"So am I," she smiled.

"It rather overshadows this stupid written warning," I said.

"I'm glad you're getting all this into proportion. Look, Harry. You're a professor. You're in *Who's Who*. You've published lots of books. You have no money worries. I simply can't see why you care what Little Miss Bossyboots thinks, or that boring Head of Department, or Barraclough for that matter."

"I suppose you're right."

"Of course, I'm right. Just look around you. You live in this beautiful mill-house full of pretty things; you have a lovely office at the university with Gothic windows and a seventeenth-century icon; you can go up to London whenever you want and dine at your club. You have the nicest cats in the world and, most important, you have me. Just what are you complaining about?"

Sheepishly I couldn't think of an answer. "Then why don't we go out to dinner and spend some of the money you earned?" I said. What about that country house hotel that got such a good write-up in *The Times*?"

The Goat and Goose Hotel was located about ten miles from St Sebastian's in a small, picturesque village that was frequently used by the BBC for historical dramas. The village green was surrounded by timber-framed houses. When we entered, we were shown into the dining room by a silver-haired gentleman wearing a dark suit who was clearly the owner. The prices were astronomic. I realized I would soon be sending another huge cheque to Christian Aid.

After we ordered, I told Victoria about Catnip. I explained that when I turned my computer on, there was a picture of Wanda and a caption explaining that she had been awarded a Chair and was due to give an inaugural professorial lecture.

Victoria seemed surprisingly interested. "She's to give a lecture?" she asked.

"You remember the lecture I gave?" I said. "Well, it's like that. All professors do it when they get a Chair. I don't normally tell you about it, because you wouldn't be interested. They talk about their speciality. It's usually terribly boring."

"But I'd like to hear Catnip. I've never heard her lecture." She embarked on a wickedly accurate imitation of Wanda's Northern vowels.

I interrupted. "Why? I have no intention of going. It will be horrible. And after what I've endured, I don't see why I should. Certainly Magnus isn't going to go."

Victoria looked out the window as I went on to explain why our attendance would be entirely inappropriate. "So, I'm not going," I concluded.

"Oh Harry, you mustn't let the side down. You really do have to go."

"But why?" I asked. "It's not as though she's done anything for me. What she and Pilkington have done is to make my life much worse. Why should I do something for that horrible woman?"

"Harry, you're supposed to be the Professor of Christian Ethics. Forgive and forget! All that sort of thing! So, you've got to practise what you preach."

"Why?" I said indignantly. "It's all very well in theory. But in practice it isn't very appealing. She doesn't like me. And I don't like her. And she tried to get me to leave. So, I'm not going."

"You must go, Harry," Victoria persisted. "It will be fascinating."

"If Magnus won't go, I'm not going. Why should I?"

"Well, if Magnus is willing to go, will you, too?"

"I don't see why I should. But OK. If Magnus goes, I'll go." I felt very safe.

"Good," Victoria said, as she polished off her salad niçoise. "You won't want to miss it!"

Several days later I had tea with Magnus in the SCR. Magnus ordered two tea cakes and a mug of coffee. He looked very pleased. I wondered why. "Why are you looking so cheery?" I asked.

"Oh no reason," he said as he plonked three sugar cubes into his coffee.

"Come on, Magnus, how come you're not your usual glum self?"

"Glum? Am I usually glum?"

"What's going on, Magnus?"

"Nothing," he said. "Really." And with that he picked up *The Times*.

"Oh, Magnus," I continued. "You're not going to Catnip's lecture are you? I told Victoria I definitely didn't intend to. But for some reason she seems to want to go. I can't imagine why. Anyway, I told her I would go if you went. But I was sure you wouldn't."

Magnus looked up. "Actually," he said. "I rather thought I would."

"But why?"

"I thought it might be amusing."

"Amusing?"

"Seeing her suck up to Barraclough. Why not?"

"I can't understand you, Magnus. This is totally inconsistent. You think she's ghastly. Why in the world would you want to hear her give a lecture?"

Magnus giggled as he went back to *The Times*. What, I wondered, was going on?

Both Magnus and Victoria refused to discuss the lecture further. Magnus avoided the issue whenever I mentioned it. Victoria simply insisted that I had promised to go if Magnus went and Magnus was going. I couldn't understand why they were so intent on the matter.

The day before the lecture I told Victoria I had a bad cold and would stay in bed. She refused to listen and told me to get up. Eventually I gave in. On the day of the lecture I saw Magnus in the SCR at lunch time. He was sitting next to Agnes, chatting amicably. This was most suspicious; he always looked morose when Agnes was around. Her new book with a university press unnerved him. She was telling him that she had just been granted study leave so she could work on her next volume. He smiled and said something polite. When I sat down, he picked up the *Times Higher Educational Supplement* and avoided looking at me. Then Agnes asked about the title of Catnip's lecture. I wasn't sure and Magnus mumbled something inaudible.

The occasion was to start at five o'clock. Victoria arrived at my office at 4:30. She was looking wonderful in a silk suit and her face was glowing. Several minutes later Magnus knocked on the door. He sat himself down on the sofa next to Victoria. "Look," I said. "I've changed my mind. I really don't want to go. I have no interest whatsoever in seventeenth-century land tenure. If you both want to attend, that's fine with me. But I'm staying behind. Anyway, I've work to do"

"But you promised..." Victoria protested.

"I've changed my mind."

"Well, you can't. You've got to come. Magnus and I insist, don't we Magnus?"

"Come on Harry," Magnus said. "You said you'd go."

"I've changed my mind."

"You can't," Victoria spoke quite sharply, "I've made a special effort to be here. If you don't come, you can't expect me to do all the things you want me to do."

I knew when I was beaten. "You two are up to something," I said.

Magnus looked conspiratorially at Victoria, and stood up. "Get up, Harry," he said, "Don't be a wimp. We don't want to be late."

"I'm not a wimp. I don't want to listen to Bossyboots. And I can't see why you would."

Victoria pulled me up out of my armchair. "Get up, Harry. We're going." Magnus grabbed my other arm, and they frog-marched me out the door. On the way to the Great Hall, I saw Barraclough striding out in our direction. He was wearing his gown and a mortarboard. "Good," he said. "I see you're coming to the lecture."

"Hello, Vice-Chancellor," Victoria said with her best smile. He softened visibly and doffed his mortarboard with a flourish. He had always had a soft spot for Victoria. Magnus was convulsed in giggles.

"OK," I said. "What's going on?"

"Nothing...", said Magnus airily. Victoria was silent. She frowned and walked faster. There was no choice. I had to follow.

A small crowd had assembled by the time we arrived. On the stage was a row of chairs. In the background was a banner with the crest of the university. Most of my colleagues were scattered in the audience. I sat in the back between Victoria and Magnus. Magnus continued to chuckle and stared straight ahead. As the cathedral bells struck the hour, everyone stood up. A trumpeter wearing a red academic gown and a floppy Tudor hat marched to the stage. He began Purcell's voluntary.

A procession consisting of the Visitor, the Vice-Chancellor, the Registrar, and various other dignitaries marched in. Wanda Catnip entered last. She was dressed in her University of Hull doctoral gown. They all sat on the stage except for the Vice-Chancellor who stood behind a podium. He was resplendent in his black and gold Vice-Chancellor robe. He read several lines in Latin, and then translated them into English. Magnus continued to giggle throughout. Victoria stared straight ahead. I looked at them both – I felt disaster was looming.

Catnip blushed with pleasure as the Vice-Chancellor praised both her scholarship as an economic historian and her invaluable efforts for the university as Dean. He explained that a group of assessors had recently agreed that she should be appointed to a personal Chair. They had particularly commended her contribution to our understanding of land tenure in the seventeenth-century. He then held up a copy of her recently published book. This study, he explained, was the fruit of years of sustained and dedicated research and was of seminal importance. In fact it was based on her PhD thesis which she had written twenty years earlier. I happened to know that the revised version had been rejected by several university presses before being taken on by an obscure American publishing house. However, it was no secret that Barraclough was adept at ignoring realities for his own purposes.

There was polite applause when Wanda stood up and walked up to the podium. In her hand was a depressingly thick wad of paper. I wondered how long we were going to have to endure all this. The Vice-Chancellor sat down in a large wooden chair at the edge of the stage, and rearranged his gown. He nodded to a photographer sitting in the front row who stood up and took Catnip's photograph. She smiled. Then she started. We were clearly in for a very dull hour.

I looked across at Victoria. Her face was raised toward the speaker with every appearance of absorbed interest. Magnus was fidgeting. I settled myself in my seat and sighed. How had I got myself into this situation? I closed my eyes and tried to think about something else.

Suddenly there was a commotion at the back. The door swung open and a huge man wearing a hairy brown gorilla costume entered. He bellowed as he lolloped toward the stage. Barraclough looked stunned. Sloth stood up, and then sat down again. Wanda looked pale, but she stood firm by the podium. He stopped in front of her, swung around, beat his chest and bellowed again. Then he took two bananas out of his pocket and presented one to Wanda. "Congratulations," he said. He peeled open his own banana and proceeded to eat it while he capered about the stage. Then he beat his chest again and threw the banana skin on the floor. He bellowed again, blew Wanda a kiss and snatched the lecture off the podium. Catnip tried to grab it back, but he held it above her head and, still prancing, proceeded to screw up individual sheets and throw them among the audience. There was another photographic flash from the front.

Initially the audience seemed stunned. Then Barraclough started patting his pockets underneath his robe and eventually he brought out a mobile telephone. He seemed to have some difficulty turning the machine on, but after a few seconds he started speaking urgently into it. The gorilla leapt into the air and off the stage. He threw the remaining lecture sheets onto the floor. Still beating his chest and bellowing, he cantered out of the hall. Wanda was left holding the banana.

The audience slowly came to life and the Vice-Chancellor stood up. He put on his mortarboard and strode to the podium. Under cover of the audience chatter, Magnus was convulsed with laughter. Victoria hissed at him to be quiet. We waited to see what would happen next.

Wanda left the banana on the podium and sat down in her chair. Barraclough leaned over her in discussion. She was clearly shaken by what had happened and showed signs of becoming tearful. I saw her say, "But I haven't got my paper! He took it!"

After several minutes, Barraclough walked to the podium. "This has been an outrage," he fulminated. "As Vice-Chancellor, I will not tolerate such behaviour in my university. Whoever is responsible will be subject to the most severe discipline." Wanda snivelled as he continued. "I'm afraid this event will have to be cancelled. Given the circumstances, I think it will be better for Professor Catnip to deliver her most interesting lecture at a later date so she can be spared such an unforgivable interruption. Can I ask you all to leave quietly after the procession."

He swept off the stage and the rest of the university officers tried to reassemble their dignity. Raggedly they followed Barraclough out of the Great Hall, leaving the audience in a state of happy confusion. Magnus was weeping with joy. I had never seen him so elated. Victoria poked him with her forefinger. She spoke severely. "Pull yourself together, Magnus," she said. "Poor Wanda. What a terrible thing to happen!" I looked at her. She gazed back at me. Her face was completely expressionless.

Victoria, Magnus and I left quickly and went directly to my room. Magnus stretched out on my sofa, convulsed in giggles. Victoria poured us all a drink. I sat at my desk. "OK," I said, "Explain!"

Victoria poked Magnus. "Oh, joy! Oh joy!" he gurgled. "The happiest day since I came here."

"You two are responsible, aren't you?"

Victoria smiled. "It was good, wasn't it?"

I sighed. "You'd better tell me all about it."

"Magnus didn't do anything," Victoria explained. "It was all my idea. I saw an advertisement in the back of *Private Eye* for kissograms. So I called them. Well, they do various kinds of things: kissograms, stripograms, and gorillagrams. It all sounded intriguing, so I went up to London a few days ago and spoke to the person who runs the organization."

Magnus couldn't stop chuckling. He rolled over and buried his head in the sofa. "So," Victoria continued, "I didn't want anyone to know who I was. I borrowed a blonde wig from a Women's Institute friend, got a 52 bus from Knightsbridge to Willesden, and pretended I was Welsh. I used my best Welsh accent. Anyway, the place was located in a little room up the stairs from a greengrocer. I spoke first to a receptionist and then to the person who dresses up as a gorilla. He was splendid. I told him that my son was a student at St Sebastian's and was having endless trouble with the Dean. I explained in detail what I wanted, and paid in cash. I stressed that there was to be no stripping, or kissing. Everything had to be respectable. But I also said that, without actually stealing it, the Dean had to be separated from her lecture. I paid him with the money I got from the article in *Country Life*. It cost a hundred and seventy-five pounds plus VAT."

"Don't worry, Harry," she emphasized, "no one will ever know it was me."

"You're a genius, Victoria," Magnus said looking up from the sofa.

The following day there was a photograph of the gorilla and Wanda on the front page of the *St Sebastian's Gazette* with the headline 'Gorilla Disrupts Lecture'. Clearly the photographer had been busy. The article explained that Professor Catnip had just been appointed to a personal Chair, and she was to deliver her inaugural professorial lecture. Just as she began to speak, a gorilla jumped up to the podium, handed her a banana, and then tore up her lecture. It quoted Barraclough who expressed outrage that anyone could have behaved in such a way. He declared that if this prank were done by students, they would be sent down from the university. If staff were responsible, they would be dismissed. The article went on to say that Professor Catnip was deeply shaken by this incident and would be taking sick leave for an undetermined period. The lecture would be postponed to a future date.

The Senior Common Room was buzzing with gossip. Magnus and I sat next to Wendy Morehouse who was talking to the History department secretary. She said that the gorilla had left a card with the porter. He asked if it could be put on the noticeboard. The Registrar had been trying to reach his organization all day, but there had been no answer. The Vice-Chancellor was determined to find the person who paid for the gorillagram. I asked about Wanda. Was it true she was going on sick leave? The History secretary nodded. She had been so disturbed by what had happened, that she was unable to concentrate on work. It had been agreed that she would come back as soon as she recovered. Wanda had sent her an email, saying she was going to see the doctor and would send in a doctor's certificate later in the day. "It is a great tragedy," she sighed. Magnus spluttered behind his newspaper.

Pilkington was at another table near us. He was lamenting what had happened with several members of the department. He shook his head as the others looked on sympathetically. I tried to overhear what he was saying. Like the secretaries, he related that the gorilla had left his calling card. The organization was called Kissogram UK, and he had looked it up on the internet. Alongside pictures of a naked woman wearing a g-string, there was a photograph of the gorilla. London based, it listed costs. Pilkington was puzzled that students would be prepared to pay nearly two hundred pounds, and he suspected that the gorillagram might have been sent by a member of staff. The VC was determined to interview any possible culprits. The question was: who had a grudge against Wanda?

CHAPTER EIGHT

What Kind of a Deal Can You Offer Me?

Rumours were circulating throughout the week about Catnip's lecture. The Vice-Chancellor was determined to discover who had hired the gorilla, and he had eventually contacted Kissogram UK. Initially the owner refused to give out any information. But after threats of police investigation, he revealed that a Welsh woman with blonde hair had paid in cash for him to visit the university. She was the mother of a student who was currently having difficulties with the Dean.

The Registrar had then been given instructions to look through the entire undergraduate body for all those with Welsh names, and the names and addresses of all students from Wales had been compiled as well. It emerged that over two hundred students were possible suspects. They had all been emailed asking if they knew anything about the prank. To the Vice-Chancellor's dismay, there were so many possibilities that the task of uncovering the culprit seemed impossible, but he insisted that he was leaving no stone unturned.

Victoria was delighted with the outcome of her adventure, but I felt guilty about Wanda. It was true that she had plotted against me, and that I had been given a written warning. She and Pilkington had conspired and connived with the Vice-Chancellor to see if I would take early retirement. Yet, Wanda was a lonely, rather sad figure whose only consolation was her career. She lived in a drab house on an estate on her small income. We had robbed her of her great triumph, and I was wrestling with my conscience.

Several evenings after the lecture, I told Victoria that I would prepare dinner. I found it difficult to concentrate and I cut my finger while making salad. Then I accidentally spilled water over the Aga while cooking spaghetti. Victoria couldn't understand why I was being so clumsy. When I told her that I felt bad about what she had done, she refused to listen. "She got what she deserved," she said

"I suppose so. But compare our lives with hers."

"That has nothing to do with it. She's responsible for your troubles, and she ought to have a few of her own. You're being silly, Harry. My father fought in the Second World War; he was part of the D-Day landings. His colonel was shot in front of him and half his men were wounded. He didn't sniffle and say he couldn't go on. He improvised. He had only just left school, but he rallied his troops and they captured the German guns. That's how he got his DSO. And it's what you'd have done! If someone had disrupted your lecture, you'd have eaten the banana, made a joke and kept the audience amused for an hour anyway. Little Miss Bossyboots is totally pathetic. She can't even give a lecture without notes. And then she goes off sick. That's not the kind of behaviour that put the Great into Great Britain!"

"But that doesn't make it right." I sounded feeble even to myself.

"You're not being rational. You're an expert on ethics, right? And you've always described yourself as a Christian utilitarian, right? That means you believe in the greatest happiness for the greatest number. Well, do the calculation. Magnus was thrilled. I was thrilled. The audience was certainly happier with the gorilla than they would have been with a boring exposition on seventeenth-century land tenure. The university has something to talk about for a change. The gorilla was delighted to receive his fee. Barraclough has a chance to be even more pompous than usual. Even the Personnel Officer can now justify her existence contacting all the Welsh students. The *St Sebastian's Gazette* was pleased to have a sensational story. And the students themselves are enjoying the extra attention. So Wanda's misery is trivial besides all this. It was clearly the right thing to do."

"But she's on sick leave," I objected.

"That adds even more happiness to the calculation. Think how restful it is for everyone without her!"

"They're still looking for the person who hired the gorilla. Once they've exhausted the student population, they'll probably start on the staff."

"Well, if you're asked, all you have to say is that you didn't know anything about it. That's the truth. And if they ask if you know who did it, just lie."

"I suppose I'll have to."

"Good grief, Harry. It's just a little white lie. Just concentrate on the huge amount of happiness the whole episode has given the university. There was even publicity."

On the Friday following the lecture, a small article about the gorillagram had appeared in the *Times Higher Educational Supplement*. The column featured a picture of the gorilla. (Victoria pointed out that the photographer would have been happy with his fee.) Underneath there was a headline: 'Professor Pooped by Primate.' The item went on to explain that Professor Wanda Catnip had just been promoted to a personal Chair, and that her inaugural professorial lecture had been disrupted by the arrival of a gorillagram. The Vice-Chancellor was quoted at length. He used all the usual clichés about weakest links and bad apples, and he declared his determination to discover the person or persons responsible. The next week there was a two line reference to the event in *Private Eye*. ("Still more happiness!" said Victoria.)

In a severe email sent out to all staff, Barraclough instructed them not to speak to any member of the press. All inquires from newspaper reporters, he stated, should be directed either to him or to the Registrar. Any infringement of this instruction would be treated in the most serious manner.

Several days later, yet another letter arrived in my pigeonhole from the Vice-Chancellor marked Private and Confidential. With a sense of dread I opened it. The Vice-Chancellor, it said, would like to see me for a brief interview on Wednesday at four. It was to be an informal meeting to discuss my future. I debated whether to take Penelope. But I resolved to say no to any offer that might be made.

On Wednesday I arrived early. Barraclough greeted me warmly and showed me into his office. I sat in a wing armchair across from his desk. His secretary came in carrying a tray with a silver teapot, cups and saucers, and a large coffee and walnut cake. The Vice-Chancellor poured out the tea and handed me a slice of cake. I had never seen him so amiable.

"It's a pity about Wanda's lecture," he began. " The poor girl is very upset. We'll have to reschedule it sometime."

"How is she?" I asked.

"In rather a bad way. Very weepy. Unfortunately we don't seem to be having much luck catching the culprit. Whoever it was covered their tracks. Anyway, in the circumstances, she deserves some study leave. I've decided that she ought to have a full term next academic year."

"Now Harry," he said as he munched his way through two large slices of cake, "I know we recently had a conversation about early retirement in less favourable circumstances. But something has emerged that I need to talk to you about."

I noticed that Barraclough was wearing his Acropolis tie. "Vice-Chancellor," I interrupted. "Is it true that the Registrar doesn't want to be a member of the club?"

"Well, I think it's more complicated than that," he replied. "There's been some difficulty with the election committee, and I was advised to withdraw his name."

"Oh dear," I responded. "I hope he's not too distressed?"

Barraclough fiddled with a folder on his desk and avoided my question. He took out a letter and adjusted his spectacles.

"I have just received this note from Mr Gold," he said. "Let me read it to you:

Dear Vice-Chancellor,

You will remember that we have had recent correspondence about my daughter who is a student at your university. I am glad to report that she has recovered from the unfortunate ordeal of last term. She seems much more settled and is happy with her studies.

The reason I am writing to you is to inform you of my intention of making a donation to the university as I indicated previously. However, rather than wait until Lisa graduates, I would like to make this benefaction at an earlier stage while Lisa is with you. My proposal is to establish a Lectureship in Ethics in remembrance of my dear mother.

I know it would have given her enormous pleasure to honour the institution where her granddaughter is a student. I would like the lectureship to be in her name, and I am prepared to fund it for three years in the first instance.

I would be grateful if you could let me know if this gift might be suitable.

Yours sincerely,

Freddy Gold, MBE

Gold and Gold Manufacturers"

"That's very generous," I said.

"It is indeed. Particularly given the difficulties of last term. I phoned Mr Gold yesterday and we discussed his proposal at length. There is one condition that I want to explore with you. It appears that Mr Gold intends to give this donation on the understanding that the person appointed would take over all teaching of ethics in your department."

"But I do the ethics teaching."

"Yes. That's just the point. The condition of the gift is that the new lecturer takes over all your courses."

"That's outrageous." I was furious. "He's just trying to get rid of me by the back door."

"Look, Harry. We are most grateful for all you've done here. You have made a real contribution to the university. But surely you do see the merits of accepting this gift. It really is a lot of money!"

"You can't expect me to take early retirement just so Mr Gold can replace me with a junior lecturer."

"I do have a proposal for you, Harry. The university is prepared to enhance your pension and offer you a quarter-time contract for the next five years. This would enable you to have more time for research and travel and still retain your links to St Sebastian's. It would also enable you to develop your teaching interests outside the field of ethics. Of course you will need some time to think this over . . ."

"That's not necessary," I said. "There's nothing to think over. The answer is no."

"Please be reasonable, Harry. This is a generous offer which would save the university a great deal of money."

"I don't want to take early retirement, Vice-Chancellor. And I do resent the whole proposal. I assume Mr Gold intends to be involved in the appointment."

"Well, yes. That is another condition of the bequest."

"And I suppose he intends to appoint young Ronald Grundy, my research student. You are aware, aren't you, that he's going out with Mr Gold's daughter."

"I didn't know that," said Barraclough. He looked embarrassed. "Mr Gold did mention his name as a promising young scholar."

"What does Gold know about ethics? Promising young scholar indeed! He's just trying to buy a job for his daughter's boy-friend!"

"It isn't like that at all, Harry. If this lectureship were established, the job would be advertised in the normal way. Candidates would be selected on the basis of their qualifications, and there would be interviews."

"But Gold will be on the appointment committee, and he will make it clear that young Ronald is the only candidate he will pay for." I put my cup of tea on Barraclough's desk and stood up. "Thank you Vice-Chancellor for letting me know about this. But I have made up my mind. I am happy here and have no intention of leaving. Now if you'll excuse me, I have work to do." Barraclough sat at his desk as I walked to the door. As I shut it, I noticed that he cut himself another slice of cake and was reaching for the telephone.

Victoria was horrified when I told her about my interview with Barraclough. Magnus was less surprised. "Sneaky shit," he said. "All he can think about is money. No standards. And as for Gold, that man is a menace to scholarship."

I was determined to stick to the point. "But look Magnus, is there anything I can do?"

"I think you've done it. You said no."

"I'm afraid it's not going to be the end of the matter."

I was due to have a supervision with Ronald the following week. No doubt he'd heard from Lisa that her father's scheme had met serious obstacles. I wondered how he would react. On the day, he arrived fifteen minutes late. He was flustered when he knocked on my door. I offered him a cup of coffee, but he refused.

Seated on my sofa, he spread out papers on the floor. "My computer has been acting up," he said. "That's why I'm late. I wanted to print out my last chapter, but the printer wouldn't connect up. Anyway, I finally managed to get it printed. Do you mind if I make a call?" he asked. He took his mobile telephone out of his jacket pocket and dialled a number. "Hi," he said. "Yea, I finally got it to work. So I don't need yours. Look, I'm with Professor Gilbert now. Can we meet at the Student Union in an hour?"

I looked over his chapter as he spoke. When he finished, I asked him when he thought he'd be ready to submit the thesis. "It's nearly finished," he said. "Just this last chapter and the conclusion. If you think it's OK, I should be able to complete the whole thing by June."

"Very good," I said. "Have you thought what you'll do next?"

"Actually," he sounded awkward. "I have just got engaged to Lisa Gold. Not formally, but we plan to get married this summer."

"Congratulations," I said.

"So, I've got to look for a job. There doesn't seem much at the moment. There is a lectureship at Aberdeen in systematic theology; I saw the advertisement in the *Times Higher Ed* last week. But it isn't really my field. And anyway Lisa has still got another year to do here."

"I see. It's a problem." I tried to sound as neutral as possible.

When the supervision ended, Ronald packed up his papers, put on his coat, and left. I watched from my window as he made his way to the Student Union. He looked downcast as he walked across the campus.

Rumours were still circulating about Wanda. There was no announcement about her lecture, but Barraclough sent out a note to the department saying that she was planning to return at the beginning of next term. I had a pile of essays to mark, and I was busy reading them when Magnus arrived at my door one afternoon. He was wearing a new Harris tweed jacket, and a dashing red and yellow bow tie.

"You look very jolly," I said. He dropped into my armchair and handed me a letter. "You won't believe this," he sounded excited. "You know my aunt gave me a present at Christmas of a few premium bonds. Well, they worked." The letter was from the office of National Savings, announcing that Magnus had won a quarter of a million pounds. Normally a cheque for small prizes arrives in a standard envelope, but winners of large sums are informed individually.

"That's amazing, Magnus. I don't know anyone who has ever won a big prize. My father-in-law has been trying for years; I think he has the full quota of premium bonds, but he's never won more than a hundred pounds at one time." I phoned Victoria and told her Magnus's news. We arranged to have dinner to celebrate in a small Indian restaurant in town. Magnus insisted it would be his treat and he booked a table.

He was waiting for us when we arrived. We had onion bahjis to begin, and Magnus ordered pints of lager all around. Lifting his glass, he said, "Destruction to our enemies! And Happy Days!"

"Happy days at St Sebastian's?" Victoria inquired sceptically.

"You must be joking," he said. "I'll be giving in my notice as soon as I can. But don't tell anybody. I have an appointment with the VC and Sloth next week. I want to get the best deal I can. There's no need for them to know I just won a big prize. I plan to plead poverty . . . got to squeeze them dry. And then I'm off!"

"Off?"

"I'm going around the world." Magnus pulled a brochure out of a Marks and Spencer bag that he had put next to his chair. As he flipped through the pages, he enthused about the Queen Christina. He had circled the cabin he wanted to have: it was the cheapest first-class accommodation, but would entitle him to the first-class dining room. There were pictures of elegant, grey-haired couples playing shuffleboard, dancing and swimming in the indoor pool. Some of the men were wearing dinner jackets and their partners were dressed in ball gowns and diamonds. "What do you think?" he asked.

"You'll love it, Magnus," replied Victoria. "But do you have a dinner jacket?"

"Mine had the moth decades ago. But I thought I'd be able to find a used one at a charity shop."

"What about dancing?" I asked.

"Actually, that might prove something of a problem. My aunt insisted I have lessons when I was about eleven. I even learned the tango. But I can't remember a thing. If I just jiggle about will that be OK?"

"No, Magnus," Victoria sighed. "It won't. If you plan to be a hit with the grandmothers, you'll have to brush up on the fox-trot and waltz. Do you want me to teach you?"

"You wouldn't mind?"

"Of course not," Victoria said. "At Cheltenham we had classes with the gym teacher."

"Do you think I could learn?" Magnus asked shyly.

"Anyone could learn, even Bossyboots."

"You know," I said. "I've heard she's actually quite good at ballroom dancing. I understand she won some competition."

Magnus had ordered a vast quantity of food including tandoori king prawn, chicken korma, and lamb vindaloo as well as a variety of vegetable dishes. I thought I would forget my diet and enjoy myself. After several pints of lager, Magnus looked glazed. "Look, Harry," he said. "I've got to see the VC and Sloth next week to tell them I'm going to leave. I need a friend to come with me. Would you mind?"

"I'd be delighted," I said. "But what are you going to say?"

"Wait and see," he replied as he tackled the After Eight mints.

On the day, Magnus arrived half an hour early. He was wearing an old tweed jacket that had a large hole in one sleeve. He smelled of whiskey. "How do I look?" he asked as he slouched into my armchair.

"Terrible," I said. "What happened to your jacket?"

"I poked a hole in the elbow with a fork."

"Your breath is quite awful. What have you been drinking?"

"Scotch. Actually, I soaked my jacket in it this morning."

"Why? The VC will think you're a tramp."

"That's just the idea," he smiled. He pulled a whiskey bottle out of his brief case and handed it to me. "Want a drink?"

"No thanks, Magnus. But I don't get it. What are you up to?"

Without answering he stood up. "You know," he said, "I'm not sure I can stand wearing this jacket. It really stinks of drink. Come on, let's go."

When we arrived at Barraclough's office, the door was open. He was speaking to Sloth and ushered us in. Magnus thrust out his hand; the Vice-Chancellor looked dismayed. He shook it and then stepped back coughing. "You'd better sit down," he said.

Magnus staggered into an armchair. I sat next to him on a dining chair that had been pulled up to Barraclough's desk. Sloth sat on the sofa. He was holding a small calculator and had a pile of papers spread out next to him. The Vice-Chancellor looked disapprovingly at Magnus. "I see you've had a bit to drink," he said.

"More than a bit. Actually quite a lot."

Sloth stared at Magnus's jacket. The hole had got bigger and his elbow was even more visible. Barraclough shifted uncomfortably. "I understand you want to talk to us about early retirement," he said.

"I do." Magnus looked exceedingly tipsy. "I can't cope, Vice-Chancellor. I'm simply exhausted. I feel on the verge of a breakdown..."

"I see."

Magnus leaned forward; the fumes wafted from his jacket and Barraclough moved his chair backwards. "The idea of summer school is the final straw," he declared. "Can't concentrate on teaching or anything. When I look at the students in my classes, I feel sick. That's why I'm here."

Sloth began doing some sums on his calculator. Magnus stretched out and sighed. The Vice-Chancellor took out a file and made notes. Magnus belched noisily. "What kind of a deal have you got to offer me?" he asked.

Sloth looked up from his work. He passed over his pocket calculator to Barraclough. The Vice-Chancellor made a note and handed over a piece of paper to Magnus who dropped it. I reached down and handed it to him. He looked as though he was going to pass out. Drunkenly he read out the note: "'Enhancement of five years. No part-time teaching. Beginning October.'"

Magnus looked stupefied. "Vice-Chancellor," I said. "Perhaps we ought to discuss details when Magnus is in a better state."

"I'm fine," Magnus belched again. "But not too frisky after so much whisky!" He took out a pen, crossed out October, and added: 'One year study leave on full pay.' "Think I deserve it," he said. "Anyway, I won't get my full pension if I retire in the autumn. I'm only sixty next year. So I need five full years enhancement after that." He winked at Barraclough and passed him back the note.

The Vice-Chancellor shook his head. "I'm not sure...."

"It's non-negotiable," Magnus interrupted. "Take it or leave it. A one day offer. It expires at midnight. Otherwise, I'll stay here and endure it for six more years, and you'll have to pay me until I'm sixty-five. Is that what you prefer?"

Barraclough shook his head. "No, Magnus. You've got to go."

"Then you've got to pay me. It's not exactly a golden handshake. You're getting off lightly. Most academics want part-time teaching. I want to leave for good."

Sloth passed a note across the desk. The Vice-Chancellor read it and sighed. "All right Magnus. It's not unreasonable. But no part-time teaching. After next year, you'll be fully retired. I hope you make profitable use of a year's sabbatical. Perhaps you'll manage to get something written for the RAE."

Magnus brightened. "Good," he said. "If you'd care to sign your note, then I'll consider the matter done. I'll sign it too as a goodwill gesture. The Registrar and Harry can witness the deal. That will constitute my notice as well as your guarantee about the sabbatical and the five years' enhancement. You can draw up the formal letter later."

Barraclough looked puzzled, but signed anyway. He passed the note to Sloth who scribbled his signature and then gave it to me. Both Magnus and I added our names "Shall we celebrate?" Magnus asked, taking his whiskey bottle out of his briefcase. It was followed by four tumblers which he put on the desk.

Barraclough recoiled, "Not today," he said.

"If not now, when?" Magnus asked.

"Perhaps later. I'm sure your department will have a retirement party. You can celebrate then."

Magnus packed up his glasses, leaving the whiskey bottle on Barraclough's desk. He stood up. "Now, Vice-Chancellor, is this absolutely legal?" He sounded far more sober. "Can I come back if I change my mind?"

"No Magnus," Sloth said. "You can't. I'm afraid you are definitely going. There's no coming back."

"And you can't renege on your part of the bargain? I get five years' enhancement to my pension after my one year's paid sabbatical?"

"That's correct," said Barraclough.

"Right. Well, then there's one thing I want to mention to you on this happy occasion. I thought you might like to know that my aunt Ursula gave me some premium bonds for Christmas.

And I won one of the big prizes. A quarter of a million to be precise. Just got the letter last week."

Barraclough looked shocked. He opened his mouth and closed it. "So," Magnus continued, "I think I can spend next year quite profitably on a round-the-world cruise. Actually, I just booked it. Reserved a snazzy little first-class cabin. Harry's wife promised to give me some dancing lessons so I can tango with the old ladies."

Barraclough stared at Magnus as he stood up and did a little jig. "Come on Harry," he said, as he made his way to the door. As he danced out, he slipped out of his sport jacket and slung it over a coat hook on the back of the door. "Perhaps you can find a good home for my jacket. Give it to one of your wage-slaves," he said. "I'm off to see my tailor!"

Later in the afternoon Magnus and I caught the train to London. We took the underground to Bond Street, and walked to a small antique shop near Berkeley Square that specializes in leather luggage. Magnus found a very heavy trunk with brass fittings and arranged for it to be delivered to the university. We then went to Jermyn Street where he bought a selection of silk ties. "Got to be equipped for the voyage," he announced as he gathered up his purchases.

In the evening we went to the Acropolis for dinner. Afterwards, as we walked up the stairs to the drawing room, I saw the Bishop of Bosworth, my old friend Charles, talking to the Lord Chancellor. He joined us for coffee later and I introduced him to Magnus. "Charles and I were at Cambridge together," I explained. "Now he's a bishop!"

"How very grand!" Magnus said slyly.

"Magnus is off on a round-the-world cruise." I said. I explained that he was going to have a year's sabbatical and then would retire from St Sebastian's. Charles looked envious. "And how are you, Harry?" he asked. "Is that little difficulty with the undergraduate sorted out?"

"Not exactly," I said. I explained that even though the matter with Lisa had been dropped, I was having difficulties with my Head of Department and the Dean. Magnus made snide remarks as I recounted the story of Pilkington and Catnip. "But that prissy fusspot got what she deserved," Magnus affirmed. "Upstaged by a gorilla."

"I think I read something about that in *Private Eye*," Charles said. "But I've got some good news for you, Harry. Of course, it's strictly confidential," he whispered.

"Can Magnus know?" I asked.

"Well, he shouldn't. You shouldn't either for that matter. But I suppose it won't do any harm. You're going to get an award in the Queen's Honours List. I rounded up some of my fellow bishops and we sent in a recommendation along with suggestions of referees. It'll be for your contribution to Christian ethics."

I was elated. "This isn't a joke?"

"No really, Harry. It's in the bag. I had a word with the Archbishop at Cannonbury last week. He's one of your referees."

"He's to be a knight?" Magnus was impressed.

"Well, not exactly," Charles said. "More like an OBE."

"Oh dear," Magnus said. "Well, you've got to start somewhere!"

I was a bit disappointed: I wasn't going to be called 'Sir', and Victoria wasn't going to become a Lady. But at least an OBE was something. "Thanks Charles," I said. "Very kind of you."

"Don't mention it old chap. I felt you needed a treat after the nonsense with that student." Charles got up to greet a fellow bishop and disappeared into the library. Magnus finished his glass of port, picked up the *New York Review of Books* and settled into his armchair. He was elated. "Well, Harry," he said. "That'll make Barraclough even more angry. He's been longing for a gong, and he won't like the fact you got one. Pilkington and Bossyboots will be furious when you go to Buckingham Palace to pick up the thing. You'll get to meet the Queen and shake the royal hand. I can't wait to see their faces!"

Both of us had too much to drink and were rather bleary-eyed on the way home. The train was late and we arrived after midnight. We took a taxi and out of curiosity passed by Catnip's house; her lights were on, and we heard familiar voices at the door. I told the driver to stop. Pilkington and his wife and my postgraduate Ronald Grundy and his fiancée Lisa Gold were just leaving. I looked at Magnus. "What's that all about?" I asked.

"Doesn't look good to me," Magnus said peering out the window. "We'd better not get caught staring." And with that the taxi sped off into the darkness.

Victoria was waiting for me in the drawing room when I arrived home. She was curled up on the sofa reading the latest P.D. James novel; Cleo and Brutus were asleep by her feet. They looked a picture. "Did you have a nice time with Magnus?" she asked. I had phoned her in the afternoon to tell her about our meeting with the Vice-Chancellor and Sloth.

"Lovely," I said, as I collapsed into the armchair opposite. "Now, look, Victoria, I've got some good news. I saw Charles at the club. He told me I'm going to get an award in the Queen's Honours List."

"A knighthood?" she asked hopefully.

"Just an OBE, I'm afraid."

"Poor Harry. Well, at least it's not the bottom."

"I'm rather pleased about it,"

"And just what will you do with your medal – wear it on your dressing gown?"

"Actually," I said, "that might look quite fetching."

"Why don't you wear it at graduation pinned on your hat."

"It's not a joke, Victoria."

"No, no joke. Sorry. Very serious. Actually, that's very nice, Harry. By the way, what's it for?"

I wasn't going to tell her it was because Charles sympathized with me after I had been propositioned by a student. "Charles said it was for my contribution to ethics."

Victoria laughed. "Very suitable, given the gorilla's treatment of Catnip."

"That's not fair. It was your idea."

"Yes, but you loved it. And so did everyone else. Yes, contribution to ethics," she mused. "Just right!"

114

CHAPTER NINE

Can I Take You Dancing?

Victoria thought we needed a break and had arranged for us to go to the Cotswolds over the weekend to visit the Mandril-Fortescues in their new house. We set off early on Saturday and arrived after lunch. James was trimming the hedges when we drew up. Their Georgian double-fronted cottage was located just outside Upper Buttercup. There was a large magnolia tree in bloom in the front. James showed us to our room overlooking the garden. Like their Chelsea house, the cottage was full of exquisite furniture and old Oriental carpets. Their golden labrador, Maximillan, bounded about and demanded attention.

After we unpacked, we had tea and delicious fruitcake in their pretty drawing room. Vanessa enthused about life in the country and told Victoria about several of their school friends who lived nearby. As our wives gossiped, James explained that he was keeping going doing some part-time consultancy. He had set up an office in their garden house which was connected to the internet. There was no difficulty in getting on the web and sending faxes. Email, he continued, was also no problem:

he pulled a Blackberry out of his jacket pocket, turned it on, and explained that all communications arrived without even having to dial up an internet service provider.

Vanessa turned the conversation to her grandchildren. One reason they had settled in the village was that their daughter, Camilla, lived five miles away. She was married and the mother of three children. Victoria was intrigued. She remembered that Vanessa had not altogether approved of her son-in-law.

"Well," said Vanessa, "he is a bit minor public school, but you won't believe the money he's made. I don't know what he does. He talks about something called commodities. But it certainly brings home the bacon." Then we heard that the eldest grandchild would be participating in a gymkhana over the weekend, and it was arranged that we would go with the family.

After tea, Victoria and I walked into Upper Buttercup. Near the village green there was a row of delightful shops including an estate agent. Victoria insisted we go in. We were greeted by a smartly dressed middle-aged woman wearing a grey flannel skirt and a Guernsey sweater. From her accent it was obvious that she had been expensively educated.

We emerged with a batch of brochures about local cottages for sale. The prices were similar to St Sebastian's; we could easily afford to move into the area, and Victoria was persistent. "Harry," she said as we walked along a narrow lane lined with charming golden cottages, "I think we would be happy here. Vanessa and James love it. We'd fit in. There would be lots of people like us. Haven't we had quite enough of that boring university?"

I felt increasingly guilty throughout dinner. James and Vanessa had asked their neighbours, David and Julia Seymour, to join us. David was a retired barrister; a bencher at his inn-of-court, He regularly journeyed up to London for dinners. His wife was active in the local Red Cross and was chairman of the village Women's Institute. Victoria and she compared notes. She was also having an ongoing quarrel with the lady-vicar over the new services in church.

"I never understood why we abandoned the *Book of Common Prayer*!" she complained.

I knew that Vanessa had had little academic education beyond the age of seventeen, but her parents had ensured she had gone to a first-rate Swiss finishing school. Consequently our dinner was wonderful. We began with asparagus soup made from local produce, followed by guinea fowl coated with honey. Pudding was my favourite, jam roly-poly. There was also a fruit tart which was a work of art and a magnificent selection of cheese. My trousers felt tighter and tighter.

Victoria was animated throughout. With glee she described in detail the gorilla's appearance at Catnip's lecture. The table was convulsed. Later Julia and Vanessa told stories of their own children's experiences in various establishments of higher education. It was clear that the Cotswold upper-middle classes thought their children were being short-changed by the modern university system.

"It's not like it was when I was at Oxford," said David. "When Archy was at Exemouth, there was no proper individual attention. The groups were bigger than his classes at Winchester. When I met his tutor at graduation, he didn't even seem to know who he was."

I tried to remind the company that we were trying to educate a far larger proportion of young people than in the past. "That's just the point," boomed Julia in a voice designed to carry over three hunting fields, "Everyone knows, More means Worse!"

On Sunday we joined Vanessa's family and the Seymours for the morning service at their local church. The incumbent, the Rev. Kathleen Volefield, was a predictably mousey woman. The congregation used *Common Worship* much to Julia and Vanessa's outspoken dismay. "Such dreary prayers," they said loudly.

After the service, James introduced me to Ms. Volefield I was flattered when she said that she had used my textbook on Christian ethics at Salisbury Theological College. "You certainly charmed her," James commented on our way to the car.

"Rather a good sermon," I said. "I've always liked the parable of the sheep and the goats."

"Too much talk about doing things for people," Vanessa objected as we drove home to lunch. "People have got to learn to stand on their own feet. No backbone, that's the trouble

117

nowadays." I restrained myself from pointing out that not everyone was fortunate enough to have feet to stand on.

In the afternoon we met Camilla and her husband Richard at the gymkhana. Their eldest child, Pandora, was entering for the first time on her fat little pony. The creature's name was Smudges, and he had been very obstinate about climbing into his horse-box. Both Camilla and Richard were in a state of exhaustion. Their two youngest children, both boys, were in the care of their Australian nanny. Little Pandora was thrilled – she was bouncing up and down on Smudges's back and demanding that we all look at her. She calmed down somewhat after she had been round the course. Smudges had knocked down three fences and had refused a fourth. When she came out of the ring, Pandora was in tears and was only consoled by sitting on her mother's lap with a very large ice-cream.

Victoria was in her element. I watched her drifting around with Vanessa in her oily green jacket and old gum boots. It was like an informal reunion of Cheltenham. She seemed to know an enormous number of people. I saw this was her world, the life she had grown up to lead. Ultimately the fact she was so intelligent, had been to Cambridge, and was an expert on art history was irrelevant. Here in the Cotswolds she was with her own people. I could hear her chattering and laughing in a way that she never did at St Sebastian's. I wondered if I perhaps should give up academic life and let her be herself in a Cotswold cottage.

In the evening we went to Camilla and Richard's house for dinner. We drove through imposing stone gates and up their drive; at the top of a hill was a vast Georgian mansion. Richard was standing on the steps waiting for us to arrive. He showed us into a magnificent drawing room with wood panelling where we were all given drinks by two Polish au pair girls. On the walls were hung an array of oil paintings including a large portrait of one of Vanessa's relations. He was clearly a general and was dressed in a military uniform with a red sash. Pandora greeted us carrying a massive, white stuffed rabbit.

Victoria asked Richard about some cottages bordering the estate which looked in poor repair. She was always quick to notice such things. One reason her father's castle was so cold and uncomfortable was that her family had traditionally regarded keeping the estate cottages in first-rate order as a higher priority. She was shocked to discover that young Richard appeared to have no sense of responsibility for his tenants.

Later we had dinner in the dining room around a long Regency table. Camilla and Richard had just returned from a trip to the United States where they were visiting a Mandril-Fortescue cousin who lived in Virginia. Victoria was interested. "We're supposed to go to Virginia soon," she said. "Harry has been invited to give a lecture at Sweetpea College – we met the president skiing in Colorado and he asked us to come."

"What an amazing coincidence! James's cousin is a trustee of Sweetpea," Vanessa said. "He lives in an old plantation house about two miles away. Sweetpea is a charming little college town. Full of delightful clapboard colonial houses. I understand everything is fearfully expensive, but it's full of the nicest people. They gave you a very good time, didn't they, Camilla darling?"

On Monday we returned to St Sebastian's. It seemed very far from the pleasant world of the Cotswolds. On Tuesday morning I arrived early, picked up my post, and went to my office. Amongst a pile of letters was one from Pilkington. It was a summons to see him urgently. Since he hadn't arrived, his calls were being transferred to Wendy Morehouse. I asked if she knew why John wanted to see me; she said it had something to do with a postgraduate. Later in the morning I got an email from Pilkington. He explained that Ronald Grundy had come to see him on Monday. He was apparently disappointed about his supervisions. Pilkington wanted to see me straightaway and asked if I were free to come round immediately.

I wasn't sure whether to phone Penelope. If this were a formal meeting, I might need help. But I decided I should find out what was going on first. When I arrived, Pilkington was seated at his desk; he gestured for me to sit down. He was wearing a green sports jacket and a striped blue and yellow polyester tie. He handed me a long letter from Ronald outlining numerous deficiencies in his supervision. It alleged that I was largely ignorant of his topic, and that I had made little effort to direct him to the right source material. Our meetings, he

119

stated, were of marginal help and he suspected I didn't bother to read drafts of the chapters he submitted. In his view, there were too few supervisions, and he accused me of trying to put him off whenever he wanted to get together. He also said that my comments about his writing were skimpy. He concluded the letter asking if he could have a new, more conscientious supervisor.

"I'm sorry, Harry. But yet again, there is a formal grievance. It is my duty as Head of Department to investigate this matter. So, could you please write to me about these charges." He handed me a copy of Ronald's letter and the procedure for dealing with student complaints. "We will have to have a formal disciplinary meeting to discuss this once I have your response," he continued. "Of course, you have the right to bring a representative to the meeting. Perhaps you might want to bring Penelope... but, if you do, please tell her to leave her cat at home."

I was outraged. I took a lot of trouble with all my research students, but Ronald had been particularly favoured. To say I didn't know anything about his topic was absurd. I had written a well-received book on the subject. I had introduced him to the people who I thought would be useful to his future career. I even arranged for him to be in touch with the Archbishop of Cannonbury. He had had lengthy supervisions. I had read and commented on all his work in detail. I thought back to the glimpse I had had of him and Lisa leaving Catnip's house. It was clear that this affair was being engineered to get rid of me and to give Mr Gold's future son-in-law my job.

When I got back to my room, I phoned Penelope. There was no answer, so I called Morris O'Murphy in London. His secretary told me he was driving to Birmingham; when I reached him, he was having lunch at a pub en route. I explained what had happened and asked what I should do. He told me to put together every dealing with Ronald including his application to do research, references, written work and any records of our meetings. He stressed that it was vital I could demonstrate that I had been a conscientious supervisor. I arranged to meet him on Thursday at the Acropolis for lunch. "Don't worry," he said.

"As long as you have plenty of evidence, there shouldn't be a problem."

Early on Thursday I took the train to London. I promised Victoria I would do some shopping for her at Fortnum and Mason: I was to choose a hamper as a thank you present for Vanessa and James and arrange for it to be delivered. In addition, she was anxious for me to buy presents for our hosts in Sweetpea. I found a bottle of vintage port for the Billstones, and a large jar of Welsh honey for Thomas Jefferson Porpoise. I also purchased a box of marron glacé as a little surprise gift for Victoria. I arrived at the Acropolis at one.

Morris was waiting for me in the hall. "Bloody hell," he said pointing at the porter. "He said I couldn't come in without a tie, so he gave me one." Morris was wearing corduroy trousers and a checked sports coat with a green flannel shirt. The striped red and gold Acropolis tie looked most peculiar with them.

"Sorry, Morris. I should have warned you."

On the way into the dining room, I saw Charles with a group of Commonwealth bishops hovering around the lavatories. We waved at each other. As we sat at our table, Morris looked around the room. "Grandest place I've ever been," he said. "Can't imagine what I'm doing here. Bugger!" he observed, "isn't that the Vice-Chancellor of Wellington?" In the corner by the window, there was a group of elderly men in grey suits. I had never seen any of them before.

"I don't know him," I said.

"I do," Morris said. "Had a fight with him two months ago about a professor who was accused of trying to seduce the department secretary. Damn stupid thing to do. Anyway, the whole thing died down."

"What happened?" I asked.

"The guy got a very good deal: five years' enhancement to his salary, plus sixty per cent part-time teaching for three years. More than he deserved! Nearly killed me!"

We ordered the set meal, and Morris opened up his briefcase, took out a file and put his mobile phone on the table. "Morris," I said. "I'm afraid we can't look at anything dealing with my case in the dining room."

"Place is bugged?"

"No, Morris. I'm afraid it's against the rules. And, you'll have to put away your phone."

Morris looked bewildered. "What kind of establishment is this?" he asked. "They make me wear this ridiculous tie, won't let me discuss anything important, and ban my mobile."

"It's a gentlemen's club," I smiled.

"Right. Right. OK. But does that mean we can't talk about your predicament?"

"We can talk. But it can't look like business."

After we had finished the three-course set lunch, Morris still looked hungry. I ordered the cheese board. He ate most of it.

We went to the drawing room for coffee. Scattered around the room were elderly men reading newspapers. Several were asleep in large green leather armchairs. A fat ginger cat wandered around the room, hopped on to a sofa near a window, and went to sleep. I poured out coffee for both of us, and we settled in the corner near a library table covered with newspapers and magazines. Morris looked perplexed. "I don't get it," he said. "Who are these people? Why aren't they at work?"

"They're mostly retired," I said.

"Place looks like a geriatric day-care centre," Morris observed. "Is there a television set somewhere?"

"No, just books."

I was reassured by my conversation with Morris. As it happened, I had kept very full records of my meetings with Ronald. By any standards I had been more than conscientious. He told me he would brief Penelope who would go to the meeting with Pilkington.

On the way back to St Sebastian's, I took out *The Times*. In the supplement there was a long article about settling abroad. One of the couples interviewed had moved to the United States. They had been living in London, and sold their house in Fulham. They went to Rome, Georgia, where they bought an old colonial house which they had restored. It was filled with English furniture as well as American silver. They were photographed standing in the garden with the house in the background. It all looked rather tempting.

Pilkington had arranged the disciplinary meeting for a week from Monday. I phoned Penelope, told her about my conversation with Morris and arranged that she should accompany me. On the day, Penelope came to my office. She had taken photographs of Rufus with her mobile telephone, and showed them to me. He was much better, she said, and appeared to have recovered from his trouble with hairballs. Pilkington opened the door when we arrived; Sloth was seated at a small table waiting for us. He had assembled several papers on the table including Ronald's letter. Pilkington sat at the head of the table. Penelope and I sat next to each other across from Sloth.

"Before we begin," Pilkington said, "I want to say something off the record. This is the fourth meeting we have had to discuss your behaviour, Harry. I hope it will be the last. Yesterday, I had a long conversation with the Vice-Chancellor, and we are anxious to ensure that there will be no further complaints." Sloth shifted uncomfortably and nodded his head. "So," Pilkington continued, "I hope you will recognize the gravity of this meeting..."

"I'm sorry," Penelope interrupted. "There can be no off-the-record comments. We are here simply to investigate this postgraduate's allegations about Harry as his supervisor. Nothing more."

Pilkington was undeterred. "I think you fail to recognize the seriousness of Harry's position," he said. "And I must tell you, in addition to these formal complaints, other students and members of staff have been complaining about Harry."

I was furious and was about to demand concrete details, but Penelope cut across me: "We are not here to discuss anonymous grievances, John, Can we get down to the matter at hand?"

Sloth was making notes as Penelope spoke. She was wearing black trousers and a violet turtle neck sweater. As usual she was covered in cat hair. Her mascara on her right eye had smudged, and her lipstick was uneven. I wondered if Pilkington and Sloth noticed. Pulling a folder from a large Tesco bag, she embarked on my defence.

"Now," she began, "there are strict guidelines laid down by the university for the supervision of research students. As you will see, Harry has carried them out rigorously." One by one she ticked them off. Pilkington shifted uncomfortably; Sloth stopped writing. Penelope handed over Ronald's thesis with my corrections as well as a list of all the meetings I had since Ronald began. Eventually she concluded by emphasizing that there was no foundation for any complaint, and that if a warning were given the union would advise me to appeal and would ensure the case attracted the maximum of publicity.

Pilkington turned a dull shade of red. He asked if I had anything to add; I shook my head. Triumphantly Penelope stood up. "Right," she said. "So we are agreed that there is no substance whatever in the complaint?"

Pilkington looked at the file glumly. He turned over the pages and peered at all the documents. After three or four minutes, he closed it and sighed. He shrugged his shoulders at Sloth and shook his head.

"So, are we agreed that this was a specious complaint and the matter be dropped?"

Pilkington nodded reluctantly. "All right," he said. "But, Harry, I must say ... "

Penelope was having none of it. "There is nothing to say. Harry was falsely accused by a malicious student who wanted his job. We all know what really happened." Sloth squirmed in his seat. "I hope you ensure Ronald Grundy apologises." Penelope continued, "Come along, Harry!" I got up and followed her out the door.

"Tremendous!" I said as we walked across the lawn.

"Piece of cake! It was a good thing you had kept such thorough records. Not everyone's so careful. That's what they were hoping. They won't trouble you any more. But you must indicate that given the circumstances, it would be inadvisable for you to continue as Ronald's supervisor."

Penelope strode off, and I made my way to Magnus's room. When he answered the door, I was shocked. He had a blue bruise around his eye. "What happened?" I asked.

"Damn women," he said. He removed a pile of papers from a chair, and gestured that I sit down. He paced as he recounted his latest encounter. "I got in this morning and saw I had a flat tyre. Well, I saw that butch car mechanic who lives with that colleague of ours. I was standing there looking hopeless, holding the jack. I didn't know what to do. Anyway, she asked if I wanted some help. I was jolly relieved. The girl's a genius – had the tyre off and put the new tyre on in about two minutes. I didn't think I could give her a tip, so I said: "Look, can I take you out dancing?" If she could fix a flat like that, I figured she might be a whiz at the tango. I know Victoria is doing her best, but I need some more practice before my cruise. I thought I would take her to the dinner dance that is advertised in the White Hart Hotel."

"Magnus," I said. "What were you thinking of? She's a militant lesbian."

"Well that shouldn't stop her dancing. Anyway, she lashed out completely without provocation and hit me in the eye. Then she called me a male chauvinist pig. I couldn't believe it! And now I've just found this note in my pigeonhole". He handed me a folded piece of paper.

Dear Dr Hamilton,

I am writing to you because I have just been informed that you propositioned my partner after she fixed your flat tyre. I cannot understand why you behave so inappropriately. We both regard this as an insult and insist on an apology.

Yours sincerely,

Patricia Parham

(Reader in Twentieth Century History)

"Handbags at dawn!" I remarked.

"Look at my eye," Magnus sighed. "It will take months to go away. How am I going to explain this to the ladies on my cruise?"

Two days later I received a short letter from Pilkington, telling me that the complaint from Ronald had been dropped. He had sent him a detailed account of my interview, and it had been agreed that a new supervisor would be appointed in my place. This, he thought, would be the best resolution to the problem.

With a sense of elation, I phoned Magnus and told him the result. He sounded morose. The bruise, he said, was now a deep purple. He had gone to the pharmacist who told him there was nothing that could be done – he would simply have to wait for it to go away.

Later in the day I received an email from Barraclough requesting that all research-active staff provide a brief description of the work they intended to submit for the Research Assessment Exercise. These reports, he explained, would be sent to external assessors who would make a preliminary judgment. He was anxious to have this information by the end of the week.

Magnus refused to go to the Senior Common Room because of his black eye, so we agreed to meet at a small teashop in St Sebastian's. He was sitting at a table in the front wearing his new Harris tweed jacket and a pink bow tie. A black eyepatch covered his right eye and hid most of the bruise. "What do you think?" he asked.

"Good grief!"

"Rather fetching, I thought. Like a pirate!"

"Ridiculous! Everyone will think you lost an eye."

"Nearly did! Still can't believe it! All because I wanted to take her out dancing!"

"I think you rather misjudged the situation."

Magnus pulled out a batch of papers from his pocket. "Just got my ticket," he said. "They gave me an upgrade. I'm set to sail on the 14th of June." He handed me a brochure with a picture of an elderly couple drinking champagne. The woman was dressed in a blue velvet ball dress. Her husband was wearing a dinner jacket and black tie. "That's what my cabin will be like," he said.

"Do they also supply a companion?"

"I'm afraid that's up to me. Do you think the eyepatch might help?"

The next day I received a surprising letter from Rabbi Wally Wachman. Several weeks ago, he explained, he had met with Lisa Gold and her fiancé, Ronald Grundy. It appeared that Ronald was anxious to convert to Judaism as soon as possible. Because he lived in St Sebastian's, it was difficult for him to attend conversion classes, and he hoped to study on his own. He listed me as a referee, and the rabbi wanted to know something about him.

Given recent developments, I was anxious to avoid further difficulties. I wrote back, indicating that perhaps it might be more suitable to ask someone who knew him better than I did. I emphasized that although I had been his supervisor, I was in no sense a personal friend.

Two days later I had a telephone call from Rabbi Wachman. He apologized for bothering me, but he thought it might be possible to have a brief conversation about Ronald. I hesitated. But, after some prompting, I told him about Ronald's recent complaint about me as a supervisor.

"That has all the marks of a Freddie Gold campaign!" Wally said consolingly.

I was sure, I said, that he would no longer wish for me to act as a referee. Rabbi Wachman then explained that it was not the normal practice to rush someone through conversion, but that enormous pressure had been applied by Freddy, who wanted his daughter to have a sumptuous wedding over the summer. I then told him about Gold's scheme to pay for a lectureship in ethics for his future son-in-law. Rabbi Wachman sighed. "That family is a nightmare. Quite frankly, I don't think Gold will come through in the end. That's what keeps happening to the synagogue. Promises are made, but seldom kept."

Before we finished the conversation, the rabbi asked about our holiday plans. I told him I had been invited to give a lecture at Sweetpea College in Virginia. He was amused. It turned out that his brother, Manford Wachman, was the major luxury car distributor in Sweetpea. He specialized in Rolls-Royces. He had started with one tiny outlet, but there now were branches of Manford's Motors all over the southern states of the USA.

"He really is a living example of the great American dream, unlike his poor rabbinical elder brother! He married a charming American girl and they settled there to be near her family. I'm sure he'll give you a good deal on a hire car during your stay," he told me. "Just give him a ring and mention my name."

"I'll do it this afternoon," I said.

Later that day, I had an email from Wally's brother. It would be his pleasure, he said, to lend us a car at a discount. He also asked if Victoria and I might be free one day to come to lunch during our stay.

When I told Victoria about the rabbi's brother, she was apprehensive. "Really Harry," she said, "you can't go around Sweetpea in a Rolls-Royce, even if it's only for a few days. They'll think you're incredibly vulgar."

"It's only for three days," I countered, "I've always wanted a really posh car and I've never driven a Rolls."

"Still, what will the Billstones think? You're there as a guest, not a celebrity."

"Actually," I said. "I think I will be regarded as something of a celebrity. And, I understand from the dealer that the president of the college has a black Bentley. So what's wrong with a Rolls?"

"If you can't see, there's no way I could explain. But, trust me, it's not the done thing."

"It probably is in Virginia. Remember, it is the land of the brave and the free."

When I told Magnus about the Rolls-Royce, he was elated. "Maybe I should get one myself," he mused. "But if it's new, it will cost a fortune. And if it's old, I won't know how to fix it. I'm certainly not going to ask Parham's friend again." He shifted his eyepatch. "Then of course, I wouldn't be able to drive it with this thing on. Absolutely wrecks one's sense of perspective. I'd have to wait until the bruise heals. And that could take months."

"You'll also be on the high seas," I reminded him.

"You're right. It will have to wait. Pity! A convertible Rolls-Royce with this eyepatch would slay everyone."

The last week of term I was busy marking a pile of essays, when I received an email from the administration saying that Wanda Catnip would be returning at the beginning of next term. We were all wished a good holiday, and the urgency of completing the report about our RAE submissions was emphasized. There was also a similar missive from Pilkington. He encouraged everyone to complete their submission report, and he included a note from Sloth about university finances. It read:

Salary and Income

The Senior Management Committee, consisting of the Vice-Chancellor, Registrar, Dean and Heads of the Departments has recently discussed the policy of generating income for the university. It was agreed that each Head of Department will be responsible for calculating the income brought in by each member of staff. It is the aim of the university that for all those capable of generating income, the following rule should apply: All members of staff should be responsible for generating an income equal to their salary. In doing this calculation, Heads of Departments are reminded that all income is top-sliced at forty per cent to pay the university administrative costs. This calculation will serve as a vital element in the management of the university.

Pilkington indicated that these complicated sums would be done over the vacation and would be reported back to each member of the department. It was his aim, he said, to use this information in all future appraisals. He concluded by stressing the importance of RAE income for each research-active member of staff. Currently, he stated, all those whose work had been submitted received twenty thousand pounds every year which formed part of their total yearly contribution. Anyone left out of the future RAE would need to compensate for this loss of revenue by doing extra teaching.

I had a phone call from Magnus later in the day. "What do you think of Pilkington's stupid note?" he asked.

"I don't think I understand this business about income," I replied.

"They think the university is a factory and we're the workers. The Senior Management Committee should be taken out and shot. If I weren't leaving, I'd have to teach double the number of students all year."

"Can they get away with this?"

"Barraclough thinks he can get away with anything. But, look, Harry, you might have a problem. If you're not in the next RAE, your income will plummet and they'll make you teach summer school."

"Why won't I be in the RAE? I was in last time and we got a very high mark. And my stuff this time is at least as good. Why should I have to do summer school?"

"I just have a nasty feeling about it. They're certainly trying to get rid of you. Anyway no one wants to do summer school and I'm leaving, remember. They'll dump it on whoever is excluded from the RAE. So you better fix up your submission."

"If Wanda and Pilkington are in charge, I'm not sure it will make any difference."

"Got to go, Harry," Magnus said. "I'm off to the medical centre for some jabs. This time it's for diphtheria. Can't imagine where they intend to take us on this cruise. My rear is still sore from the cholera injection. How do the grandmothers endure it?"

CHAPTER TEN

The English Education System's Shot to Shit

Over the weekend, Victoria and I went to the annual cat show at Chelsea in London. After admiring the Siamese, none of whom were as handsome as our two, we went upstairs to the section for moggies. To my astonishment, I saw Penelope standing in front of a cage with Rufus inside. There was a pink ribbon pinned on the side; Rufus had won first prize and Penelope was glowing with pleasure. Victoria was anxious to look at the Norwegian Forest cats, and set off downstairs again while I talked to Penelope.

We were due to fly off to the States immediately after term. I wanted to ask her about my former research student. I explained that I had been pondering whether to do anything about his allegation. He had clearly been put up to making a formal grievance by Wanda and Pilkington, and I was annoyed about it.

Visitors passed by us and poked their fingers in Rufus's cage. He snarled back. "Look," I said, "I think I really ought to submit a formal complaint about Ronald. What he said was malicious and totally without any foundation. I don't think I should let this pass. I want Pilkington and Catnip to know they won't be able to get away with trying to set me up in the future."

Penelope took Rufus out of his cage and stroked his ears. He purred ecstatically "You won't have any more trouble," she said. "They got the message, and so did your student. He's lost you as a supervisor and he knows you will never give him a reference. That's quite serious. Forget about the whole thing."

"I can't forget, and I certainly don't want to forgive. I taught that little shit everything he knows about ethics; I took great pains to get him a fellowship and a bursary. He made extensive use of my contacts. And he knifes me in the back."

"Look, Harry, you were lucky that you had such full notes about your meetings with him. Sloth would be proud of you. He's always going on about risk management. Anyway you demonstrated beyond reasonable doubt that you had read all Grundy's stuff. There was a solid paper-trail. The matter's over. Don't cause any more trouble, you'll only be laying yourself open to more criticism. And, I hate to mention this, but you are a clergyman. You're meant to set an example."

"You are aware he's trying to get my job."

"Of course, but you always knew academia was a cut-throat business. Anyway, the scheme backfired. You'd be well advised to put the whole thing out of your mind. Concentrate instead on your vacation. Are you going anywhere?"

"To Sweetpea, Virginia," I replied. "I'm going to give a lecture there."

"Rufus won't let me go on holidays," she said holding him up. "Isn't that right, Rufus...Mummy can't go anywhere without you." Rufus looked down disapprovingly. When I tried to stroke him, he bit my finger.

"Sorry," Penelope said, "he gets a bit jealous."

The next week, after term ended, we set off for Heathrow and stayed overnight at an airport hotel. In the morning we had breakfast and took the bus to the terminal. After making our way through immigration, we settled down in the British Airways lounge. When our flight was called we walked to the gate, went through security, and stood in a long queue. Eventually we filed into the aeroplane and found our seats near the back. Every place was taken; inevitably there was a small child behind us who wailed and kicked the back of my seat at frequent intervals.

Victoria took a sleeping pill, put on black eyeshades, and fell asleep before the plane was in the air. I had purchased a classic car magazine and looked at advertisements for Rolls-Royces as we began our flight. Later I watched a Batman film and eventually dozed off. When we landed in Washington DC, after interminable waits in the immigration line, we went through customs.

Standing outside the visitors' entrance was a youthful red-haired woman wearing a Sweetpea blazer holding a sign with our names on it. Mary-Lou Bradley was the name on her lapel and she was the President's PR officer. She led us to a bright red Chevrolet with the college crest on the door. Victoria sat in the front chattering while I gazed out of the back window. We were driven all the way to the college which was located in a small picturesque Southern town.

The college buildings, clad in ivy, were designed in a mock Gothic style. In the centre of the town overlooking the college green was a handsome colonial church built in the early nineteenth century. There were students everywhere. They all seemed to be dressed in bermuda shorts and loafers. Some were even sunbathing on the lawn.

Mary-Lou took us to the Sweetpea Inn, an old hotel near the college. Our room overlooked the campus; filled with colonial antiques and Persian carpets, it was a welcome relief from our long flight. Victoria took a bath, and I stretched out on the bed. There was a bowl of fruit and a box of chocolates on the sidetable. I ate an apple, opened a magazine about Virginia which had been placed in the room, and fell asleep. Two hours later we were awakened by a phone call. "Hello," I said.

It was our host Oscar Billstone, the President of the College. He asked about our trip, checked that the hotel was comfortable, and invited us to join him and Nancy for dinner at their house.

He explained that Mary-Lou would deliver the Rolls-Royce and we could drive it to the President's Lodge, which was located next to the Faculty Club in the centre of town. Dinner, he said, would be informal. My lecture was to take place the next night, and would be followed by a formal dinner at the house of Thomas Jefferson Porpoise. I asked if I should wear my dinner jacket. "It's not necessary," Oscar said, "but no doubt Thomas will."

At six o'clock Mary-Lou arrived in the red Rolls-Royce I had hired from Manford Wachman. It was very splendid indeed. Victoria made scornful remarks, saying it betrayed my nouveau-riche tendencies and that my father had been in trade. I was thrilled with it. Mary-Lou handed us a letter from Mr Wachman explaining that we should keep the car over the next few days, and leave it at the Sweetpea Inn where it would be collected. He also invited us to join him for lunch in two days' time if we were free. I drove in style to the President's house.

This was a large square mansion. Oscar and Nancy were standing on the doorstep as we swung into the drive. We were ushered into a marble black and white check lobby with portraits of previous presidents of the college on the wall. In an oval drawing room lined with gold and white striped wallpaper were seated several guests including Thomas Jefferson Porpoise himself. In the corner of the room was a large mahogany pedestal desk and an eighteenth-century American longcase clock. It was all very impressive. There was obviously a great deal more money at Sweetpea than there was at St Sebastian's.

Victoria and I were placed on a burgandy sofa. Scattered throughout the room were several Hepplewhite chairs and a large tallboy. Nancy introduced us to everyone. Thomas Jefferson bowed to Victoria and kissed her hand; he turned out to be a spare, silver-haired gentleman in his mid-seventies.

"How was your trip?" Oscar asked as he poured us drinks.

"Tiring. But delightful to be here," I said.

Thomas Jefferson picked up his glass. "A toast to our English friends," he said. Throughout dinner, the conversation was animated. Thomas Jefferson Porpoise was seated next to Victoria, and he was obviously much taken with her. He told her in detail about his family. There had been a branch of the Porpoises in

Virginia since the seventeenth century. They had owned great plantations. But he believed his ancestors had originally come over to England with William the Conqueror. Because of their bravery at the Battle of Hastings, they had been granted several estates on the Welsh border.

"My family has a castle on the Welsh border," said Victoria.

"In Monmouthshire?" asked Thomas Jefferson eagerly.

"No, in Shropshire," Victoria said. "That's in the north. Your family come from south Wales, but you're Welsh like me. All the best people are Welsh!"

"Well, gee," Thomas Jefferson said, "I never knew that. Does your family have a coat of arms?"

"Of course. And a crest. And a motto. People like us do!"

"I think we've only got a coat of arms." Thomas Jefferson was crestfallen.

"Oh don't worry about that," Victoria was very reassuring. "I'll design you a crest and motto. I know all about heraldry. Crests are generally based on people's names. My maiden name was Dormouse and our family crest is a fat dormouse couchant. Now let me see..." She fished about in her bag for her diary. On a blank page she drew a very rotund fish with a friendly expression. He was standing upright balanced on his tail.

"There you are," said Victoria. "A porpoise rampant. What could be better?"

"Do you think I could have a motto, too?"

"Of course. Now my family's inscription is in Latin. But that's because we are a rather late family. A bit new-money. And we like to show off. You must have a proper original Welsh motto. All the really old Welsh families do. She drew a scroll underneath the porpoise and inside she printed: *Heb Porpoise, Nid Pwrpas*.

"What does that mean?" Thomas Jefferson asked. His voice was awestruck.

"It means: Without a Porpoise, There is no Purpose..."

"Gee! That's great! What can I do with it?"

"Well in my family, we have the crest engraved on all our silver."

135

"Gee!" said Thomas Jefferson Porpoise again, "I'd like that. We've got a load of old silver! I gave quite a lot of it to the college..."

Victoria looked alarmed. "I don't think you should put it on old silver. After all it's a new crest. Why don't you commission a new piece. A punch bowl, or a loving cup or something. I'm sure there are some excellent young designers in Virginia who should be encouraged."

Thomas Jefferson was delighted with this idea. 'I'll get my people to see to it straightaway. I suppose I couldn't have that piece of paper could I?"

"No, no," said Victoria, putting the scrap back in her bag, "I'll draw it for you nicely and send it to you from England."

Thomas Jefferson nodded. "You won't forget, will you?" he said anxiously.

The next day Victoria and I drove around Sweetpea in the Rolls-Royce. We parked the car in front of the President's house as he suggested, and strolled along Main Street. Students jostled past us on their way to lectures. There were a variety of small shops including the Sweetpea College Shop where I bought a purple and gold Sweetpea bow tie. Victoria was insistent that I wear a black tie for the formal dinner in our honour, but the President told me that he would be wearing the university model instead. On the way back to the Sweetpea Inn we passed a real estate office. "Let's go in!" I said.

A jovial male assistant greeted us. In a deep Southern drawl, he asked what we were looking for. I explained that I had come to give a lecture and we would only be staying for a few days. But we were curious to see what property was available. He showed us brochures of several country houses outside Sweetpea – they were all over three million dollars. Vanessa was right: houses were expensive. Later we had lunch in the dining room of the Sweetpea Inn. Afterwards, we sat in a delightful room next to the entrance where we were served coffee and home-made chocolates. I was uncomfortable to notice that, as at the President's house the previous night, all the serving people were black.

Both of us were jet-lagged and took a nap before dinner. When we were dressing, I noticed with misgiving that my trousers were even tighter than when I had last worn them and the dinner jacket itself did not do up comfortably. For the hundredth time I resolved to go on a diet.

At six Oscar and Nancy picked us up from the Sweetpea Inn and drove us to the Porpoise mansion just outside Sweetpea. We drove through enormous gates. The drive was at least a mile long and at the end there was a vast white building with tall Corinthian columns. In the front was a marble fountain with a stout golden porpoise spouting water. The path to the house was lined with cherry trees. There was a large brass knocker on the front door also in the shape of a porpoise. Oscar banged it. A black butler opened the door, but Thomas Jefferson was close behind. He was splendid in a white dinner jacket with a Sweetpea College tie. He ushered us into the drawing room which was lined in mahogany and covered with engravings of American presidents. The lecture was scheduled for seven o'clock in the ballroom.

We were poured drinks from a crystal decanter and another black maid served canapés from a silver salver. "That was made by Paul Revere," Nancy whispered. Victoria was hugely impressed. In the distance we could hear guests arriving who were taken by the Porpoise butler to the ballroom. Oscar, Nancy, Victoria and I sat on two Federal sofas opposite one another while Thomas Jefferson went to check on the arrangements. Just before the lecture was due to start, Oscar put on his Harvard PhD gown and mortarboard and led our party to the white and gold ballroom where more than a hundred guests were assembled.

Oscar showed me to my seat and stood at a podium. After an effusive introduction in which he mentioned all the books I had written, he sat down. Then it was my turn. I walked to the podium and delivered my lecture. The topic was 'The Paradox of Selfishness,' the title of my new book which was due to be published at the end of the month. I tried to be entertaining and there was no sign of a gorilla.

The audience seemed to enjoy it. After I had finished, they clapped enthusiastically and there were several questions.

Thomas Jefferson then gave a lengthy vote of thanks. He obviously liked the sound of his own voice. Oscar introduced me to the Mandril-Fortescue cousin who said how much he appreciated the lecture. Then various members of the religion department were brought over to meet us, but by this stage I was tired and they all merged into each other.

Afterwards, Thomas Jefferson led Victoria and me and several members of the audience to the dining room where there was a vast mahogany table set with places for twelve. The silver gleamed and again all the servants were black. When everyone had taken their places, Thomas Jefferson asked me to say a prayer. I recited the St Sebastian's grace in Latin. We all sat down and turtle soup was served. I was seated next to Nancy who presided at one end of the table. On my left was an elegant, well-groomed woman who was wearing an enormous emerald necklace. Nancy introduced us: she was the wife of the French Ambassador to Washington. Victoria was seated next to Thomas Jefferson himself at the other end of the table. The Ambassador's wife told me that Victoria's neighbour was the editor of the *Washington Post*.

A string quartet, who were seated in the shadows, played Schubert. After the first course, tall fluted glasses came round. They were filled with champagne sorbet. This, the Ambassador's wife explained, was to clear the palate. The main course was sea bass served with exquisite vegetables. For pudding there was pecan pie. The dinner did nothing for my diet.

After dinner we adjourned to the library, a circular room lined with leather volumes. Oscar and I sat next to one another in large Queen Anne armchairs which, Thomas Jefferson said, he had purchased in London. Oscar lit up a large cigar and offered me one. A bottle of vintage port had been placed on the table in front of us with a bowl of walnuts. A magnificent Paul Revere silver nut-hammer lay on top.

"I much enjoyed your lecture," he said. "Now, Harry, there is something I would like to talk to you about. I've had a word with Thomas Jefferson. As you know, he has been a very good friend of the college. It is his intention to establish a Chair here to honour his great-great-great-grandfather: Thomas Jefferson Porpoise I. He has asked me to inquire whether you might be interested in coming. There would be few duties attached to the position since it would be a Distinguished Professorship. I know this is rather sudden. But we would very much like you to consider the possibility. It would be an honour to have you on the faculty, and to have your wife among us. Think about it. Talk it over with Victoria."

"That's very kind of you," I mumbled. I looked at Victoria who was chatting to the French Ambassador. She looked very elegant in her simple silk dress and was clearly having a lovely time. It was the Cotswolds all over again. She fitted in perfectly. I felt a pang of guilt. Oscar followed my glance and smiled. "She has made a huge hit with Thomas Jefferson," he smiled. "Let me know what you think," he said as he stood up to talk to the Ambassador's wife.

After dinner we drove ourselves home. I loved the Rolls-Royce. As we undressed for bed, Victoria told me about her conversation with the editor of the *Washington Post*. "You know," she said. "He's read some of my articles about English antiques. How I can't imagine. Through the internet I suppose. He wants me to meet the antiques editor of the newspaper when we go to Washington. I'm supposed to have lunch with her to discuss the possibility of writing some pieces."

"That's splendid," I said. "How are you supposed to get in touch?"

"I'm to ring before we leave and arrange to meet. Really, Harry, this place is astonishing. There seems to be no end to the Porpoise influence."

I sat on the bed in my striped pyjamas. It was a relief to be out of my tight trousers. "You won't believe this," I said, "but I think I've been offered a job. They want me to come here as a Distinguished Professor. Thomas Jefferson wants to establish a Chair in honour of one of his relations. Oscar told me."

"A job? With a salary? Did he really offer it to you just like that?"

"He asked me if I was interested. We didn't discuss any details. But he suggested I talk it over with you. I think they really want me."

Victoria took off the cameo necklace she had inherited from her grandmother. She put it in its Victorian leather box and locked it up. "I don't know, Harry. They are very nice. It's a far cry from Little Miss Bossyboots and that awful Barraclough, isn't it? But it is far away. And Daddy wouldn't like it. I don't know anyone in Sweetpea."

"You know Thomas Jefferson," I countered.

"Yes. Thomas Jefferson. And the Billstones. And Vanessa's cousin. And we're going to meet Manford Wachman of Manford's Motors," she giggled. Then she looked thoughtful, "I don't know . . . We'll talk about it tomorrow."

The next day Manford Wachman took us for an early lunch at the Tam O'Shanter Country Club. Located outside the town, the club was exclusively for Jews. Mr Wachman picked us up in a new black Rolls; on the way he explained that in the past Jews were not allowed to be members of the Sweetpea Country Club. As a result, a group of his wealthy co-religionists had bought a derelict rambling colonial house with one hundred and thirty-six acres of land. They refurbished the property, created one of the best golf courses in the South, and built an Olympic-sized swimming pool and tennis courts. They used the adjoining lake for sailing. We parked in the parking lot which was crowded with Cadillacs, Mercedes, and Jaguars.

Like the Porpoise mansion, which it strongly resembled, the entrance was framed by Corinthian columns. In the lobby there were exotic flowering plants and marble statues of Greek gods. The dining room was lined with Scottish tartan wallpaper. We sat at a small table near the window overlooking the golf course. Again all the serving staff were black, but this time they were dressed in tartan kilts.

"Choose whatever you like," Manford said, as he got up and went to other tables to greet friends. We were surprised to notice there was ham and shellfish on the menu. It seemed that the Jews who belonged to the Tam O'Shanter Club were not rigorous about the Old Testament dietary laws. The dining room was full of middle-aged men and women dressed in sports clothes. Some of the women were wearing short tennis skirts; children ran back and forth in swimming dress dodging the waiters. Next to us was an elderly couple; the wife, dressed in pink slacks and a pink tee-shirt, was in a wheel chair.

"Not quite the Acropolis," Victoria commented. 'How appalling that Jews were segregated and had to found their own club. I can't believe it goes on still. I wonder how this establishment survives."

Manford came back to the table with his blonde youthful-looking wife, Sherrie, who had been playing canasta. Dressed in white shorts, she was wearing white socks, and a white top with rhinestones. Her nails were exquisitely manicured and painted a deep pink. I stood up and shook hands. Victoria smiled as we were introduced. The waiter re-emerged and took everyone's order. "I've heard so much about you from Manny's brother. He's just my favourite rabbi!" Sherrie said. "How long are you staying?"

I explained that I had come to give a lecture at the college, and we were leaving later in the day for Washington. "I know, we were there," she said. "Manny says you're planning to come live here."

I looked at Victoria. Did Manford's wife know about Oscar's suggestion that I come to Sweetpea as a Distinguished Professor already? Manford leaned over. "Nothing in Sweetpea is a secret," he said. "I'm one of the trustees of the college, and Thomas Jefferson has already contacted all of us this morning to suggest it. You'd like living in Sweetpea. And if you came, maybe we could do some sort of deal on the Rolls," he winked. "Just the thing for the Professor of Christian Ethics!"

After lunch we returned to the Sweetpea Inn. I phoned Oscar at the college, and thanked him for his generous hospitality. I told him that Victoria and I had discussed the suggestion about coming to Sweetpea, but had come to no conclusion. He said he would be in touch. Mary-Lou Bradley picked us up at three and drove us to Washington. I had made a reservation at the Union Club, which had reciprocal relations with the Acropolis. We checked in and Victoria phoned the antiques editor of the *Washington Post*. They arranged to meet for lunch the next day at an establishment called the Lazy Daisy Club.

Our room was at the back of the building overlooking a courtyard. We were both exhausted by the events of the last few days and had a nap. At seven we went downstairs for a drink. As we walked to the bar we passed through a room lined with pictures of Pulitzer Prize winners. "Quite a show!" Victoria was amused. In the Acropolis there was a scrapbook of club members who were Nobel Prize winners, but it was not on public display. "Maybe we ought to do something like this," I suggested. "Good grief!" Victoria sighed.

The next day after breakfast Victoria and I went to the National Gallery. There was an exhibition of paintings by Chagall. He had painted several oils of the Crucifixion, and I was curious to see them. I stayed for lunch in the gallery while Victoria had her meeting with the antiques editor. We arranged to meet for tea later in the day at the Union Club. At three I took a taxi, ordered tea, and waited for Victoria.

She came in carrying a stack of magazines looking excited. "It was wonderful," she said putting the magazines on a chair. "The Lazy Daisy Club is charming. It's in a narrow town house in Georgetown. Lovely Sheraton chairs and they have the most exquisite collection of Georgian teapots."

"Who did you have lunch with?"

"A lady called Elizabeth Lizard. And you couldn't call it having lunch. She was incredibly thin, like an X-ray. We both ordered Caesar salad, and if she ate a single mouthful, well I didn't see it. She just pushed it around on her plate. I ate the lot. And was longing to have pudding. They advertised the most elaborate ice-creams. Sundays I think they're called. But after Elizabeth's performance, I felt it would be too greedy. I'm ravenous, how many of those muffins do you want to eat?"

"So what happened?"

Victoria piled both buttered muffins onto her plate. "Why don't you order some more?" she said. "Anyway, I think I've been offered a job," she continued. "They want me to do a regular column on English antique furniture and porcelain."

"A column?"

"Well, a feature for their magazine every month. I'm to write about the major antique fairs in the States. They're prepared to cover my costs which include plane fares and accommodation and they'll pay two thousand dollars an article."

"That's tremendous," I said. "You were right. The Porpoise millions do extend far and wide!"

"*Heb Porpoise, Nid Pwrpas!*" declared Victoria solemnly. "They all seem to have the impression we really are coming to live here."

"Even Ms. Lizard the X-ray?"

"Oh yes...She knew all about it. Apparently your lecture was a great success!"

"Did you tell them nothing's certain?"

"I wasn't sure what to say."

"Well, I haven't even been formally offered a job. And we haven't decided anything."

"True," said Victoria, "And I can't imagine how I would break the news to Daddy."

In the evening we set off for London, arrived the next morning, and then took the train back to St Sebastian's. I didn't sleep much that night and the next day I was jet-lagged. I went to the college earlier than usual, collected my post, and retreated to my office. I had left behind a massive PhD thesis which I should have read weeks ago. It was entitled *Metanoia in the text of the Synoptic Gospels and the Acts of the Apostles*. It had been supervised by Pilkington, and I had agreed to be the internal examiner. Presumably as an expert on Christian ethics, I was supposed to know something about repentance.

I stretched out on the sofa, made a cup of coffee, picked up the thesis and immediately went to sleep. A couple of hours later I woke up. I made another cup of coffee, blacker and stronger this time, and turned over a few pages. I scanned through the thesis. There was no Greek at all in the text. How, I wondered, could the candidate write a scholarly thesis on the concept of 'metanoia' without using any Greek?

At that moment the telephone rang. It was my fellow-examiner. Professor Timothy Titus was a Professor of Biblical Exegesis at the University of Blenheim and the current President of the Association of New Testament Scholars. We had been ordained from the same theological college at Cambridge and occasionally we met at conferences. He said he had been desperate to reach me. I explained I had been giving a lecture in Sweetpea, Virginia.

"I can't understand this thesis," he said. "Despite the title, it's clear he has no idea of the Greek text. He's missed numerous references to *metanoia* and some of what he says only makes sense if you are reading the English translation. Sometimes he even talks about repentance when a Greek word other than *metanoia* is being used. It's nonsense once you look at the original text. I don't know what his supervisor was thinking of. Presumably your university demands a knowledge of Greek if candidates intend to write a thesis on the New Testament?"

I explained that biblical studies was not my area, but that I was sure we did. Anyway I would check what was going on with the supervisor. Later in the day I phoned Pilkington. I told him that I had just returned from the States and that I was reading his candidate's PhD thesis. Both the external examiner and I were concerned that the candidate seemed to have no knowledge of Greek.

"But that can't be right," I insisted. "Timothy Titus wants to know if we demand a knowledge of Greek for students writing theses on the New Testament text and of course I said we had the same standards as everyone else."

There was silence. "You discussed this with Titus?" he asked angrily.

"Of course I did. We're the two examiners of the thesis."

"Look, Harry, I don't care about that. It is imprudent to discuss university policy with outsiders."

"What are you talking about John? What university policy?"

"It's none of Titus's business what we demand or do not demand from our students. That's our affair. You're the internal examiner. Your job is to make sure that our candidates get through."

"Wait a minute, John," I said. "The role of the internal examiner is to make a scholarly judgement about the thesis. That's what the regulations state."

"I don't care what the regulations state. You're there to make sure external examiners aren't too harsh. You're to be a moderating influence. You shouldn't stir things up. I suppose you brought up the subject of Greek."

"No. As a matter of fact, he did. But I was equally concerned about it. We were both worried..."

144

"Look, Harry," Pilkington interrupted. "I bitterly resent this. Your prime responsibility is to the university. And to your colleagues for that matter."

"My chief obligation is to scholarship by examining the thesis properly," I said angrily.

"Not as far as I'm concerned. As a matter of fact, this candidate is dyslexic. It was unrealistic to expect him to learn Greek. And, as an employee of the university, which pays your salary, you must do the very best you can for him."

"But you can't write a PhD on the text of the New Testament if you can't read the text..." I was aghast.

"Don't be naive Harry. The university needs the money from postgraduate students and it is our duty to see them through."

"But you can't write a thesis on *metanoia* in the Greek text if you can't read the Greek. It's nonsense and he's made loads of mistakes. The word 'repentance' in the English translation is not always a translation of the word *metanoia*, and he doesn't seem to realize that. I don't know why you, as the supervisor didn't pick it up."

Pilkington was furious. "Perhaps if you contributed a little more to the administration of the university, I might have more time to give to my research students."

I wasn't in the mood for a fight. "I just don't know what I'm supposed to do."

"Well, it's your job to sort the matter out and keep Titus quiet. Make a list of all the mistakes. Then the candidate can correct them, resubmit the thesis and get the degree."

"This is ridiculous. You mean we have no standards at all?"

"Of course we have standards. But we also have responsibilities towards the university and our colleagues. The university will go bankrupt if you go on like this."

The next day I received an email from Pilkington. It had been sent to everyone in the department. It read:

> Dear Colleagues,
>
> It has come to my attention that there is some uncertainty about the role of internal examiners of PhD theses. I want to clarify the university's view. As you know, the department is dependent financially

on the successful recruitment of postgraduate students. It is vitally important that we appear to have a flourishing research culture. Increasingly a university is being judged on its MA and PhD completion figures and success rates. In this light, the internal examiner should do everything possible to help our candidates. When writing his or her report, the role of the internal examiner is to present the thesis in the best possible light and to direct the external examiner away from any defects. Under no circumstances should the internal examiner write anything which can in any way be interpreted as a criticism of the thesis supervisor.

John Pilkington,

Head of Department

After reading this missive, I phoned Magnus. "Did you see Pilkington's email?" I asked.

"He's a complete crook. I always knew it," Magnus said.

I explained about my conversation with Pilkington the previous day. "Look, Harry," Magnus said, "I know all about this. I was supposed to be the supervisor four years ago. But the student is mentally defective..."

"I think he's dyslexic," I interrupted.

"That's what I said," retorted Magnus, "mentally defective. He refused to learn Greek. How can you claim to have a PhD on the Greek New Testament when you can't even read the language? I told Pilkington to get stuffed."

"Well, I'm not sure what I'm supposed to do about this."

"If you want my advice, you'll pack your bags like me."

"It seems to me that PhD degrees are no longer worth the paper they're written on. Presumably, they'll soon be scores of people walking around with doctorates who can't even read the text they're supposed to be experts on."

"It's the same everywhere." For once, Magnus spoke seriously. He sounded weary. "All the universities are desperate for PhD money. No one under the age of fifty has learned the ancient languages properly. You and I have been learning Latin and Greek since we were eight. We were put down to it when we first went off to prep school. But it's all different now. Nowadays it's all sex education and self-expression in the schools. As a result the children can't even read and write English correctly, let alone Latin or Greek. What it comes down to is the English education system's shot to shit!"

CHAPTER ELEVEN

The Judgment was Reached in an Open and Transparent Manner

The summer term began in late April. I had just received an advanced copy of my new book. The publishers had sent out press releases, and my editor told me that she had been contacted by the BBC. I was to appear on *Start the Week* on Radio 4. On Wednesday the producer phoned to discuss my views. After a lengthy conversation, she told me that I would need to be at the studio at 8:30 a.m. to meet the other guests – a leading conductor and a well-known playwright. The interview was arranged for next Monday. I told the publicity officer of St Sebastian's about the programme. When I turned on my computer, the university homepage included a notice about the interview and a description of my new book.

Later in the afternoon I went up to the Senior Common Room. Magnus was seated in the corner reading *The Times*. I ordered a cup of tea, resisted a flapjack and joined him. I saw

Pilkington and Wendy Morehouse at another table; Pilkington glanced at me and said something to Wendy. "How's the dancing?" I asked Magnus.

He looked up and grinned. "Well, well, the radio star has emerged."

"Very funny, Magnus."

"Won't make you popular, you know."

I showed Magnus my new book. He flipped through the contents page and read the blurb on the back. "*Paradox of Selfishness?*" he asked.

"The point is that by looking out for oneself, one can in fact be altruistic. That's the paradox. Of course it's a bit more complicated than that."

Magnus looked unconvinced. "Selfishness is selfishness," he said. "Can't see what you're talking about. Think you're in a bit of a muddle, old chap." He bit into his flapjack with enthusiasm. It looked delicious. Arguably by being selfish and eating it, he was supporting the factory which made it, was thereby helping the British economy and thus contributing to the social welfare of society. I wasn't sure I was convinced.

Agnes approached us carrying a cup of coffee. "Can I join you?" she asked. "Nice announcement on the web, Harry," she said. "May I look at the book?" I passed it to her.

Magnus was absorbed in the Court Circular Page. "Bugger!" he said. "Look at this!" He handed me the newspaper. "I had no idea Anthony Leopold was still alive. Or at least was until last week." There was a long article about Professor Anthony Leopold, FBA. "We went to the same prep school. He was a sneaky little shit. Raided my tuckbox and stole my aunt's biscuits. I heard he had a double by-pass operation. Thought he'd popped off years ago."

Agnes looked horrified. "Really, Magnus. How can you say such things?"

Magnus grinned, "No trouble! Actually, I'm being altruistic. Ask Harry. It's a paradox."

To my astonishment on Sunday, there was a lengthy article in *The Observer* about my new book. Titled 'Greed is Good', the piece outlined my views, and contained comments by a number of critics including the Archbishop of Cannonbury. There was a photograph of me taken from the university website.

Victoria's father phoned in the afternoon to tell us he'd seen the piece. "Daddy doesn't agree with you," Victoria announced. "He thinks the problem nowadays is that everyone is too selfish and has no idea of proper responsibility. He's dedicated his own life to fulfilling his duties as a landowner."

Our next door neighbours brought us a copy of the article along with a freshly-made sponge cake. In the evening I had a call from the local radio station. They wanted to interview me the next morning.

When I went into the university the next day, I was greeted by the Head Porter. "Saw your picture in the papers yesterday," he said. "Jolly good. I agreed, but the wife wasn't sure if you were right though."

In my pigeonhole there was a brief note from Pilkington. He wanted me to know that in view of my negative attitudes, it was thought better if there were a different internal examiner for the PhD thesis I had discussed with him. He asked if I could return the thesis and the relevant forms. In addition, he told me that a new supervisor for Ronald Grundy had officially been appointed. Magnus had also scribbled a note on a postcard with a painting of a hissing cat: 'Saw the article. Many congratulations. Bossyboots and Pilkington will be furious! Happy Days, Magnus.' Finally there was an official envelope containing the tickets for the OBE ceremony at Buckingham Palace.

Victoria dug out her best garden-party suit for the occasion and found a delightful black hat with a veil at one of the St Sebastian's charity shops. Even though it was very tight, I had an old morning coat I had bought years ago for weddings at the Oxfam shop which I thought would be suitable. We planned to go to London on the train, have lunch at the Acropolis, and then take a taxi to the Palace. I had sent a note to Barraclough telling him that I was to receive an award; he wrote back a curt note thanking me for letting him know. There was no whisper of congratulation. The event was to take place in two weeks' time.

Magnus and I met in the Senior Common Room for lunch. Wanda was ahead of us in the queue. Several members of the department had gone up to welcome her back. She looked more relaxed, but rather thin. When she walked by us, I smiled. "Welcome back," I said. Magnus grinned to himself. Wanda nodded and went over to join Pilkington and Wendy Morehouse. "Doesn't look like a happy bunny to me," Magnus said.

"I wonder if they've rescheduled her lecture."

"No one will go," Magnus said.

"Not unless the gorilla makes another appearance. *Nid Pwrpas, Heb Primate!*" I said to myself.

"What?"

"Just a private joke. You're not planning to do it again, I hope?"

Magnus sighed. "Wasn't it wonderful? Maybe it ought to be a stripogram next time."

"Come on, Magnus."

Magnus picked up a copy of *Country Life*. "I say, Harry, have a look at this pile. Can you see me as country squire?"

There was a two page spread of a Regency country house in Oxfordshire. The price wasn't mentioned. "You didn't win that much," I said.

"Not this time. But I'm still in there with a chance."

The next few weeks were uneventful except for my appearance on *Start the Week*. I got up at six, and took an early train to London. We assembled at half past eight as planned, and were taken into the bowels of the BBC. Sitting around a small table, the three of us plus the presenter engaged in discussion; I don't think anyone agreed with my views, but it was a pleasant occasion.

A fortnight later, the award ceremony took place. As planned, Victoria and I travelled up dressed in our uncomfortable clothes. We had lunch at the Acropolis and found a taxi to take us to Buckingham Palace. We showed the guards our pass, walked across a courtyard, and through an archway where we were checked. Victoria and I then separated. She went to the grand ballroom; I followed a group of those who were to receive awards into a separate long room. There we were roped off into groups, Knighthoods (I would have liked one of those!), DBEs, CBEs, OBEs and MBEs were strictly segregated. We heard music in the distance. I spoke to several others in my gilded compound.

Eventually it was my turn to enter the ballroom. The Queen was standing on a dais on a higher level from where I stopped. The ballroom was crowded with visitors. She looked down and smiled. I bowed. The equerry next to her whispered something. Leaning forward, she asked about my latest book. "I understand you think being selfish is a virtue," she said.

"Not exactly a virtue," I stammered.

"But a good thing?"

"Well, sort of . . . Sometimes."

The Queen pinned a medal on my jacket. With a tiny pushing hand gesture, she made it clear I was to move on. I walked to the other side of the room. Afterwards, I sat down in the back of the ballroom and watched the other recipients go through the same ceremony. When it was over, I joined Victoria.

"Well, well," she said taking my photograph with the disposable camera she had bought at Boots for the occasion. "An Officer of the British Empire."

I thought briefly of Lisa and why Charles had got me the award. "I'm exhausted," I said. I put the medal into its black box. "Let's go have tea at the club." We walked down the Mall. Tourists stared at us as we strolled up the Duke of York steps. The porter at the Acropolis smiled as we walked in. We climbed the stairs, and I collapsed in an armchair. The Provost of St Sebastian's Cathedral was sitting in the corner. He waved and came over. "Mind if I join you?" he said.

We ordered teacakes. Victoria told him where we had been. "Show him your medal," she said.

I pulled the box out of my pocket and opened it. "Many congratulations," said the Provost. "How was Her Majesty?"

"I don't know how she does it," I replied. "She asked me if selfishness was a virtue." The Provost looked amused. "The equerry must have told her about my new book."

"No doubt she has read it," said Victoria slyly.

"Perhaps not," said the Provost.

"Anyway, I wasn't sure what to say."

"It's not in the Sermon on the Mount," Victoria commented. "But it is in Harry's book."

"Not exactly the same thing," I said.

"No indeed," the Provost looked longingly towards our teacakes. "Those certainly look delicious!" he said.

A few days later Magnus and I were having lunch in the Senior Common Room. Penelope joined us, looking irate. She had brought her lunch in a large purple handbag. She took a cheese sandwich and a pack of cheese and onion crisps out of a plastic container and poured a cup of coffee out of a thermos.

"Harry," she fumed, "you won't believe what happened. That girl Lisa – the one that caused you so much trouble – is a little sneak. She handed in an essay about three weeks ago for my Women and Literature course that was copied from the web. I was suspicious and found it using the new plagiarism detection software. When I confronted her, she denied it flatly and said she'd written the essay entirely herself. Honestly, it was practically word for word off the web. So I went to Wanda and told her all about it. The next week I got a note saying that Lisa's father was intending to sue the university for defamation of character, slander, libel, hurt feelings and I don't know what else!"

"But if you found the essay..."

"I did," Penelope interrupted. "But it wasn't absolutely identical. She had made a few changes, all of which, I may add, made the essay worse rather than better. But nonetheless there was no doubt that the lazy little toad had just lifted it."

"I wish we had had the benefit of the world wide web when we were students," said Magnus. "It would have saved a lot of bother..."

"Anyway," continued Penelope, "I went to see Wanda. She knew perfectly well what Lisa had done, but she said that Mr Gold was an important parent. There was the possibility of a donation or something. And since the essay wasn't absolutely word for word, she would be grateful if I would ignore the matter. I would get no support from the administration if I proceeded."

I had a queasy feeling at the thought that Wanda still expected an endowment from Mr Gold. "So what did you do?" I asked.

"What could I do? I had to drop the charge. And because it was a very good essay, I had to give it a first-class mark."

"Sickening," I said

"You haven't heard the worst." Penelope became positively shrill in her fury. "What's happened now is that little bitch is asking for a concession on the basis of stress. She says that the incident caused her so much anxiety that she has been unable to concentrate on her work. She has a doctor's note from some quack in Harley Street to say she can't take the exam and must have a concession instead. Well you know the rules as well as I do. If students can't take the exam, they get the mark for the essay as their final course assessment. So that little cheat is going to get a first for my course. She's done no work at all; she blatantly cheated and she's going to get away with it because she can hide behind her odious rich daddy and his slimey doctor."

"Was the essay really that good?"

"The bits she didn't write were superlative. That's why I knew immediately she hadn't written it. It was full of quotations from Levinas, Derrida and Kristeva. One of the best pieces of work I've had in years."

Magnus put down *Private Eye*. He looked amused. "You know," he said, "when I was at Oxford, nobody had heard of concessions. Now everybody wants them. Last year there were more concessions than students taking the exams."

Penelope looked dumbfounded. "But how could that be?"

"Some students wanted more than one concession. Their granny has a hernia; their guinea pig has just died; they're recovering from an abortion; they've just fallen off their bicycle and, in any case, they have serious learning difficulties. That makes a total of five concessions... You see how it works," Magnus smiled. "It's a complete racket."

Magnus got up and went over to the servery. He returned carrying another mug of coffee and three sugar donuts and handed one to each of us. "You know," Magnus said, "I tried to get a concession last year just like the students. I claimed I was under such stress that I couldn't concentrate on marking essays."

"Did it work?" Penelope asked.

"They were completely unsympathetic. Threatened to take disciplinary action if I didn't mark them. Made me quite cross. Why can't I have a concession if the students can?"

"Stress for what?" Penelope asked.

"General stress. No specific reason. Never got promoted. Made to teach too many students. Too many classes. Too many essays. Not enough money. Lousy colleagues ... "

"You don't look particularly stressed, Magnus," Penelope observed.

"'Not now," Magnus laughed, "I'm off on a world cruise.'

"During term?" Penelope asked.

"Starts this summer. I've got a year's sabbatical. Sailing on the *Queen Christina*. And then I quit."

Penelope was wide-eyed. "Gosh," she said. "How did you ever get a whole year's sabbatical?"

"I made Barraclough an offer he couldn't refuse," he said, standing up and doing a little soft-shoe shuffle. Got to go. I'm off to the medical centre. Got to get more jabs for the journey."

Later in the day, I had an interview with a reporter from the *St Sebastian's Gazette* about the OBE. Victoria had sent the newspaper the photograph she took with her camera. They asked me about the day and what the Queen had said. On Thursday there was a short article and a photograph of me standing in Buckingham Palace wearing my medal. It was on the front page.

Several days later, I received an email from Oscar Billstone in Sweetpea. He had seen the article on the internet and had sent a copy to Thomas Jefferson Porpoise. They planned to reproduce the picture in the *Sweetpea Alumni Magazine* with a report of my lecture. He asked if I could write a short piece describing the ceremony and an explanation of the British honours system. He added as a postscript that he was discussing the details of the Thomas Jefferson Porpoise Distinguished Professorship with the Board of the College and would be in touch soon.

One afternoon a few days later I was marking essays in my room. There was a knock on the door. To my amazement it was the Vice-Chancellor. "I hope I'm not interrupting you," he said. He was carrying a large file and sat in the armchair opposite my desk. "Lovely office," he remarked. He glanced at the icon of

St Sebastian. "You know, that would be a wonderful legacy for the university. Now, Harry, there is something serious I want to discuss with you. As you are aware, we have had external assessors evaluate the submissions for the Research Assessment Exercise. This was a trial run. This morning your Head of Department came to see me."

Barraclough frowned. "We discussed your case, and I'm afraid both John and I think there are problems with your submission. You see, this new book of yours has caused quite a stir. I saw the article in *The Observer* and I understand you've been on *Start the Week*. While this is all very nice publicity for the university, and I'm sure it helps your royalties, it is obvious your book is for a general audience. It's not the kind of thing the RAE favours. What they like is much more scholarly. Top marks are awarded for serious original research in learned journals. The more obscure, the better. So, you see, this makes the situation very difficult."

I was shocked. "Look, Vice-Chancellor," I said, "I was in the last Research Assessment Exercise. And we got the highest marks. I can't understand. That's not the only book that I've written. There is my textbook on ethics. It broke new ground, was very well-reviewed and is used widely in universities and theological colleges."

Barraclough looked at his papers. "Yes, I know about the book. But, Harry, it's a textbook. Not a scholarly monograph. You know the RAE takes a dim view of introductory books unless they are in some sense original."

"This one is. There are also several articles in scholarly journals. And three chapters in books. You can't ignore everything."

Barraclough shifted in his chair. "I'm sorry, Harry. I'm not an expert. I'm taking advice from John."

"But what about the outside assessor?"

"John has based his decision on the assessor's view as well."

"What did he say?"

"As you know, this information is confidential. No one is to see it other than myself, the Registrar, the Dean and the Head of Department. So I am not at liberty to say."

"This is ridiculous. It's clearly a conspiracy against me."

"Don't be absurd, Harry. I just wanted to let you know before there is an official report. But if you do object, you can appeal against the decision. There is an appeal panel consisting of Wanda, the Registrar, and the Provost of the Cathedral in his role as Visitor."

"Look," I said, "I'm a senior professor. I have the right to be included in the RAE. I can't understand what you're thinking of."

"No one has the right to be in the submission. But you do have the right to appeal." Barraclough stood up and looked again at the icon. "That really is a most splendid painting. It would look just right in the chapel."

When Barraclough left, I went to see Magnus. When he opened the door, he was wearing a dinner jacket. "What are you doing?" I asked.

"Trying on my new outfit for the cruise. Just got it at Oxfam. What do you think?"

Magnus's room was cluttered as usual. There were piles of paper on the floor and books stacked on every chair. He turned around so I could see the fit. "It's very short," I said. There was a three inch gap between his socks and his trousers.

"If I wear long black socks, no one will notice."

"And the sleeves are too long." They came over his knuckles.

"I don't think anyone will care."

"Otherwise it's not a bad fit. But it does look a bit loose in the waist." Magnus was holding his trousers up with his left hand.

"That can be remedied if I wear braces," he said.

"Frankly, I think you'd be better off buying a new one."

"It's only for the evening. I thought it was rather fetching. Look," he said, "it's got buttons on the fly. And you can button up the sleeves. Must have been tailor-made for someone."

"Perhaps for your friend the gorilla," I said.

Magnus pushed books off a chair and sat down. His trousers exposed his ankles and about five inches of his legs. "So, what's new?" he asked.

"I just saw Barraclough. He told me I'm going to be left out of the RAE."

Magnus looked stunned. "Gosh, they do want you to go! Did he say anything about summer school?"

"He didn't mention it. Why?"

"Well, now that I'm going, someone's got to do it."

"But I'm a professor."

"That won't make any difference if you're not in the RAE. Without the RAE money, you won't be earning your salary just by term-time teaching. You know how fixated they are on it. So they'll make you make it up elsewhere." Magnus looked at his ankles. "Do you really think the trousers are too short? Maybe Victoria could lengthen them for me."

I was desperate to reverse the Vice-Chancellor's decision. It was humiliating not to be included in the department's research submission as a professor, and I saw all too clearly what it would mean in terms of other duties. Therefore I contacted Morris O'Murphy. He was on his way to Sheffield for a complicated case dealing with bullying and harassment and told me to discuss the matter with Penelope. When I phoned her she was in the middle of a supervision with a graduate student. She advised me to look at the regulations concerning launching an appeal.

Without much difficulty I found these on the university website. They stated that two references should be sought from outside experts, and that the appeal would be heard by the Registrar, the Dean, and the Visitor. I then sent an email to the Regius Professor of Divinity at Bosworth and the Archbishop of Cannonbury asking them if they would be willing to write references about my work. Later in the day I received emails from both of them. They indicated their shock and bewilderment at the university's decision and they agreed unreservedly to act on my behalf. I then wrote a letter to the Registrar, stating that I wished to appeal and listed the Regius Professor and the Archbishop as my referees.

For a week I heard nothing. Then I received a brief note from the Registrar, telling me the date of the appeal. It was to take place in the Registrar's Office in two weeks time. I was allowed to have a representative attend. I sent Penelope an email asking if she would accompany me. In the meantime there was a general memo to the department from Pilkington listing those who were to be included in the RAE submission, and asking if they would send him copies of the works they planned to submit. I noticed that three other members of the department besides me were not included. One had recently been appointed; the others were Magnus and a senior lecturer in patristics who only published book reviews in theological journals. This was profoundly embarrassing. I wondered what the other members of the department made of my exclusion.

On the day of the appeal, I arrived early wearing my best suit and dog-collar. Penelope looked nervous as we waited outside the Registrar's office. "Look, I don't know anything about theology," she said.

"I know, but you can make sure they act fairly."

"I can do that," she said hesitantly. "But I'm not an expert. Still you do have very impressive referees."

Sloth opened the door and ushered us in. The Provost of the Cathedral was sitting at the head of the table. Wanda was on his right. Sloth sat opposite Wanda and gestured towards a couple of hard chairs. Wanda had a notepad in front of her as well as a file of papers. Sloth began by outlining the procedures. I was to speak first, and then Wanda and the Visitor would ask questions. The appeal would last no more than half an hour.

I began by explaining that I had been teaching Christian ethics for over thirty years, and that I had been included in the last Research Assessment Exercise in which the department had achieved high marks. My new book, I stressed, was designed for a wide audience, but had ample footnotes and a bibliography of relevant works. I explained that my textbook on Christian ethics was highly innovative, was widely used in universities and theological colleges and contained substantial original material. I also handed out a list of my other publications including articles in prestigious scholarly journals and the book chapters. In addition I circulated a number of favourable reviews of both books including the article in *The Observer*.

Wanda made copious notes as I spoke. The Visitor looked uneasy. When I finished, he commented that my most recent book was not entirely in accord with the teachings of the Church of England. I pointed out that that was not the criterion used in the RAE exercise. "Nonetheless, we wouldn't want people to be led astray," said the Provost.

"But the Archbishop himself is supporting my appeal," I said indignantly.

The Provost sighed. "Yes, it's all very awkward, very difficult, very embarrassing. I'm thinking we should be trying to find a middle way." He wrung his hands.

"There is no middle way, Provost," said Sloth firmly. "Either Harry is to be included in the St Sebastian's RAE submission, or he is not. I vote that we follow the advice of the outside assessor."

"But what did the outside assessor say?" I asked.

"That is not your affair," snapped Wanda. "The judgment was reached in an open, transparent manner and that is sufficient. And it is entirely confidential. I agree with the Registrar."

The Provost looked uncomfortable. "Oh dear," he said. "I am most reluctant to go against what the dear Archbishop recommends."

"Well, it really doesn't matter," boomed Sloth. "The committee already has a majority."

"In that case," the Provost said, "I want to put on record how very impressed I was with the references of the Archbishop and the Regius Professor of Divinity. But of course, I cannot describe myself as an expert. It is always unwise to go against the advice of an external assessor – although, of course, I haven't seen that . . . "

I was aghast. "You mean they haven't let you see the external report?"

"It's confidential," said Sloth. He was wide awake.

"But Provost," I said desperately, "then you only have the word of these two. You don't know what the assessor said, nor do I. What I do know is that there is a long history which I am very willing to describe to you of these two trying to get rid of me. What is happening is they are hiding behind confidentiality to drive me out of my job."

"I deeply resent the implication," said Wanda. "How dare you suggest that the system is anything but completely fair!"

"Oh dear, oh dear," lamented the Provost. "Unpleasantness is always to be regretted. I think, Dr Sloth, if you will excuse me, I really must leave now. I have an appointment later in the day to talk the cathedral sacristans."

It was the end of the meeting. I knew I was defeated. Penelope shook her head but she remained silent. She knew there was nothing she could say. I walked in the direction of my office fuming. Magnus was waiting for me by the chapel. "Well?" he said.

"Hopeless!" I said. "They wouldn't even discuss the references. They just said they had to follow the assessor, whose report the Provost of the Cathedral hadn't even seen."

"Did they mention summer school?"

"Not yet."

When I arrived home, I told Victoria the saga of what had happened. Cleo was sitting on my lap as I recounted the interview; Brutus was chasing his paper ball.

In the middle of my furious exposition, the telephone rang. It was Oscar. He told me that the Sweetpea Board of Trustees had approved Thomas Jefferson's offer of the Distinguished Professorship and were in the process of sorting out details. The salary for the Chair was to be one-hundred-and-fifty-thousand dollars a year and the duties would be minimal.

Thomas Jefferson had also offered the use of a small cottage on his estate which was fully furnished. There would be a token rent of a hundred dollars a year. The cottage had previously been used as a museum for the Porpoise estate, and contained antique furniture dating from the colonial period. It was very much hoped that I would take up the offer and begin in September. The Board would be writing to me officially within the next few days. He concluded by emphasizing how much Thomas Jefferson wanted me to accept the position. He planned to have a inaugural ball in our honour when we arrived.

"Well, Harry," Victoria said, "that's quite an offer. Double your salary, free housing and nothing to do. And the cottage sounds charming."

"Would you really like it?"

"It would be wonderful for you. And I am interested in the offer from the *Washington Post*. I've heard from them too. They really do want to have me on the books. Do you want to go?"

161

"Well, after what has just happened it does sound tempting. But what about your father?"

"That is a problem, but he could come and stay with us. He'd love the United States and he's never crossed the Atlantic."

"And what about our house?"

"Look, Harry. We don't have to make any decisions. But we should think about it. Now, what would you like for supper?"

When I told Magnus about Oscar's offer, he was astounded. "One-hundred-and-fifty-thousand-dollars for doing nothing. It's not fair!"

"But Magnus, you just won a quarter of a million pounds for doing nothing."

"That's different. And they're giving you a house to live in? On an estate? With colonial antique furniture?"

"That's what the President said."

"And a car?"

"Well, I was thinking I might buy the car we used when we visited last month. I was offered a deal on it."

"The Rolls?"

"Do you think I shouldn't?" I asked sheepishly.

Magnus put his head in his hands. "This isn't fair!"

"You could visit us on your cruise, once we've settled in Virginia," I said.

"So you've decided?"

"No we haven't, but the tide is turning against St Sebastian's. The only real objection to Virginia is the thought that that horrid little Grundy will get my job. That does put me off. Not to mention the fact that the ghastly Gold will have won."

Magnus shook his head gravely. "But you must be forgiving toward your enemies. That's what our school padre used to say."

"Oh, shut up, Magnus!" I responded.

CHAPTER TWELVE

The Union Will Not Tolerate It

The last few weeks of the summer term were devoted to examining. In the midst of marking exam scripts, we were contacted by the UCU. The union and the university were anxious to communicate information about the new pay scale, and a meeting was to take place before the examinations finished. Penelope sent an email out to all members informing them of the date. I emailed her back. Everything that had been happening this past year had been designed to persuade me to take early retirement and I was livid. I was determined not to let the matter rest:

Private and Confidential

Penelope,

Thanks for your email. I will of course attend the meeting. But I want to give you my reaction to the recent UCU appeal and also to say something about the events of the last year. I am very grateful indeed to the union for its support, but unfortunately it demonstrates that very little can be done against the systematic corruption of the university. It is clear that the authorities have been united in trying to drive me out of my job. In my view, the Vice-Chancellor will do anything for money. The Registrar (and his wife) are idle and incompetent. My Head of Department, John Pilkington, cannot see beyond his own suburban prejudices. Wanda Catnip is a sad, embittered women who finds compensation for her personal inadequacies only by making the lives of her colleagues miserable with her bossy officiousness. Even the Visitor, the Provost of St Sebastian's Cathedral, is weak and entirely devoid of principle. I was given first an oral and then a written warning without any justification. My research students have been encouraged to make unjustified complaints against me. My exclusion from the RAE is the result of naked discrimination. On top of all this, on several occasions I have been urged to take early retirement, even though I have made it crystal clear that I have no desire to do so. The more I stood firm, the more determined the university managers have been to evict me. I have reached the end of my tether. I would very much like to meet with you and Morris O'Murphy in the very near future to discuss what more, if anything, can be done.

Best wishes, Harry.

Later in the day, I had an hysterical call from Penelope. "Harry," she said. "You've made a terrible blunder. Your email has gone out to all members of the UCU."

"I don't understand." I was bewildered.

"You replied to my email about the meeting. That was sent to the entire UCU. By emailing me back, your reply went out to everyone on my list."

I gasped. "But it was marked Private and Confidential."

"That doesn't make any difference. By replying to my email, the whole UCU received what you sent."

"So anyone could read it?"

"Everyone has read it. I have been answering the telephone all afternoon. Harry, you said the Dean was officious. You accused the Vice-Chancellor of corruption. You said John was prejudiced. You labelled the Registrar incompetent. You maintained that the Provost has no principles. You are in deep shit, Harry."

I was aghast, but also a little amused. I laughed.

"Harry," Penelope went on desperately, "I don't know how the union is going to defend you. You have libelled the entire administration. This is now potentially a legal matter. We don't deal with defamation of character."

"It's only libellous if it's untrue," I said meekly.

"But how are you going to prove it? Oh dear, Harry, I don't know what to do. I have to see the Vice-Chancellor in an hour. He's already contacted the university lawyers. Really, what were you thinking?"

"But I didn't know it would go out to everyone. I never did understand how email works."

"Anyway, I've got to go. I'll talk to you after I see the Vice-Chancellor."

I put the phone down. It rang again; it was Magnus. "Magnificent!" he said. "Best email I've ever had! They deserved it! The whole lot of them! Wish I had done it!"

"I'm in the shit," I said.

"Of course you are! But what a way to go! Have you heard from the Vice-Chancellor yet?"

"No, from Penelope. She's meeting Barraclough with the university lawyers."

"Oh dear."

"I think they'll probably sack me."

There was a pause. "I doubt it," said Magnus stoutly. "If there's one thing they hate, it's bad publicity."

"What should I do?"

"I'd sit tight. See what happens. Keep me informed. Wonderful email! I think I'll frame it."

I felt terrible and rang Victoria. She roared with laughter. "Terrific mistake! How hilarious! Daddy'll adore it! They'll never sue you. There's too much justification on your side."

There was an examiners' meeting the next afternoon. I didn't want to go, but I had to attend since all my courses were being discussed. I came in late and sat at the back. Everyone stared. John looked extremely hostile. Magnus had kept a seat for me. He looked radiant and passed me a note: 'Everyone's talking about your email. I think you've shocked their bourgeois sensibilities. But don't worry, they're all enjoying themselves. The greatest happiness of the greatest number, remember!'

At the end of the meeting, Magnus and I walked to the Senior Common Room for tea. Standing in the queue, I sensed everyone looking at me. I heard colleagues whispering as we made our way to a table in the corner. Magnus poured us both tea and handed me a teacake. "Any news?"

"Nothing yet," I said.

"What did Victoria say?"

"She was delighted. She thought it was the funniest thing she had ever heard. She doesn't think they'll sue."

"Of course they won't. But they will summon you."

"I know."

"Have you decided about the American job?"

"Maybe I ought to take it."

"Of course you should! You have no choice now. But make them sweat first. Be sure to get the best retirement deal you can from St Sebastian's."

"But I won't be retiring. I'll be going to another job."

Magnus looked at me as if I were an idiot child. "Really, Harry! You're so unworldly! How your father made a fortune in fish fingers is beyond me. Didn't you pick up any of his financial skills?"

" I was always hopeless. That's why I went into academic life," I said meekly.

"Listen to me," said Magnus, "You'll be retiring from the English university system, so of course you can get a deal. What you do in America is your own business. As far as the university is concerned you'll be an old age pensioner like the rest of us."

"What kind of deal are you thinking of?"

"They're not going to want bad publicity. In the end they'll pay you to go away. Insist that they enhance your pension to the maximum and make them give you a paid year's sabbatical.

166

After all, I set a precedent. If they did it for me, they will have to do it for you." Magnus thought for a moment and then he whispered, "But don't let them know you are going to another job, whatever you do. If they think you are going to leave anyway, they won't give you a thing. You know what they're like."

"So what should I do?"

"They're bound to set up some kind of disciplinary panel. They'll huff and they'll puff, but they won't dismiss you. You're too well known, too many friends in high places. There'd be too much bad publicity for the university. Once they give you another warning, go and see Barraclough, looking desperate. Tell him the stress has got to you and you might think about leaving if he offered a good enough deal. Then wait and see what comes up. You've got to be firm with those bastards. This is no time to for Christian charity or forgiving your enemies or any nonsense like that..."

"You think it will work?" I found it hard to believe.

"Trust me." Magnus was very positive. "I know it will."

After tea I returned to my office. There was a call from Penelope. "Sorry I didn't get back to you sooner," she said. "But I wanted to get in touch with Morris. The Vice-Chancellor is planning to set up a disciplinary panel under Provision 35 of the university regulations. There's a real danger here. Potentially they could sack you on the spot for gross misconduct. Morris doesn't think they will and he will fight them if they do. He wants to be your representative. The Vice-Chancellor will let us know the date of the meeting. In the meantime, Morris wants you to write a letter about the email. You've got to explain that it was sent out by mistake. And, he says you must retract what you said."

"But every word of it was true!"

"I know that and you know that, but Morris thinks you have no choice."

"I see. And what does he think will happen?"

"In the end, they'll give you another written warning. So you'll have two written warnings. I have to say you are near the ejector button, but Morris insists that it'll all right."

"Well, that's comforting."

167

"Sorry, Harry, but that's the way it is. It was a very stupid thing to do."

That evening Victoria and I discussed the future. I was still waiting for the official letter from Oscar and I was uneasy about the decision. Victoria was much more upbeat. "Look, Harry," she said. "It's only for a few years. You're over sixty already. At most you only have four more years here, and do you really want to endure any more time with that loathsome lot? They really want you to come to Sweetpea. You'll be popular, which would be a nice change for you. We don't have to sell the house or anything. We can just lock it up for the duration and hire someone to look after it. You should look on it as an adventure. It's a wonderful opportunity."

"But what about our life here? And your family?"

"We can come back for vacations. And, really, Harry, they want you to do so little, you'll be free to come back during term if we want to."

"Are you sure Victoria? It would be a big change for you."

"Well, I've been looking up the American antique fairs on the internet. They sound splendid. There's a big one in New York at Christmas. Oh come on, Harry," she said impatiently, "You'll love it."

The next day I received the letter from Sweetpea formally offering me the Chair. If I accepted the job we could move over the summer and my class would begin in August. Apparently, Thomas Jefferson Porpoise was anxious to organize a ball in our honour. He understood Victoria's birthday was in July and that would be another thing to celebrate. The letter was sent by the President of the Board of Trustees.

I showed it to Victoria and she was astonished. "How did Thomas Jefferson find out about my birthday?" she asked. "That settles it! Of course we must go!" It seemed that the decision was made. I wrote back immediately, but I stressed that my acceptance must be confidential until I had given in my notice to St Sebastian's.

The next week I had a short letter from the Vice-Chancellor. The disciplinary hearing was to take place the first week of June. The panel, he wrote, would consist of the Visitor, the

Vice-Chancellor and the Dean. I had the right to bring a representative to the meeting. The Registrar would handle all correspondence and would be in the chair. Following the meeting, the panel would make a report to the university council, but I did have the right to appeal against its decision. After I read the letter, I emailed Morris O'Murphy. I asked if he would be able to come on the suggested date. He emailed me back to say he was free, but he insisted I come to see him as soon as possible to discuss strategy.

When I arrived at Morris's office in Paddington, I was greeted by the same receptionist in African dress. She offered me a cup of coffee and handed me the latest UCU newsletter. Morris, she said, had been in since seven working on a complicated case. It was now nearly one o'clock. Looking bleary-eyed, he staggered into the waiting room. "Bloody mess," he announced. He was wearing a Hawaiian shirt and a cotton blazer. "Want a doughnut?" he asked holding out a sugary bag.

I had offered to take him out to lunch. We set off for a nearby Italian restaurant. Morris was clearly well known – the waiter asked if he wanted his usual table. We both ordered spaghetti vongole and a green salad. Morris ate several bread sticks as he told me about the latest case. "Man's a complete idiot. Exposed himself to one of his postgraduates. She's on a Fulbright scholarship, and now the American Embassy is up in arms. He said it was a misunderstanding. To make it worse, she's the daughter of a Baptist minister." He shook his head. "I'll never understand academics."

I smiled wanly. Our spaghetti arrived. The waiter sprinkled parmesan cheese on top. He gave twice as much to Morris as he did to me. "Now," said Morris, "Your case. Look, Harry, you've got to learn how to send out emails."

"I know," I said.

"Damn big blunder."

"You're right," I said humbly.

Morris caught the waiter's attention. "Could we have some garlic bread?" he asked. "I imagine the Vice-Chancellor's quite upset."

"I think so. I haven't seen him recently."

"You did imply he was corrupt."

"He is, but it was supposed to be confidential."

"Nothing's confidential, Harry. Particularly if you send an email to every member of the UCU."

I sighed. "It was stupid."

"Well, you'll have to argue it was a mistake."

"It was."

"And you'll have to retract your allegations."

"But they're true!"

"You'll never be able to prove it. But, they won't sue you. They won't want even to try. The publicity would be too dreadful. So, they'll give you a warning. It will be unpleasant. But, I'll be there to defend you. We'll have to plead incompetence."

"Wanda will love it. So will the Registrar. And Barraclough will want vengeance."

Morris finished his spaghetti and picked up the menu. "You don't mind if I have a look at the desserts," he said. "The chocolate profiteroles are particularly good here." I made a mental note to send another large cheque to Christian Aid.

The next few days were devoted to examining, but I told Magnus that I had accepted the offer from Sweetpea and I swore him to secrecy. The day before the disciplinary meeting he came to my office. He was wearing a new blazer with an Oxford crest. "Where did you get that?" I asked.

"Ordered it from Harrods and asked them to sew on the badge."

"But why?"

"Thought the ladies on the cruise would be impressed."

"Magnus!"

"What do you think?"

"Victoria will think it's ridiculous. You're nearly sixty."

Magnus stretched out on the sofa. I noticed he was wearing new brown brogues. "So, new shoes, too."

"Got to get used to the part."

"What part?"

"Snappy dresser! Flashy dancer! Anyway, we've got to talk about the disciplinary meeting."

"Morris O'Murphy is coming. I've got to explain that the email was sent by mistake. And retract what I said."

"That's a pity. Still, can't be helped. You're bound to get a warning. Accept the punishment. Look chagrinned. And then, two days later, go and see Barraclough. Tell him you're under stress. That if he makes you a decent offer, you'll go."

"It doesn't seem very honest . . ." I began,

"Oh nonsense," said Magnus. "The university owes it to you. You are giving the administration the chance to do the right thing."

"You mean by being selfish, I'm really being altruistic!"

"That's the spirit!" said Magnus.

"Anyway the Vice-Chancellor will be thrilled!"

"Absolutely . . . The greatest happiness of the greatest number, remember! But then you've got to say that you can't leave without an enhancement to your pension. Make sure he agrees. And then ask for a year's sabbatical. Remind him that that's the deal I got, so it's only fair. Point out that it would be far more expensive if they have to keep you on until you're sixty-five. That means four more years on full salary. He'll agree just like he did with me. Make sure he writes it all down. Get him to sign it. And then walk out the door."

"Just like that?"

"Don't mention Sweetpea. Tell him you need a formal letter. And once that arrives, that's it. You can tell everyone about your new job. They'll be furious. I can't wait!" he chortled.

"That's good, Magnus."

"I know!" Magnus was pleased with himself. "I'm experienced in these matters!"

He stood up, did a few steps of the tango and with a flourish swept out the door.

Once examining was over, most of the department disappeared. Some went abroad on their holidays. Victoria and Magnus continued with their dancing lessons. Magnus, she said, was a quick learner and was doing rather well. I began packing up books and the other things we planned to take with us. Victoria informed her father about our plans. This was something we dreaded, but he was surprisingly enthusiastic about it all. He told us that he had always wanted to go to Disneyland and would now have an excuse. To our astonishment, he booked a holiday in California in the New Year with stopovers in Washington and Las Vegas.

I wrote a lengthy letter for the disciplinary panel in which I explained that the email was intended to be private; only by accident was it sent out to all the union members. I stressed that it was written after a series of unpleasant and upsetting encounters and perhaps the balance of my mind was disturbed.

Morris O'Murphy arrived the night before the meeting, and stayed at the White Hart Hotel. In the morning, I picked him up. He was waiting in the lobby, wearing a turquoise sweater, a brown sports jacket, and an UCU lapel badge. He was eating a sandwich.

The meeting was to take place in the Registrar's office. Together we waited in the lobby outside. At eleven, we were ushered inside. Sloth was wearing a grey suit and a St Sebastian's tie; Wanda was garbed in a severe green flecked suit; the Vice-Chancellor wore his usual dark suit with a silk spotted red tie and the Provost looked suitably clerical. Morris and I sat down opposite.

Sloth assembled a stack of papers in front of him and began. "This," he announced, "is a formal disciplinary meeting. We are here to consider the latest in a series of unfortunate events." He then introduced Morris to the other members of the panel. Morris smiled. The Vice-Chancellor grimaced.

Sloth continued, "Now, Harry, I think you will understand that the Dean, the Provost, the Vice-Chancellor and I have been extremely upset by the email you sent out. I know that your Head of Department is equally disturbed. This was a most unfortunate incident, and we fail to understand how you could have acted in the way you did. We have read the explanation you sent us, but personally I find it impossible to understand how you could have failed to appreciate that in responding to Penelope's email, your message could be read by the entire membership of the union. But, we will not quibble about this. We accept your apology. And I am glad to see that you have retracted what you said."

Sloth took off his glasses and stared at me. "However, there are other matters the panel needs to consider. As you know, you have had two warnings about bullying and harassment this past year. There was also the encounter with one of the undergraduates. The panel is particularly concerned with the incident concerning my wife, and the subsequent conflict with the head of the IT Unit. In both cases, you acted less than professionally. What we are witnessing is a lack of judgment and a degree of arrogance which simply cannot be tolerated."

Sloth paused and looked at Morris. "I am pleased that you could join us this morning; it is important that the union is satisfied that justice is not only done, but seen to be done." Morris blinked and said nothing.

Sloth continued: "We have had a discussion already about the proper course of action to be followed, and there is unanimity in our decision. I regret to inform you, Harry, that the panel feels that your tenure here should be terminated. We do not believe you have acted in the best interests of the university. You have been guilty of gross misconduct. As you know, the regulations of the university specify that in such a case as yours, it is permissible for the panel to terminate a contract. This is the course of action we plan to follow, and we will be making a recommendation to the council to implement our decision . . ."

Morris interrupted. "I'm sorry Registrar," he said, "The union will not tolerate this. I would advise you to be very careful what you say next. Harry and I will leave the room and give you a moment to consult with your colleagues, but I must warn you that your decision could have very serious consequences for the university." He got up from his seat and left the room. I followed.

Outside he looked shaken. "This is more serious than I thought," he said, "Attitudes have hardened, but don't worry Harry, we're not at the end yet."

Within a couple of minutes, Wanda came out. She was flushed and clearly angry. Her spectacles swung on their chain against her jacket as she walked. "They want you to come back," she said.

Morris immediately took charge of the meeting. Ignoring Sloth, he turned to Barraclough. "Now Vice-Chancellor," he said, "You must know that I have consulted fully with my superiors on this. Everything I am going to say next is supported and endorsed by them. I must warn you that the union will not tolerate your proposed course of action."

"Professor Gilbert," he continued, "is one of the most distinguished scholars in his field. He has been awarded the Order of the British Empire for his contribution to Christian ethics." Barraclough winced. Morris was not to be deterred. "He has served the university well during his time here. The union was most unhappy with the disciplinary actions that have already been taken against him. They were clear cases of victimization." Sloth went a dull shade of red. "And," continued Morris, "the fact that the university has been offered a significant endowment on the condition that Professor Gilbert leaves his job calls into serious question the motivation of the administration throughout this whole episode. This is just the kind of situation which will be of great interest to the *Times Higher Educational Supplement.*"

Wanda shifted uncomfortably in her seat, but Morris had not finished. "The email you refer to was sent out by mistake. Harry did not intend anyone other than Penelope Ransome to read it. As you will note, it was prefaced by Private and Confidential." He stood up dramatically. "I must warn you, Vice-Chancellor, that if you follow this course of action, the UCU will have no option but to black-list the university and initiate formal strike action. Now if you will excuse us, I think there is nothing further to add."

Morris beckoned to me to follow and with considerable dignity he walked out of the room. We left a profound silence behind us.

Morris hummed as we walked down the corridor. We sat down on the nearest window-sill. I was awed. "You were brilliant, Morris."

"All in the day's work. I think we gave them something to think about!"

Behind us, we heard the Registrar. He was out of breath when he caught up with us. "Now, look here," he said, "there is no reason for you to walk out. The Vice-Chancellor would like you to return."

Morris stared at Sloth. There was a long pause. "All right," he said, and we headed back to his office.

Barraclough looked distraught when we entered. "Gentle-men," he said, "There is no reason for such precipitate action." He looked at Wanda who was staring out of the window. There were two red patches on her cheeks. Morris and I sat down. The Vice-Chancellor ruffled through his papers and took out the Staff Handbook. "You will see," he said, "that the regula-tions provide for an appeal against the decision of this panel. If you are dissatisfied with the outcome, you have the right to protest."

Morris turned his stare to the Vice-Chancellor. "I don't think that will be necessary," he said. "When I leave today, I will report to the General Secretary of the union about this meeting, and recommend the action I have already outlined. The union is determined to protect the jobs of its members. I will also advise Professor Gilbert to publicise the injustice of your decision through the press. As you are aware, he has considerable contacts. In addition, I am sure that the Archbishop of Cannonbury will take a dim view of what you propose. He is a personal friend and supporter of Professor Gilbert."

There was silence. At the mention of the Archbishop, the Provost looked anguished. "I think we must have further discus-sion," he said. "With your permission Vice-Chancellor, could I ask for a short adjournment?"

"Certainly," Morris said obligingly. We stood up again and left.

Again we waited outside the office. This time Morris took a chocolate bar out of his pocket. "Must keep my strength up," he said.

After about ten minutes the door opened and we returned inside. Wanda was clearly furious. Sloth looked even more gloomy than usual, and the Provost was obviously relieved. Barraclough cleared his throat. "We have now had an oppor-tunity to reflect on what you've said. In the light of the union's objections, we are willing to defer making any final decision. But, I must emphasize that the panel will treat any future indiscretion with the greatest severity."

Morris glared at the Vice-Chancellor. "And, the union will be equally vigilant about any future infractions. The possibility of black-listing remains on the cards. The union takes a very serious view of victimization. If there are any further unwarranted accusations against Professor Gilbert, the university will be facing industrial action." The Vice-Chancellor opened his mouth, but Morris was like a bulldozer. He was not going to stop. "I will of course be reporting back to the General Secretary on the outcome of this hearing, and he may wish to correspond with you directly. We will be watching the activities of St Sebastian's University very carefully in the future. In particular, we are profoundly unhappy about the offer of an endowment from Golds' Corsetry. While Professor Gilbert is at the university, there can be no more negotiations with Mr Freddie Gold. I hope that is clearly understood. Now I think we have finished our business. Thank you for your time."

Barraclough looked agonized as Morris and I left the room. As we walked down the hall, Morris smiled. "Rather got to him, don't you think?"

"Morris, you're a genius," I said. "I haven't even got another warning."

"I should think not." Morris sounded indignant. "You're the victim remember."

"Look, Morris," I confided. "I didn't want to tell you until this was over, but I've got a new job."

Morris stopped in front of the chapel. "What?"

"Well, it's really a secret. I'm not supposed to tell anyone yet."

"What kind of new job?"

"Actually it's a job in the States. At Sweetpea College in Virginia. I'll tell you about it at lunch."

Victoria picked us up outside the university gates and we drove into St Sebastian's town centre. She was delighted with Morris's account of events and giggled throughout. "Daddy would have loved it," she said.

I had made reservations at the local Indian restaurant. On our arrival, Victoria insisted we celebrate. In view of what I had observed of Morris's appetite I ordered the Taj Mahal special meal for four rather than three. "So," Morris began, "what's this about a new job?"

I explained about our trip to Colorado, meeting the Billstones, the lecture at Sweetpea and Thomas Jefferson's offer of a Chair. Morris hooted with joy when Victoria told him about the new Porpoise crest. Meanwhile he ate four popadoms and I told him the details of the Distinguished Professorship. "You cheeky buggar!" he said. "They're giving you double your salary plus a free house. All for doing practically nothing. That'll put the cat among the pigeons at St Sebastian's."

"I'm supposed to teach an hour's class every week during the first semester," I said sheepishly.

Morris took out a pen and did some calculations on his napkin. "Let's see," he said. "A semester in the States is about fifteen weeks. And you're supposed to give an hour's lecture each week. So that's fifteen contact hours altogether. If you divide one-hundred-and-fifty-thousand dollars by fifteen, that's ten-thousand dollars an hour."

"Not bad money," said Victoria, "And don't forget I've been given a little job with the *Washington Post* as well ..."

"The only thing," I interrupted, "is that now the university will accept the Gold offer, and that frightful man will buy a job for his horrible new son-in-law."

"Well, win some and lose some," said Morris philosophically, as he embarked on two enormous stuffed parathas.

"But what about St Sebastian's?" he asked with his mouth full. "Why didn't you just say you'd accept early retirement?"

"Because Harry wants a proper retirement deal. He's going to get a year's paid sabbatical. Plus all the increments for his pension," Victoria said.

"But you can't be on the university payroll, even on sabbatical, if you have another job."

"You can if you are completely outside the British system. What I do in America is nothing to do with them." I said triumphantly.

"You cheeky bugger!" said Morris again.

"In two days time," I explained, "I'll go back and see Barraclough, tell him that I'm under stress and say that I want to leave, but that I can only do so if I can have all the increments for my pension plus a year's leave."

"Wait a minute," Morris said. He could hardly believe it. "You plan to have paid sabbatical leave, starting this September. And then your pension will start the following year. So you'll have your pension plus a full salary from Sweetpea, plus an extra year's salary from St Sebastian's."

"Well that's what I want to talk to you about..." I began.

Morris was speechless for a moment. Then he laughed. "You wouldn't let me do the negotiation for you? I'd love to see that Registrar's face when he finds out!"

"Actually," I said, "I want to ask you something. Does the UCU have a fighting fund or a hardship scheme or something?"

"Yes. Like everyone else we're desperate for money, but we do have a little put by to help victims of real injustice."

"Well the union has done a lot for me. I don't need the extra year's salary. Could I give it to your fund?"

Morris was overwhelmed, "Of course you could. Are you sure? That's really very generous."

"That's fine," I said. "No need to say any more. I'll write you a cheque as soon as I've dealt with Barraclough."

Victoria giggled. "Can you imagine the Vice-Chancellor's reaction? He'll never forgive you Harry!"

"Dear me!" I said.

By this stage Morris had eaten nearly three-quarters of all the food we had ordered, and he asked the waiter for another pint of lager. He paused and his expression changed. "Your VC will be furious," he said. "Particularly after today's performance. But what you're asking is not unreasonable. It's what anyone else would get and by leaving you are saving the university a lot of money."

Victoria and I couldn't eat anything more, but Morris was transfixed by pictures of the puddings. At last he ordered a chocolate ice-cream concoction sprinkled with hazelnuts. Although he tucked into it with enthusiasm, he was silent for a few minutes. Then he spoke thoughtfully. "You know," he said, "your Vice-Chancellor is not as evil as you think. He's entirely at the mercy of the government who have starved universities of funds for years. He is forced to take more and more students, and he has to educate them on less and less money. So he puts his managers under pressure. All Vice-Chancellors do it. He can't afford to train anyone properly and, in any case, most academics are not natural managers. They're too much like prima donnas. So it ends up a mess. It all comes down to money in the end. Universities simply don't have enough of it. They'll do anything for cash, like getting involved with that shark Gold. And there you are. Everyone suffers...'

There was a pause while Morris licked the last trace of his ice cream off his spoon regretfully. Then he grinned. "Still the UCU will be delighted with the money. Thanks!"

As planned, I went to see the Vice-Chancellor two days later. I told his secretary that I would only need to meet for a few minutes. Remembering Magnus's performance, I arrived at four o'clock, looking haggard. When I entered his office, he was seated at his desk. "Yes, Harry," he said, putting down his fountain pen.

"I'm sorry to trouble you, but I must talk to you about an important personal matter."

Barraclough frowned. "I only have a few minutes," he said as he urged me to sit down.

"I've been thinking over what you said during the meeting... I'm afraid I simply don't think I will be able to continue under the circumstances."

Barraclough looked surprised. "Not continue...?"

"No, Vice-Chancellor. I have not been sleeping. I am showing every symptom of stress. The last year has been terrible. If you would be prepared to make me some sort of offer, I might think about early retirement after all."

Barraclough visibly brightened. "You think you might want to leave us?" he asked.

"Yes, Vice-Chancellor. For my own good, and for that of St Sebastian's. But I will need to have an enhanced pension. I can't afford to go otherwise."

Barraclough took out a notepad and wrote down some figures. "Up to sixty-five?" he muttered. "Let's see, that's a four-year enhancement. What about part-time teaching?"

"I really don't think in my present state of health I could do justice to the students."

"Good! No part-time employment..." He became notice-ably more jovial.

"But I would like a year's sabbatical. I'm due for some study-leave."

"A year's sabbatical on full pay?" He sobered up a little.

"Like Magnus," I said firmly.

"I see." Barraclough did further calculations. "Yes," he went on, "it could be arranged. But it must be understood in return that you won't block Freddie Gold's gift."

"No. That's all right. But...if I don't go you will have to have me on the books for four more years."

"I realize that." The Vice-Chancellor looked grim. "The union is clearly going to be a complete menace. So...when would you plan to leave?"

"This autumn," I said.

Barraclough got up and shook my hand. "You're making the right decision, Harry."

"Would you mind writing this down," I said. "So we have some kind of record?"

Barraclough scribbled a note on his official writing paper, signed it, and handed it to me. "Once I get a formal letter," I continued, "I'll send in my notice."

"Of course, of course...I'll ask my secretary to do it this afternoon. It's a good decision. The right decision," Barraclough smiled affably. He was himself again. "We'll have to arrange a retirement party before you go. I'll get in touch with Wanda."

"Thanks, Vice-Chancellor," I said, as I walked to the door. Barraclough shook hands again.

Magnus was waiting for me outside my office. He was wearing his new clothes. "You were right Magnus," I said. I showed him Barraclough's scribbled note. Magnus reached into a brown bag and took out a bottle of vintage champagne. "Time to celebrate!" he declared and he did a little jig in the hall.

CHAPTER THIRTEEN

It is Always Nice to be Appreciated

As promised, a letter from Barraclough arrived the next day stating the terms we agreed. I was to be given a three-year enhancement to my pension and allowed to have a year's sabbatical on full pay beginning in October. He added a personal memo to the letter saying he would consult with Wanda about arranging a retirement party. He asked me to write back formally to give in my notice. I wrote a letter on St Sebastian's writing paper:

Dear Vice-Chancellor,

Further to our conversation, I would like formally to give in my notice from St Sebastian's. I understand that I will take sabbatical leave from October this academic year until next October. My pension will begin then.

I want to inform you that I have just been appointed the Thomas Jefferson Porpoise Distinguished

Professor at Sweetpea College, Virginia. The salary is one-hundred-and-fifty-thousand-dollars per annum and includes free accommodation. Naturally Victoria and I are thrilled. It is always nice to be appreciated.

I should perhaps also inform you that, in view of the above, I have sent a cheque equivalent to a year's salary from St Sebastian's to the UCU Hardship Fund. I am sure you agree that it is extremely important that the union continues its fight against injustice in Britain's universities,

Yours sincerely,

Harry Gilbert.

Later in the day I received an email from the Vice-Chancellor telling me that my letter had been received. There was no mention of my new job at Sweetpea, but he added that in light of my future plans, it would not be appropriate for St Sebastian's to give me a retirement party.

"Not a good loser!" was Victoria's comment.

I also sent Morris O'Murphy the cheque and let him know the outcome of my discussion with Barraclough.

He emailed me back thanking me and saying I was a lucky bugger. He asked if he could come visit when he travelled to the States on holiday.

Two days later an email from Pilkington was sent to all members of the department announcing that I would be taking early retirement. He went on to say that a new lectureship in ethics had been established by Mr Freddy Gold and would be advertised in the *Times Higher Educational Supplement* next week. It was hoped that the successful candidate would be able to begin next term so that my courses would be covered. Again there was no mention of Sweetpea and no hint of a leaving present, a retirement party or good wishes for the future. I felt sad about this. After all, I had worked at St Sebastian's for eleven years and, within my limitations, I had done my best.

Victoria and I spent the next few days packing up books, pictures and small items to be sent to Sweetpea. We booked our flight, ordered change of address cards, and wrote to Oscar Billstone and Thomas Jefferson about our itinerary. We planned to stop off in New York for a week-end en route. The cats would travel with us drugged in their basket in the hold.

In the meantime Magnus was busy kitting himself out for his world-wide cruise. We had promised to see him off at Southampton, and on the day, we picked him up from his house. The afternoon before, Penelope had collected Pushkin; he was to be a companion for Rufus while Magnus was gone. Magnus was concerned about this. He was not confident that Penelope would keep her promise about buying Pushkin his favourite, expensive cat litter and cat food, but there was no alternative.

Magnus was wearing his blue blazer with the Oxford crest, a mauve and gold striped tie and a panama hat. His leather trunk was so heavy that both of us had to lift it together. At the dock there were no porters so we had to carry it to his cabin. Located on the top deck, it had a small sitting room and a bath. Magnus took a bottle of champagne out of his trunk and a packet of crisps.

As we sat down there was knock on the door. An elderly American woman wrapped in Persian lamb introduced herself as Violet Van Graff. She asked if we could help her find her cabin. She explained that she had been staying at the Ritz and that her bags had been sent ahead and were somewhere in the ship. We found her cabin with no difficulty at all. It was just down the corridor and we asked if she would like to join us. She returned several minutes later resplendent in a purple silk dress. She told us that she just loved our accents and that she was originally from Snowdrop, Virginia. "We're going to live in Sweetpea," Victoria announced.

"Why that's wonderful," Violet said. "My first husband's cousin, Thomas Jefferson Porpoise, has a house near there.'

Victoria and I looked at each other. "I'm to be the Thomas Jefferson Porpoise Distinguished Professor at Sweetpea College," I said.

"Gee . . . No! Are you on your way now?"

"No," I replied. "Magnus is going on a round-the-world cruise. We're just here to see him off."

"So it's just Magnus! Well, I hope you are planning to go dancing in the evening, young man."

"He's a splendid dancer," Victoria said smiling. "Knows everything: cha-cha-cha, samba, tango, fox-trot... He had an excellent teacher!"

"Gee!" said Mrs Van Graff again. "Well, keep the first one for me!"

When the steward announced that the ship was to sail soon, we departed leaving Magnus with his new friend. She was telling him about her recent stay in London. I winked at Magnus when we left; he grinned and refilled his glass.

Several days later we stood in a queue at Heathrow. We had said good-bye to Victoria's family. We had locked up the house, and left our keys with neighbours. All post was to be redirected and the lawn was going to be mown once a week in summer. We were to stay at the Harvard Club in New York for two nights before flying to Washington. There was a slight worry about the cats, but we hoped they would get through customs and that the club authorities would not notice them.

Magnus was due to dock in New York during our stay and we planned to have lunch together. Everything went according to plan. When we arrived we checked in, unpacked our bags, and spent the day at the Metropolitan Museum. Victoria was anxious to look at their collection of eighteenth-century English furniture. "After all, I'm meant to be an expert," she said.

The next morning, we met Magnus at the docks. He emerged smiling with Violet Van Graff at his side. She looked tired. Magnus was wearing a loud blazer with a bright pink cravat we had never seen before. Even though the weather was hot, Violet was swathed in fur. We found a cab and drove to the Harvard Club where we had booked a table.

"Danced all evening, every evening." Magnus declared. "Do you know they have a midnight feast? You can't imagine how much lobster I've eaten!"

Violet sighed. "I'm pooped." She looked at Victoria. "Do you know I had to buy him a new tux?" she said.

"And this nice blazer," added Magnus.

"The tux he brought with him didn't fit anywhere!"

184

"A bit short in the trousers, a bit long in the sleeves. And it got a bit tight with all the eating," said Magnus calmly. "Violet insisted I got some new clothes. So she took me to the ship's shop and they fitted me out. Jolly nice present. Something to remember her by on the next leg of my journey!"

"He looked like a bum," Violet interjected.

"Perhaps more like a gorilla." I smiled.

"Gorilla?" Violet asked. "Why a gorilla?"

Over lunch Magnus told us about the crossing. On the third night there was a terrible storm and nearly everyone was sick, including the Captain. Magnus, however, had been fine and had eaten two lobster dinners since there were so many empty spaces. Every evening he and Violet went to the show and then spent the rest of the night dancing. There were not enough men on board so Magnus was in constant demand. "Beautiful women kept asking me to dance," he said. "I couldn't believe it."

"He's quite a dancer," Violet sighed. "Real stamina." I hoped she was only referring to his dancing skills. For all her cosmetic camouflage, she was at least twenty years older than Magnus.

It turned out that she lived in a big apartment on the Upper East Side, just off Fifth Avenue. Her luggage had already been sent on from the ship. "You should see her suitcases!" said Magnus. "There were about twenty of them. All matching, from Louis Vuitton." Violet looked complacent.

Magnus was due to reboard the *Queen Christina* at three, and we had to hurry back. We put Violet into a yellow cab and we promised to tell Thomas Jefferson that we had met her. Magnus looked relieved as she sped away. "Quite an ordeal. Didn't know how to escape."

"I imagine there are lots of elderly women on the ship," I said.

"Place is loaded, in every sense of the word."

"I think you've found your vocation, Magnus," Victoria teased him.

"Never been so popular!" he said.

We watched as the *Queen Christina* sailed off. Magnus waved from the top deck. He had promised to email us on his journey.

The next day, when we arrived in Washington, we were met by Thomas Jefferson's secretary who drove us to our cottage in Sweetpea. She gave Victoria a letter from her employer. It was an effusive missive inviting us to dinner and thanking her for sending him the Porpoise crest and motto. He said he had a little birthday present for her. She would see it at the ball which was to take place the following week.

Our new house was near the main gates. Built at the end of the eighteenth century, it was a small white clapboard folly and was furnished with beautiful examples of American colonial furniture. I hoped we could keep the cats from sharpening their claws on it. The boxes we had sent on were placed in the corner of one of the bedrooms. The trees were in full leaf in the small garden in the back. Parked in the drive was the red Rolls-Royce.

We found a note of welcome from Oscar tucked behind the telephone. He hoped that we had had a pleasant flight, and he and Nancy looked forward to seeing us at dinner in the Porpoise mansion. He assumed we would be able to find our own way and he included a map. Dinner was arranged for seven o'clock; dress was to be informal. Thomas Jefferson, he said, had also invited Joel and Mimi Perley. Dr Perley was the Head of the Religion Department.

"Unfortunate he has the same initials as John Pilkington . . . "

"Don't worry about it," I tried to be reassuring. "Everything'll be fine!"

"I hope so," said Victoria.

At six we arrived at the Porpoise mansion; Thomas Jefferson, wearing a navy blue blazer with the Porpoise coat of arms, greeted us at the door and led us into his private study. We had not seen this room before. The walls were lined with leather books; in the corner was a magnificent eighteenth-century walnut knee-hole desk. Oscar and Nancy were seated on a pink Regency sofa; opposite were Mimi and Joel Perley on a matching chaise longue.

Thomas Jefferson introduced us. Joel was wearing a sober pair of trousers and a polyester jacket in dark green; his wife, who was plump with long fair hair, was in a flowery summer dress. Somehow they looked shabby beside Oscar in his presidential dark grey suit and Nancy in her expensively casual silk shirt-dress.

At seven, the butler struck a gong and led us into dinner in a small dining room with dark wood panelling. Thomas Jefferson sat at the head of a large mahogany table with Victoria on his right and Nancy on his left.

During dinner, Joel told me about the department while Victoria chatted to Thomas Jefferson. Mimi described her new job at the Sweetpea nursery-school at length to Oscar and Nancy who listened patiently. Dinner consisted of Southern fried chicken with sweet-corn fritters and fried bananas. The vegetables came from the estate, and there was lime chiffon pie for pudding. I realised I was going to have even more trouble with my weight in Sweetpea.

Over coffee, Thomas Jefferson announced that he had something to show Victoria; he went into the hall and returned with a huge red box. Ceremoniously he removed a vast, new, silver punch bowl inscribed with the new Porpoise crest and Victoria's motto. He put it on the table and asked Victoria to read the inscription. "*Heb Porpoise, Nid Pwrpas,*" she declared in ringing tones.

"What does that mean?" Mimi asked in her soft, Southern voice.

"It's Welsh. 'Without a Porpoise, there's No Purpose', Victoria said solemnly.

Thomas Jefferson gleamed. "Quite right!" said Oscar.

Joel looked at his wife. I detected a slight shrug pass between them. After dinner we sat in the drawing room. Thomas Jefferson offered the men Havana cigars that he had sent from London. He also opened a bottle of vintage port and handed out glasses. Joel and his wife refused all these refreshments and looked increasingly uncomfortable. Nancy asked if I had met the Queen when I received my OBE. I told them that I had seen her briefly and had shaken hands.

"Wow . . ." said Oscar. "Did she say anything?"

"Actually, she asked me about my latest book," I tried to look modest.

"She's read your latest book?" Joel asked incredulously.

"I wouldn't think so – one of her aides prompted the question. They do their homework thoroughly."

"And you were given a medal?" Thomas Jefferson inquired.

"A small one in a black box."

"When are you supposed to wear it?" Mimi asked.

"Only for formal occasions," I said.

"Ah, then you must wear it at Victoria's birthday ball," Thomas Jefferson announced. I though the ball was meant to be in honour of the new Chair, but I let it pass.

After coffee, Oscar and Nancy stood up and thanked Thomas Jefferson for his hospitality. The rest of the company followed. As we were ready to leave, Thomas Jefferson took Victoria's hand, kissed it, and bowed. I glanced at Joel; he looked dismayed. On the way back to our cottage, Victoria looked worried. "You know, Harry," she mused, "I think the Perleys could be a lot of trouble."

"I don't think so," I said. "They're just shy."

The next day I went to the college and was shown my office. Located in yet another stately colonial building, it looked out over freshly mown lawns. I had sent on my furniture and books from St Sebastian's. All this had been arranged by the moving firm. Above my desk hung the icon of St Sebastian. The college had purchased a lap-top computer which sat comfortably on my pedestal desk. I turned it on: there was a long email from Magnus:

> Exhausted. And stuffed. But, Harry, I'm being besieged. The ship is full of old women who keep joining me in the first-class bar. After lunch, they sit at my table for coffee and tell me about their late husbands. Dinner is murder. I have to sit with five ladies who all talk at once. The average age must be over eighty. After the show, they demand I take them dancing. I hardly have a chance to sit down. But do tell Victoria that she did me proud. I'm said to be one of the best dancers on the ship. In many ways it was easier when there was just Violet. But, that was exhausting, too. I'm really not sure what to do. Perhaps I ought to move to a second-class cabin.

But I understand the food isn't as good, and you've got to sit at tables for eight. The meals remain excellent. I am rapidly growing out of my new dinner jacket. I've got to go. There's a lady sitting next to me in the computer room who wants to take me gambling in the casino. She's a millionairess, but she needs help with her wheelchair, so at least I won't have to dance! Give Victoria a big kiss.

Magnus.

While I was laughing over this, I heard a knock on the door; Joel Perley came in carrying several booklets about the college. "Thought you might like to have these," he said." He put them down on my drinks table next to the sherry decanter. "Golly gosh!" he said. "I didn't know you were bringing your own stuff. He sat down in the armchair opposite my desk. "What's that?" he said pointing at the icon.
"An icon of St Sebastian."
"It's a saint?"
"Yes," I said. "My last university was named after him."
"Are you a Roman Catholic?" I detected disapproval.
"No, no...an Anglican. What you would call an Episcopalian. I just thought the icon was beautiful."
"I might have guessed," said Joel. "Mimi and I are Baptists. You'll get to know all the smart crowd round here if you're Episcopalians."
He looked round the room. "Did you bring that desk too?" The long case clock struck twelve. "You must have shipped that as well," he said standing up. He went over to look at it.
"It was made in Shrewsbury in the eighteenth century by a local clockmaker. That's where I went to school."
"I expect it was a private school?"
"Well..." I said carefully, "it was called a public school because it was originally founded to educate poor boys, but yes, it cost my parents money to send me there."
Joel continued to look around. "This place looks like a film set," he said resentfully. "You should see my office. I'm so busy, I never have time to tidy up. Well, I'm glad you've settled in."

Later in the day Joel and I went to the Faculty Club for lunch. Next to the President's house, it was full of college staff. I was introduced to several members of the department, and we had a drink in the bar. The walls were lined with etchings of the college; the furniture was reproduction colonial with a mixture of modern armchairs and sofas. I ordered beer, but Joel had non-alcoholic lager. We shared a basket of popcorn. "I thought you'd like to know we've been invited to Spouty's ball next week," Joel announced.

"Spouty?"

"You know, the Porpoise. That's his nickname."

"Thomas Jefferson?"

"Nobody around here calls him Thomas Jefferson. I know you're living in the cottage on his estate, but it's only fair to tell you that the staff think he's a joke. One of Buffalo Bill's donors. Actually his biggest."

"Buffalo Bill?"

"Oscar Billstone, the President ... anyway, that's what we call him. Not to his face, of course. His wife is known as 'Her Royal Highness'."

I was dumbfounded. "They've been incredibly nice to us ..."

"Sure. They would be. You're their pet professor. An academic with a fancy English accent and a wife who's the daughter of a Lord."

"Baronet," I corrected automatically, but, with a sinking feeling, I wondered how he knew.

"Look," Joel continued. "I don't want you to get the wrong idea. We're pleased you've come. The department could do with some new blood. But Buffalo Bill's gang isn't popular around here. They swank around and run the place, but they pay us a pittance and have no real interest in what we're trying to do."

"A pittance?" I asked.

"Well, relatively. None of us can afford to live in Sweetpea or even in the surrounding communities. I live twenty miles away."

"I see," I said.

Lunch was served in the Faculty dining room. All the waiters were black. This continued to make me uncomfortable, but no one else seemed to notice. We ordered hamburgers and fries.

190

Joel explained that as chairman of the department, he had to be at the college over the summer. But he and Mimi planned to go away for a week later in the month. They were taking their two children to South Carolina to stay with their grandparents.

As we walked back to our offices, we went past the faculty parking spaces. "Look at that Rolls!" he said. "Some parent must have parked it there by accident."

"It's mine, actually," I said.

"You own a Rolls-Royce?"

"We bought it from the Wachman dealership," I said. "It's a demonstrator. Manford gave us a very good deal. I know his brother in England."

"No . . . ." Joel became quite excited. "Can I see it?"

We walked over, and I opened the door.'

"Jumping Jehoshaphat!" he exclaimed, "This is fancy!"

I didn't know what to say. "Would you like to go for a drive?"

"Wow . . . Sure . . . I've never been in a Rolls before!"

Joel climbed into the passenger seat and we set off. As we passed by a row of shops near the college, I saw Victoria and Nancy. They were shopping for plants for the garden. I honked and pulled over and put down the window. "Do you need a lift?" I asked.

Victoria came over loaded down with shopping bags. "Harry, would you mind taking these home? Hello, Joel."

Joel smiled wanly. I got out of the car, and put the bags in the boot. Nancy kissed me on both cheeks, careful not to smudge her lipstick.

"Nancy just took me to lunch at the most lovely little women's club," Victoria said. "She's going to take me home later. Where are you two off to?"

"Just out for a ride," I said.

Nancy and Victoria waved as we set off for the department.

Joel looked nervous. "Look," he said. "I didn't know you were so friendly with the President's wife. You won't say anything about what I told you, will you?"

"Of course not. Just between us."

Joel looked relieved as we passed through the college gates.

We spent the early part of Victoria's birthday quietly together. At six o'clock, she took her ball dress out of the wardrobe. It was long, white and very simply cut. It had originally been made for her when she was seventeen for her coming-out debutante party. I could not help but be envious. She ate far more than me, but she slipped into it and the zip went up as if it had been fitted for her yesterday.

Then, with a great deal of ceremony, she brought out a battered purple velvet case from her bottom drawer. She had carried this with utmost care from England in anticipation of this very occasion. It contained the famous Dormouse diamonds. Early in the nineteenth century the magnificent parure had been bought by her great-great-great grandfather for his young bride. In those days, the Dormouses had been rich. It consisted of a festoon necklace, pendant earrings, a hair ornament, and an indecently large brooch. To Victoria's fury, these treasures were entailed through the male line so they did not belong to her. Instead, her eldest brother Billy would inherit them. But as it happened Victoria's sister-in-law was not interested in jewellery and had always been happy to lend the set for special events. However, when we borrowed them, we had to pay the insurance. That comfortably disposed of my salary for the month.

We set off for the Sweetpea Country Club at seven. A mile outside the town, it had originally been the Porpoise tennis pavilion, but Thomas Jefferson's father had handed it over to the club committee. It was another large colonial mansion surrounded by rolling green hills. As we drove through the club gates, we passed a golf course of unbelievable greenness. Thomas Jefferson was standing between two large pillars on the steps of the club greeting guests. An attendant took the keys to the Rolls, as I helped Victoria out of the car. Thomas Jefferson stepped down, kissed Victoria and shook my hand. "You look delightful, my dear," he said. He gazed at the diamonds. "How magnificent!" He was awestruck.

"They're the Dormouse diamonds," I said. "Very historic. They belonged to Victoria's great-great-great grandparents. We brought them over from England for the ball."

Thomas Jefferson was speechless for a moment. He then turned to me. "And I see you are decorated as well." I was wearing my OBE medal pinned on my lapel and felt quite ridiculous. "I thought you wanted me to wear it," I said.

"Of course I did."

Thomas Jefferson's dinner jacket was unbuttoned. I noticed it was lined in pink silk with the new porpoise crest woven into it. He must have had it made for the occasion. As we walked up the steps, I pointed it out to Victoria. She giggled. "He seems to take heraldry very seriously," she said.

Oscar and Nancy were standing near the entrance hall and introduced us to other guests. Again all the waiters were black They distributed champagne and canapés to the company. Then a gong was struck and it was announced that dinner was served. We filed into the club dining room and found our places. Victoria was seated next to Thomas Jefferson; I sat next to Nancy. I waved at Manford and Sherrie Wachman and the Mandril-Fortescue cousin who were all placed nearby. I also noticed the Perleys at a distant table. None of my other colleagues seemed to be there. Still, over two hundred guests were seated in the dining room. The windows were draped with filmy gold material and the room was lit by sparkling chandeliers.

In the middle of our table, Thomas Jefferson had placed his new punch bowl. Victoria was delighted and said how nice it looked. Thomas Jefferson was pleased. In fact it was a twin of the one we had already seen. He had had two made and had donated one to the club. Then a rather effete young man was introduced to us as Julian Bosie. He sat on the other side of Thomas Jefferson and was described as one of the most promising young painters of his generation.

The first course was caviar served on ice with hot toast. Thomas Jefferson gazed at Victoria and gestured to his young guest. "Here she is," he said, "Isn't she perfect!" Turning to Victoria, he asked: "My dear, would you be so kind as to let young Julian paint your portrait. It will be the making of him. You must wear that beautiful dress with the Dormouse diamonds. It shall hang in the cottage. And remain there for posterity."

Victoria looked astonished. "You want to paint me?"

"Of course!"

Thomas Jefferson stood up. Hush descended on the party. "Friends," he said. "We are here today to welcome the new Thomas Jefferson Porpoise Distinguished Professor and his lovely wife to our little town. Professor Gilbert, as you all know, is a most important theologian who was recently honoured by the Queen of England." (I thought momentarily of Lisa) "And Mrs Gilbert, Victoria, is descended from a long line of English baronets. We are indeed privileged to have them among us and we must do everything we can to make them happy."

Looking directly at Victoria, he smiled. "Now, I understand today is a special day. Will you all join me in singing 'Happy Birthday' to Victoria. We must not let such an anniversary be forgotten!"

Victoria went bright pink and her smile became a little fixed as the room broke out in song. Afterwards, with some ceremony, Thomas Jefferson handed her a red leather box "This is the small surprise I promised. A little something in token of this great occasion," he declared. Victoria opened the box. Inside was a Paul Revere bleeding bowl. Victoria was overwhelmed. There was applause. I glanced at Mimi Perley as Thomas Jefferson sat down. She looked as if she were going to be sick.

After dinner there was dancing in the club ballroom. Thomas Jefferson began the ball with Victoria. I wondered if I was meant to ask the effete young artist, but I compromised by going over and sitting next to him. "Oh wow! I've never seen such beautiful diamonds," said Julian Bosie. "I only hope I can do justice to them."

"I've always rather preferred the lady," I said.

When Thomas Jefferson and Victoria came back, it was young Julian's turn to dance. I saw Victoria was going to have a tiring time. I began to feel sorry for Magnus who had to endure this every night.

Throughout the evening I was introduced to numerous guests. But other than the Perleys, they were few from the college. At about midnight I asked Mimi to dance, and asked her why.

"Some of the administrators are here," she said. "But they don't ask faculty to events like this. Except Joel because he's the chairman of your department. That's the only reason why we've been invited."

"I don't understand," I said.

"We don't count." Mimi was angry. "We could never afford to be members of the country club. The entrance fee must be about twenty thousand dollars. Spouty isn't interested in people like us."

"But there's the Faculty Club," I said.

"That's not a real club. Anybody can belong as long as they're employed by the college."

The music ended and I took Mimi back to her table. "Look," she said. "Why don't you and Victoria come over to us next week. Then you can see how the other half live."

The ball finished at one, and we drove back to the cottage. "You know," I said, "I can't imagine how Magnus does it. Every night he has to do waltzes, fox-trots, sambas, and who knows what else with total strangers."

"He's due to send another email. I wonder how he is getting on," Victoria was amused.

As she undressed, I went downstairs and turned on the computer. There was a new message. It read:

> Must tell you the news: you'll be gripped! I just heard from Penelope. She told me Pushkin annoyed Rufus and Rufus bit him. Pushkin had to go to the vet with an abscess but Penelope won't hear a word against her thug of a cat. Anyway, you'll want to hear the university news: Your job was advertised, but they interviewed only one candidate. Guess who?? Absolutely!! ... Got it in one! They hired young Grundy, and gave him a contract for three years in the first instance. The money did not come through immediately; apparently the cheque was always in the post. We soon found out why. Apparently Lisa has run off with a Harley Street

specialist. He's thirty years older than she is, has four children, and his wife is breathing vengeance. You know all about him: he's the one who gave Lisa that phoney certificate for the concession which so annoyed Penelope. That's when they met. The rumour is she took off all her clothes in his office! So the engagement with Ronald is off, and as a result, Gold wrote a snooty note to Barraclough saying, in view of the circumstances, it would no longer be suitable to commemorate his dear mother with an endowed lectureship . . . Barraclough is now stuck with paying your salary for a year, making up your pension, losing out on the money for your work for the RAE, employing Ronald for three years and having no endowment to finance any of it. Isn't that exquisite! It really feels that there is still some justice in the world . . . .

Got to go. The casino's about to open, and I've got a date with an octogenarian from California. Wish me luck.

Love, Magnus.

CHAPTER FOURTEEN

It's the Same as Everywhere Else

The following Friday, Victoria and I set off for Railroad City, Virginia. The Perleys had asked us to come to their house for dessert once their two boys had gone to bed. As we crossed the boundaries of the town, we saw rows of dilapidated houses. There were groups of black youths wandering the streets. Burnt-out cars were parked in front of derelict buildings and various appliances including refrigerators and television sets were scattered on the scrubby lawns. "They can't live here," said Victoria.

We passed by a grey granite hotel, the Railroad Inn, and we went over a maze of railway lines. Victoria struggled with the map of the town which Joel had given me. Gradually the neighbourhood became neater. We were soon driving through streets of suburban houses with well-kept gardens and freshly white-washed fences. We parked the Rolls in front of the Perleys' house on Rosebud Road. Joel was standing outside waiting for us. On the porch was a swing and a basketball hoop was suspended against the side of the house.

Joel shook hands with both of us. Mimi was in the kitchen organizing the refreshments. Joel led us into the family room. It was small and tidy with a pale green floral carpet. The walls were painted a similar colour and were lined with watercolour prints of flowers and birds. In the corner was a large flat-screen television set, a DVD player and a video. A glass cabinet in the corner was filled with dolls. Victoria and I sat on a blue leather sofa; on the wall opposite four flying pigs were arranged diagonally. Mimi came in carrying a tray with a large lemon meringue pie and mugs of coffee. Joel handed out generous slices as we discussed the ball.

"Quite a crowd," Joel commented. "But we really didn't know anyone."

"It was very kind of Thomas Jefferson," I said. "We owe him a great deal."

Joel shifted uncomfortably. "I know he's your patron and all that. And the college needs his money. But he lives in another world. Except for the Billstones and some of the administrators, no one from the college is ever invited to his house. That was the first time we've ever been to the Sweetpea Country Club."

"It was our first time, too," I said.

"I'm sure it won't be your last," Joel sounded sour.

"We're already members." Victoria spoke hesitantly. "Thomas Jefferson has organized complementary membership."

"Golly," Mimi said. "We don't know anyone who actually belongs. Faculty members couldn't possibly afford it."

"I doubt if we'll go much," I said.

Mimi went out to the kitchen to refill the coffee pot. "I suppose you're planning to go to the Sweetpea Episcopalian Church?" Joel asked.

"Actually I thought we'd support the college chapel," I said. "Oscar's invited me to preach next month. The Chaplain seems very nice."

"Oh well, if you like that sort of thing. Mimi and I don't feel that the college chapel has very much to do with Christianity," pronounced Joel. I felt uncomfortable. How could the college chapel not be Christian?

Mimi re-emerged carrying a brochure. "This is where Joel and I go," she said. "You'd be very welcome to join us." There was a picture of a modern building with stained glass windows. In bold print, it announced: 'Jesus Saves'. Apparently Railroad Baptist Church was the largest church in the area with a membership of a thousand families. Inside there was a photograph of the clean-cut minister, his wife and three children. "We're Baptists," she explained. "Joel's a deacon in the church."

Upstairs we heard the sound of a basketball bouncing, and Joel excused himself to see what was going on. Mimi poured us more coffee. "This is absolutely scrumptious," Victoria said. "I don't think I've ever had such a good lemon meringue pie before. How do you make it?"

Mimi went to the kitchen to get the recipe. She returned with a pen and paper and copied out the instructions. Joel emerged looking frustrated and angry. "I told them there'll be no more of that if they want to go on holiday. No swimming in the ocean. None of Grandma's cooking." He settled into an armchair, picked up his pie, and sighed. "It's not easy to get work done round here, as you can see."

For the next half hour Joel and I discussed details of the department while Victoria and Mimi chatted about the differences between American and British cooking. When we got on the subject of the students, Victoria turned to Joel. "There's something I don't understand," she said. "I know it's expensive to come to Sweetpea. How do the students afford it? Are most of them on scholarship?"

"Officially," Joel began, "we operate a blind admission policy. Poor students should get in as easily as rich ones. At least that's what's in the college prospectus. But it isn't as simple as that. In the first place, ten per cent of the places in every class are reserved for the children of Sweetpea alumni. Nearly all their parents can afford to send them to Sweetpea on full fees, but a few must have scholarship help."

"And they don't have to be as good as the rest of the students," Mimi added.

"The college depends on endowments, so we've got to keep the alumni happy. The kids of the big donors will always get in." Joel cut himself another piece of pie and asked if we wanted any more. "The majority of scholarship money has to be reserved for ethnic minorities," he continued. "We're under political pressure to have about twenty per cent of our student body black and chicano. But every college in America wants these students if they're any good. So we've got to finance them generously if we want them to come here. We've also got to have scholarships for football and basketball stars. Alumni come for the big games, like the annual Sweetpea–William and Mary match. The donation level goes up if the team has done well so paying for these sporting jocks is seen as a worthwhile investment, even though most of them can barely read or write. What it comes down to is if you happen to be a straightforward, studious, white kid, there isn't a great deal of scholarship money available."

"I see," Victoria mused. "So basically most Sweetpea students are from rich homes."

Joel hesitated. 'Well . . . there are others. Mimi's brother's girl is here for example. She had trouble at Charlottesville. They said she behaved inappropriately to her teachers."

"It was a pack of lies." Mimi sounded indignant. "She's a properly brought up Christian girl. They wanted to send her to some Jew psychiatrist. That would have mixed her up for sure . . ."

"So Mimi said she'd look after her here." Joel cut across his wife. "I managed to get a faculty reduction for her."

I felt I had to say something. "That was very good of you."

Joel paused for a moment and then he said. "I suppose you'll find out the true situation soon enough. We do have some clever white kids from poor homes, but they largely survive on student loans and on working their own way through."

"How could they possibly do that?" Victoria asked. "The fees are enormous and there aren't many casual jobs in Sweetpea. The town is too small."

Joel hesitated. "What happens here is no different from everywhere else. The clever kids, once they've established their intellectual credentials in class, write the papers for the spoiled rich brats and the sporting jocks. And they charge plenty for doing it."

"You mean they cheat?" Victoria was horrified.

Joel was surprised. "It must go on in England."

I thought of Lisa. "Well occasionally they copy stuff off the internet, but the latest software can usually detect that. Anyway, you can tell if some intellectually challenged student suddenly produces a first-class essay. Something's wrong somewhere. Don't these kids get caught and thrown out of the college?"

Joel sighed. "It isn't like that. The fact is the system is in everyone's interest. You can't throw out the rich kids. We need their parents' donations. We don't want to throw out the poor kids. They're what make teaching worthwhile, and if the only way they can stay is to write the papers of some black, illiterate football star, well, so be it!"

I could see from Victoria's expression that she was shocked. She made a discreet gesture to me to indicate we should be thinking of leaving. As we got up she said, "It makes me uncomfortable. Wherever we go, the people doing the manual work like cleaning or waiting at table, always seem to be black."

"What do you expect?" asked Mimi, "Most of them aren't capable of anything else."

"Well of course," I began carefully, "I know black people sometimes have to face a great deal of social deprivation and prejudice..."

"It's a very complicated situation," Joel interrupted. "Mimi grew up in South Carolina. Her family were among the earliest settlers in the town. They've never really accepted integration. She sometimes forgets that we've all got to be politically correct on the modern college campus."

Victoria began to thank them effusively for a delightful evening. We both knew it was time to go.

Joel and Mimi stood on the porch as we walked to the car. I was horrified to see that the Rolls winged victory statuette was missing. "Hey, Joel," I called out, "somebody stole my winged victory."

He walked over to look. "I'm sorry," he said. "We're too near the ghetto. This neighbourhood is plagued by a small group of boys. They're not really bad kids, but their parents make no attempt to control them. The police know all about them, but there's not much they can do unless they catch them red-handed. I'm really sorry!"

I tried not to look upset. "Don't worry," I said. "I'm sure I'll be able to get another one easily."

Joel and Mimi waved from the porch as we set out for Sweetpea. En route we saw three hooded youths on the corner near the railway. They were passing round a silver object which looked very much like my winged victory. "Do you think I should stop and get it back?" I asked.

"Don't be an idiot," Victoria said. "I'll be a widow if you do."

The youths looked up at us as we passed and grinned.

The next day Victoria was due to have her portrait painted by Julian Bosie. At eleven o'clock a white Cadillac drew up outside our front door. Julian climbed out of the back. He was followed by Thomas Jefferson Porpoise. "I hope you don't mind," he said, "I couldn't resist seeing Julian and Victoria together."

Victoria had already changed into her white dress and was draped with the Dormouse diamonds. The driver brought in all the necessary equipment. The easel was set up in the sitting room and Victoria was posed on a small Regency sofa alongside a crystal vase of roses from the garden. I retreated upstairs to my study, but through the morning I could hear bursts of laughter drifting up the stairs.

Suddenly the door-bell rang. I went downstairs to answer it and found Mimi Perley on the doorstep. She was looking untidy; her hair was blown by the wind and her blouse was coming out of the waistband of her skirt. "I'm sorry to disturb you," she said. "I just ran out of school in the lunch recess. Joel and I wanted to ask you if you'd like to come with us to the big alumni game."

"That's very kind of you," I said, "You'd better talk to Victoria." I led her into the sitting room. Victoria was still reclining on the sofa and she and Thomas Jefferson were clearly telling each other jokes. Julian was busy at the easel. Mimi went bright red and tried to retreat, "I'm sorry . . . I didn't know you had company," she said.

"Mimi wants us to go with her and Joel to the Sweet-pea–William and Mary match. That'll be all right, won't it Victoria?"

Victoria looked embarrassed. "Actually we're going with Thomas Jefferson and the Billstones. We've just arranged it. I'm sorry Mimi. We'd have loved to have joined your party."

"That's OK," mumbled Mimi, "Sorry to have disturbed you."

"And thank you for last night," continued Victoria, "We had a delightful..." But by that time Mimi had disappeared into the hall. I followed her to the front door.

"I'm sorry," I said. "Perhaps another time."

Mimi exploded. "I know he's rich, and you're very liberal and all that, but I can't believe you allow your wife to be alone with those two degenerates..." and she flounced down the garden path. Behind us there was more laughter from the sitting room.

The final great event before teaching started was the annual alumni Sweetpea–William and Mary match. The football team had been on campus for a month to train and the college was abuzz with excitement. We went with Thomas Jefferson, Julian, Oscar and Nancy. The match attracted hundreds of loyal alumni from throughout the country who made reservations at local hotels or stayed in their old college rooms. After the game there was to be a formal dinner at the Faculty Club.

In the afternoon, we drove to the college and parked in front of the President's house. The six of us then walked to the stadium. We sat in the official President's Box with several of the trustees including Manford and Sherrie Wachman. Everyone was wearing a college scarf or tie. A number held Sweetpea banners. A few even waved Confederate flags. When the team came on, the crowd stood and yelled. Throughout the game Oscar explained what was happening. It was an exciting match and to everyone's delight, Sweetpea was victorious.

When the match was over, we all made our way to the Faculty Club. Oscar introduced Victoria and me to various alumni. At dinner we sat next to the President of the Alumni Association and his wife. "Great day!" he said in his Southern accent.

"I've never been to a football game," I said.

"You know," he remarked. "We pay our coach half a million dollars a year. But he does come up with the goods."

"A half a million?" I was astounded.

"He's worth every penny. It's important for morale that the college wins at football. When we win, the donations go up. Today's match will bring in at least another million. So you see, he makes his money."

"Football's that important?"

"Keeps the college going. Pays your salary. Can't survive without it, Professor!" I felt I was in a very strange world. I wondered if Sweetpea put an equal emphasis on intellectual activities.

The following week we were invited to join Manford and Sherrie Wachman at the Tam O'Shanter country club for lunch. Rabbi Wally was visiting from London, and they thought we would like to see each other again. We parked the Rolls in the car park; I looked forlornly at the bonnet and wondered how much it would cost to replace the missing winged victory. I cheered up when I saw our hosts waiting for us in the lobby. Wally was wearing a purple polo shirt and a skull cap; Sherrie was in a white tennis outfit and Manford was dressed for golf. Sherrie led us to a table overlooking the tennis court as Manford followed behind greeting friends at every table.

Eventually Manford sat down and the kilted waiter took our order. "How was your trip?" I asked Wally, who was sitting next to Victoria. He had ordered a plain green salad.

"Tiring. Now," he paused, "I have some news for you. You'll remember the Golds, I'm sure...I'm afraid there have been some further difficulties about the daughter."

Victoria and I looked at each other. "I think we may know," I said. "A friend of mine just sent an email..."

"It's been a real crisis. Lisa has run off with one of the most prominent members of my synagogue. His wife is prostrate. It appears they've gone to the Caribbean together. I can't imagine what will happen to his patients, let alone his children. It's very upsetting and difficult."

"Wally doesn't know which side to be on," Sherrie was teasing her brother-in-law. "Both Doctor Chevre and Mr Gold have been presidents of the synagogue at one time or another. Mrs Chevre is the daughter of one of the founders of the congregation. But the Golds are richer. Isn't that right, Wally? So it's a bit of a problem who to support."

"It's nothing to do with that," the rabbi spoke with some dignity. "People's feelings are at stake; so is the welfare of the children; and it is clear that both Lisa and Sharon Chevre need help. As a rabbi, it's my duty to give a moral lead. I've got to say something."

"And if not now, when?" said Manford.

"Anyway, enough of that," Wally said changing the subject. "I understand there's been a ball here in your honour."

"It was wonderful," Sherrie said. "There was a huge crowd. And it was Victoria's birthday, too. We all sang 'Happy Birthday', and then Thomas Jefferson gave her a lovely silver bowl as a present."

"We were touched," Victoria said.

"It was at the Sweetpea Country Club?" Wally asked.

"You know," I said. "I really don't understand about American country clubs. Is it true there are restrictions on who can belong to the Sweetpea Country Club?"

Manford took a deep breath, "In the past," he said, "Jews and blacks were excluded. But that's all changed now – with a little nudge from the Supreme Court. Sherrie and I have been asked to join many, many times. But we like it here." He waved to an elderly couple who were just entering the dining room.

"So you could belong if you wanted to? You don't have to be members of a Jewish country club?"

Sherrie put her arm around Manford. "Look," she said. "You've got to try and understand. We go to all the gentile functions. And Manny is a trustee of the college. But we don't really belong and we never will."

Sherrie's tennis clothes were immaculate; her nails and lipstick matched perfectly and her hair was an ambitious shade of gold. She looked like a woman who never thought of anything more serious than the whiteness of her laundry or the decor of her bathroom. But she clearly had something important to say. She leaned forward.

205

"There's still antisemitism in Sweetpea. Everyone's very polite, but you know it's there. I think the minute Jews forget and think that the world has changed so much that there is no Jew-hatred, that's when you have problems like a Hitler. I know about this. My mother's cousins back in Hungary were in with the government. They thought they were different; they thought they'd be safe. They weren't. They were carted off like everybody else.... I'm happy to go to parties at the Sweetpea Country Club when I'm asked, but I don't want to sit round their pool. No. I'm comfortable here. These are my people and this is where I belong."

There was a silence around the table. Victoria and I looked at each other. We were both thinking the same thing. Where did we belong? Where had we ever belonged?

After lunch, we said goodbye to Wally and Sherrie. Manford walked us to our car. "Oh dear," he said looking at the Rolls. "I see your winged victory is missing. I hope nobody here at the club took it."

"No, it happened last week. We went to see some friends in Railroad City."

"You took that car to Railroad City?" Manford was incredulous. "I'm not surprised you lost your statuette. I'm only amazed you still have four wheels!"

I looked crestfallen. "Will it be very difficult to get a replacement?"

Wally laughed as he shook my hand. "I've got a big box of them. They're always getting stolen. Come by any day this week and I'll give you a new one."

Before term started, we received another email and photograph from Magnus. He was sitting on a horse wearing a cowboy hat surrounded by a group of white-haired ladies. He looked decidedly out-of-focus.

> This is me. We're in Venezuela. Damn hot. And these women are driving me crazy. I haven't had a moment's rest since we left New York. I thought Violet was trouble. But I've been pursued by a whole group for the last month. They won't leave me alone.

Because I'm listed as a doctor in the passenger list, they call me Doc and think I'm a medic. They keep coming up and asking me about their arthritis . . .

I had a chat last night with one of the gentlemen hosts. The ship employs four of them to entertain the ladies. I'm beginning to think I should be put on the ship's payroll. He told me that he initially thought he might find an elderly millionairess who would marry him and solve his financial problems. But he soon learned his lesson. They give you presents like gold cigarette lighters, but they won't get married. Their children won't let them. They don't want some old guy cutting in on the deal.

Anyway, I can hardly get out of bed. Currently I've been hiding in my cabin hoping the women won't find me. But the evenings are hopeless. I've got to go to dinner, and they're lying in wait for me in the dining room. Then they want to go see the shows and end up on the dance floor. Got to go now and rest up for tonight.

Love Magnus

Victoria was extremely amused. "Magnus is going to end up like the *Flying Dutchman*, endlessly travelling the world!" she said.

The next evening Oscar and Nancy drove us to a meeting of the Sweetpea Alumni Association at the Sweetpea Club in Washington. This was their monthly get-together, and I was to be the main speaker. Oscar asked if I would give a little talk about the award ceremony at Buckingham Palace. He wanted me to show the video of when I was given my OBE. Although I told him it would be inappropriate, he insisted I wear my medal.

The Sweetpea Club was located in Georgetown in the same street as the Lazy Daisy Club. Over the entrance was the crest of the college. Inside a group of about thirty men and women were chatting in the lobby. The walls were lined with portraits of former presidents of the college as well as watercolours of some of the older college buildings. Oscar took us to a bar in the corner of the room. A waiter handed us fruit punch and another came around with large trays of canapés. At seven we went into the dining room, which was named after George Washington Wombat who had founded the club. The Wombat Dining Room was a large circular chamber with striped burgundy wallpaper. Over the mantle, there was a large portrait of George Washington Wombat himself wearing an academic gown and mortarboard. He certainly filled the canvas.

Before we sat down, Oscar asked me to say grace. After dinner, one of the club servants brought in a large television and video recorder. Oscar introduced me as the new Thomas Jefferson Porpoise Distinguished Professor of Ethics. He explained that I was recently given an award by the Queen of England, and that my talk would be about the British honours system. I felt foolish wearing my medal, and even more ridiculous showing the video.

Afterwards, there were a number of questions. One elderly gentleman asked if I had met the Duchess of Cornwall, the erstwhile Mrs Parker-Bowles. This was followed by a heated exchange between several alumni about the respective merits of Princess Diana and Camilla. An elegant woman wearing a silk print dress asked if I had made the acquaintance of the Queen's corgis. When my talk ended, Oscar gave a profuse vote of thanks, and reminded everyone that there were pledge forms and envelopes on the table for anyone who wished to make a donation to the college. The assembled company then stood up and, with extraordinary fervour, they all sang the college song. Victoria and I felt very embarrassed and British.

On the way back to Sweetpea, Oscar praised my address and told me how successful the evening had been. He had looked at the pledge forms before we left. The elegant woman who had asked about the corgis had donated fifty-thousand dollars. Oscar explained that her late husband had graduated from the college over sixty years ago and had made a fortune in manufacturing cardboard containers.

"Harry," he urged, "this talk of yours is a winner. Everyone in this country wants to know about the royal family. We would be so grateful if you would do it again sometimes. You see there are alumni meetings all round the country, and everyone would be interested in your experiences."

From the back seat, Nancy effused about the video. "It's so colourful," she exclaimed. "All that pageantry. We have nothing like that in the United States."

As Oscar drove us to the cottage, he emphasized the importance of donations to the college. Then he went on, "I'll arrange a schedule with my secretary. You mustn't be burdened with this, but I can just see the faces of our alumni in San Francisco, Los Angeles, Phoenix, Denver, St Louis, Minneapolis, Chicago, Boston, New York, Philadelphia and Miami when you and Victoria talk to them about the Queen. They'd all just love it."

I was upset. Before we went to bed, I got a beer out of the refrigerator and some pretzels. "How can you eat anything else?" Victoria asked.

"Still hungry," I said. "Look, Victoria, I didn't come here to be a fund raiser. I thought they wanted me for my books and my scholarship."

"Don't be naive, Harry. You're here to add glamour to the college. That's why they want me, too. You heard what Thomas Jefferson said at the ball. He thinks I'm from a long line of English aristocrats."

"Perhaps we should bring your father to live over here to add to the circus."

"Come on Harry . . . you're going to have to be a sport about this. They're doing a lot for us."

"But I'm supposed to be a professor . . ." I objected.

"You are a professor. But you're a professor who's an advertisement for Sweetpea. You'll feel better once classes start."

During the first week, there were several days of orientation for the freshmen. My first class was to take place on Friday in the Old Confederate Hall. Before it began, I went to have a cup of coffee in the Faculty Club. The bar was largely empty except for a group surrounding Joel Perley. I heard him say, "Don't worry! He'll make a mistake before long and then we can make sure he goes."

As I entered they looked awkward and fell silent. I went over and joined them with my coffee, but they melted away with

209

different excuses. I was left with Joel. "I thought I'd introduce you to the first class," he explained.

"That's very kind of you," I said.

As we walked over, he told me that he had just heard from John Pilkington of St Sebastian's. Apparently they knew each other. They had met the previous year at a biblical conference in Washington. I had a sinking feeling. What, I wondered, had John told him about me.

Before we reached the hall, we overtook Mimi who was strolling along accompanying a very pretty student. She had soft golden hair and wholesome pink cheeks. On her head she wore a Sweetpea baseball cap and her dress was a pastel flower print. "This is my niece Susie-Beth," she said, "She is taking your course." She introduced us.

I smiled at her. "Yes, you mentioned her when we came over for that delicious pie," I said. "Are you enjoying the college, Susie-Beth?"

"Oh yes," replied Susie-Beth. She had a soft little voice. "Auntie Mimi has been so kind."

"Could I borrow a copy of your latest book?" Mimi asked, "It hasn't arrived in the college bookshop yet."

I was flattered. "Sure," I said, "Do you want to come and get it after the lecture?"

"I've got to get back to school in ten minutes. Perhaps Susie-Beth could fetch it. Would that be OK?"

Susie-Beth smiled prettily. We said good-bye to Mimi and the three of us went into the hall. There were at least a hundred students. They were tanned from the summer. Some had brought in drinks in large containers with ice. A few were talking on their mobile phones. Joel introduced me briefly and sat down. Then it was my turn.

I explained that the course would be about Christian ethics, and handed out a syllabus. Everyone was very attentive. Susie-Beth was sitting in the front row with her uncle and gazed at me throughout the lecture. She did not take notes. When I had finished, there was very gratifying applause, and the class filed out. Susie-Beth stayed behind and together we set off for my room. She seemed shy, but I did manage to get her to tell me that she came from South Carolina, that she had been educated in a small Christian private school and that she was the eldest of three sisters. She had found the University of Virginia overwhelming and several of the professors had been, in her own words, 'gross'. I thought it better to enquire no further.

When we arrived at my office I unlocked the door and asked her to wait for a moment. I was just going to collect my mail from the faculty office before it closed for lunch. I returned several minutes later, but she was no longer waiting in the corridor. I pushed open the door of my room. The first thing I noticed was her cardigan folded neatly on the floor with the baseball hat on top of it.

Then I saw her. She had draped herself over my sofa, her flowery dress riding high to reveal shapely, tanned thighs. "Professor," she said, in a soft little voice, "I'm so glad we can have some time alone. I want to talk to you about my credits. I'm sure you can help me, can't you? I can make it worth your while."

A Campus Conspiracy

Readers who wish to engage in discussion about the book should go to: www.acampusconspiracy.blog.com

Breinigsville, PA USA
13 September 2009
223985BV00001B/83/A